DARK HORSE

ALSO BY BILL NOEL

Folly Beach Mysteries

Folly

The Pier

Washout

The Edge

The Marsh

Ghosts

Missing

Final Cut

First Light

Boneyard Beach

Silent Night

Dead Center

Discord

The Folly Beach Mystery Collection

DARK HORSE

BILL NOEL

ENIGMA HOUSE PRESS

ISBN: 978-1-940466-76-7

Enigma House Press
Goshen, Kentucky
www.enigmahousepress.com

CHAPTER ONE

I was enjoying a sandwich for lunch and halfheartedly watching a Live 5 newscaster ramble on about what was going on in the Charleston, South Carolina, viewing area. The talking head's report of multiple shark sightings off nearby Sullivan's Island was sound clutter, until I heard her mention a dead body, and Folly Beach, my retirement home for a decade, in the same sentence. My sandwich took second place to me staring at a young reporter standing outside the entrance to the Folly Beach County Park, with the lights of three police cars alternating between red and blue in the background.

I didn't catch the beginning of the story but the reporter now had my attention as he said, "I've been told a body of a female was discovered in a gray mid-sized sedan you can see behind me." He dramatically turned his head and faced the gathering of police vehicles behind him and turned back to the camera and continued. "The body was found at approximately ten-thirty this morning by a Folly resident who was walking to the end of the island with a metal detector in search of elusive valuables lodged in the sand. Instead, he found something far worse—the body of the woman in the car."

The station cut to a taped interview with Folly's Director of Public Safety, better known as Police Chief Cindy LaMond, who said, "The body of a white female in her early forties was found in a gray Chevrolet Malibu with South Carolina plates this morning along West Ashley Avenue near the entrance to the Folly Beach County Park." Cindy paused.

Reggie, the interviewer, filled the void, "Do you know her identity and cause of death?"

Cindy nodded. "We know who she is but won't be releasing more information until next of kin has been notified."

Reggie interrupted, "Cause of death?"

The chief sighed. "It is being treated as a death investigation and there is nothing else to be said at this time. Thank you." She turned and walked away from the camera.

Cindy and I had become good friends after she moved to Folly from east Tennessee eight years ago and joined the city's small police force. She had been appointed chief a few years later, by the former chief who was now the mayor. Cindy was funny, excelled at her job, and had no use for reporters of any ilk.

The tape ended and Reggie started to say something but paused as he waited for the talking head in the studio to ask him a question. She didn't disappoint. "What else can you tell us?"

Reggie did disappoint, "That's all we know at this time."

Enlightening, I thought.

"To repeat," the newscaster said. "A body was found this morning in a car parked along the street outside the Folly Beach County Park. We will bring you updates as they become available." She went on to say we should check with the Channel 5 website for more information and to read all the latest news we should download the Channel 5 app to our smartphone and tablet. In other words, she stuck a commercial for her station in the middle of the newscast. One more reason I'm not a big TV watcher.

Folly Beach is an island located in the shadows of Charleston. It's small, only six miles long and a half mile wide, with the Folly Beach County Park anchoring the west end of the barrier island. News of anything happening on the island was big news to its roughly two thousand residents, so I wasn't surprised when the phone rang before the newscaster could say more than it was going to be a late August scorcher and to get the sunscreen ready.

"Hear about the dead bod at the County Park?" Charles Fowler said before I got to the "o" in hello.

Charles was one of the first people I met when I moved to Folly. For reasons unknown to anyone with a sense of logic, we became best friends. I worked most of my professional life in the human resource department of a large Midwestern healthcare company; Charles retired from his life of paychecks at the ripe young age of thirty-four and hadn't received a payroll check in the last thirty-one plus years. He was single, his financial needs minimal, and he met them by providing an extra set of hands to contractors, cleaning restaurants during busy season, and delivering packages for our friend Dude's surf shop. His picture can also be found in the dictionary beside the word "nosy." Don't look it up; that was an exaggeration, but only a slight one.

I said, "Just saw it on the news."

"Who was she and what happened?"

I told you he was nosy.

"How would I know?"

"You mean you haven't called Cindy yet?"

"Charles, what part of *just saw it on the news* don't you get?"

"So, you're going to call her now?"

The wise thing to do was to say yes, hang up, and call the

chief. When it comes to Charles, I don't always do the right thing, so instead of agreeing, I said, "You have a phone. Why didn't you call her?"

"The poor, misguided police chief thinks you are smarter and more sensible than yours truly. She'll tell you more than she'll tell me. Go figure."

"Charles, if I was all those things, I'd have better sense than to call the chief who's probably still at the park."

"See," Charles said, "I know none of those things are true, so that's why you should call her now. Besides, if she's still with the body, she'll be able to tell you more."

I once again asked myself why I didn't do the wise thing in the beginning. I told him I give up and hung up.

"Chris Landrum, what in the hell took you so long to butt into police business?" Chief LaMond said.

I hated caller ID. "Good morning, Cindy."

"Don't give me that morning cheery voice. My day went to hell before I had my second cup of coffee. I'm standing in the middle of a sandstorm. I've got a dead lass sitting in a car about ten feet from me. And now I must take time from my underpaid, overworked job to talk to one of my city's biggest nosy nellies."

I heard several voices in the background and the sound of a heavy truck engine. "Did I catch you at a bad time?"

Cindy laughed. "Really? You really asked that? What do you think?"

She hung up before I could respond. The answer to my question was yes.

Fifteen minutes later, the phone rang again. Gee, give me a break, Charles.

I was wrong, it wasn't Charles but someone who started with, "I saw this big hair, little brain news chick on TV jabbering about a death on your island. Who was she? What happened?"

For years, I had unsuccessfully tried to get friends to start phone conversations with pleasantries like "good morning" or with their name. Bob Howard was the perfect example of you can't teach old dogs new tricks. During his more than seven decades on this earth, the successful realtor had perfected rudeness, overbearingness, obnoxiousness, and most every profanity. Despite his drawbacks, almost too numerous to mention, he was a friend.

"Good afternoon, Bob. What do I owe the honor of this call?"

"Crap, Chris. You make sugar taste sour. Now answer my questions."

"How would I know who she was and what happened?"

"Shit, because you butt in anything weird that happens over there. Figured you'd have your nosy nose in the middle of this."

Before moving to Folly, my life could best have been described as staid, solid, and yes, boring. I went to work in a large, bureaucratic company, lived in a middle-class house in a middle-class subdivision, drove a middle-class car, had married my high-school sweetheart and we had stayed together for twenty years, childless, but had participated in most middle-class activities. Somehow when I moved across the Folly River to the city I now call home, my life turned upside down. Through luck, mostly bad, and being at the wrong place at the wrong time, I had stumbled into the middle of a murder, helped catch the killer, and while accumulating a cadre of characters, had helped the police solve several other unnatural deaths since then. In fact, Bob Howard had aided me more than once in bringing a killer to justice.

"Bob, all I know is what I saw on television; the same thing you saw. It has nothing to do with me. I'm not involved."

Bob cackled. "Not yet!"

CHAPTER TWO

I flicked off the TV, finished my sandwich, moved to the living room, and smiled about how both Bob and Charles assumed I would know something about the body found fewer than two miles from my small cottage. A few years ago, it would have never entered my mind to give more than a few seconds of thought to what happened. Yes, I had stuck my nose where it didn't belong a few times, but I only did it at the urging of Charles or when it involved a friend. While growing up and throughout my many years in Kentucky, I had paid a premium on friendships. I didn't have many close friends, two at the most, but not until I moved to Folly, and I suppose had matured and gotten a better perspective on my world, did I hold friendships as close as I do now. Seeing those friends in danger or in pain tugged at my heart and I knew unless I did something to lessen that danger or their pain, I was a failure. It led me to a few situations that I could easily have lost my life over, but I've never regretted getting involved.

A glance at the clock revealed I must have dozed. It was after three in the afternoon and my neck hurt from sleeping in the chair. I stood, stretched, and walked to the screened-in front porch. Several cars were parked in the small lot in front of Bert's Market, my neighbor on the right, and two large construction vans barreled past the house on Ashley Avenue, Folly's longest street that ran from the shuttered Coast Guard Station property on the east end, to the site of the death on the west.

To the left of my cottage was Brad and Hazel Burton's house. In a move that must have had the god of irony doubled over with laughter, the Burtons moved in next to me two years ago. Brad had been a thorn in my side for the five years before that when he had been a detective in the Charleston County Sheriff's Office. He accused me of murder my first month on the island and despite me helping the police catch the killer, he had been angry with me ever since. Every time I stuck my nose in police business, which was far more times than I had hoped to, Brad was on my case. For a time, he was partnered with Karen Lawson, the detective I had dated for several years, and I got better acquainted with the incompetent detective. To the elation of most of his colleagues, he had retired and moved next door. When he bought the house, he didn't know I would be his neighbor. When he found out, it was too late to back out and he had avoided me ever since moving in. For that, I was thankful.

Brad and Hazel's late model Chryslers were usually the only vehicles at the house, so I was surprised to see two Ford Crown Vics in the drive. I was even more surprised when I recognized the dark gray one as Chief Cindy LaMond's unmarked car. Several questions rushed through my mind. Was something wrong with one of the Burtons? Unlikely, since there were no emergency vehicles at their house, and if there had been an emergency call, members of the Folly Beach Department of Public Safety who served the dual role of police officers and fire fighters would have responded. So, no sirens, no flashing lights, no emergency. Could it have something to do with the death near the park? Was Cindy there to get retired detective Burton's help? That seemed remote, since she hadn't felt much better about Burton's competency as a detective than I had—which was next to none. Then, who did the other vehicle belong to? It could simply have been a black Crown Vic, unrelated to law enforcement. Brad and I were far from being best buds, so I wasn't about to knock on his door and ask. Let's hope Charles didn't see the cars there.

The official-looking vehicles were gone when I walked to Bert's to get supper. Eric, an affable employee, nearly ran into me as I walked through the double doors into the iconic grocery. He was carrying a stack of boxes and apologized for nearly running me down. He was stopped, so I asked if he knew what the chief was doing at the Burtons. Bert's is the go-to store for everything from beer to bait and was open twenty-four hours a day. If anyone wanted to know what was going on nearby, Bert's or the Lost Dog Cafe were the places to begin. They were hangouts for locals and nearly every vacationer who set foot on the island. I was surprised when Eric said he didn't know and hadn't noticed the cars, nor had Chief LaMond been in Bert's this afternoon. It made more sense when he said he had been in the back and this was the first time he'd seen daylight in the last three hours. He offered to ask around and let me know if he learned anything. I thanked him and said it wouldn't be necessary. My culinary skills were slightly lower than my skills at splitting the atom, so I grabbed a frozen pizza and a cheap bottle of Chardonnay. My cable television had inadvertently landed on the Cooking Channel a month ago, and in a fit of boredom, I spent a half hour watching some famous chef show how easy it was to fix some exotic recipe using the microwave. Perhaps old dogs could learn a few tricks, especially if they were easy, and I was now proficient in using my microwave. I had switched the television off before I was tempted to use my oven.

I figuratively patted myself on my back for mastering heating the pizza, took the last bite which was now cold and tasted a lot like a piece of cardboard slathered with ketchup and called Chief LaMond.

She answered on the third ring and said, "I win!"

"Win what?" I said, skipping my preferred greeting of "Hi, Cindy."

"Larry bet me ten bucks you wouldn't call until tomorrow. I said you'd be pestering me before the night was over. Poor boy will never learn."

Larry was Cindy's husband of six years and owner of Pewter Hardware, Folly's best—only—hardware store. I had known him since before he'd met Cindy and considered him a good friend.

"Congratulations, I suppose."

"Wonder when the little squirt will start believing everything I say," she said, and repeated, "Poor boy."

Larry weighed one hundred pounds, more or less, and was five foot one, but only Cindy could get away with saying anything about his diminutive size. And heaven forbid anyone use the word squirt around him unless they were referring to a toy that shoots water.

"Guess he's a slow learner," I said.

"You've made my night, Mr. Perceptive Nosy Resident. Wait until I tell him what you called him."

"I'll deny it. Now could we get to why I called?"

"Sure. I know you geezers are always afraid you'll die before you get to ask all your questions."

Since I had now reached the second half of my sixties, I consider geezer status not beginning until I reach my nineties. Cindy was still in her early fifties, but I didn't see any point in debating her.

"What were you doing at the Burtons this afternoon?"

"And I thought you called to invite Larry and me to supper, or here's another thought, you wanted to know the details about the body."

"I'll have my people check with your people about supper, and of course I want to know about the body, but…"

"The seriously deceased person happened to be a Ms. Lauren Craft, age 41. She had been in her most recent state of dead for two hours when found by a nearby resident headed to the park and its beach to find his fortune in the sand. Looks like a drug overdose, heroin would be my guess. There was a used hypodermic needle on the floorboard below her right hand."

"Are you sure it…"

Cindy interrupted my interruption, "I'm not finished."

"Sorry, proceed."

"That's more like it. I'm a big fan of citizens apologizing. Anyway, it appears Ms. Craft had been in and out of drug rehab facilities several times. My guys checked her address on East Ashley Avenue and were greeted by her two roommates. Umm, give me a sec." I heard paper rustling and Larry's voice in the background and Cindy said, "Sweetie, get out your wallet. Yes, it's Nosy Chris. Yes, I'm serious. Ten bucks, now." The phone clanked against something and Cindy said, "I'm back. The late Ms. Craft had two roommates, Candice Richardson and Katelin Hatchett. Candice works as a clerk in a Real Estate office in downtown Charleston; Ms. Hatchett said she's 'between jobs' which probably means she got fired from her last one. Think her former career was in the waitressing field."

"What did Lauren Craft do?"

"Other than take drugs and kill herself?"

I exhaled and didn't say anything.

Cindy took the hint. "Seems she didn't work. One of the roommates said they didn't know where she got her money. She never had a lot, but they said she didn't have a job."

"Are you sure it was an overdose?"

"Chris, to you every death is a murder. Gee, can't people die on their own? You don't need to get involved in everything."

"Just curious."

"Yeah, right. Anyway, it appears that way, but we won't know more until the autopsy is complete. Now to your first question, you know the one about me being next door."

"I remember, Cindy. I'm not so old that I'm forgetting everything."

"It wouldn't be hard to find some folks who would disagree. Anyway, here's the sad news. Lauren Craft was Brad and Hazel Burton's daughter."

CHAPTER THREE

O ther than being on the high side of nosy, Charles felt that if any of his friends learned anything he might have the slightest interest in knowing, the friend must tell Charles within a nanosecond of learning it. So the first thing I did after talking with Cindy was to call my friend.

After a dozen rings, I hit end call. Up until several months ago, Charles failing to answer was the norm. He had a phone in his apartment and unless he was there the call would have been wasted. He didn't have an answering machine and didn't own a cell phone until he and his long-term girlfriend, Heather, had moved to Nashville so she could pursue her dream: a career as a country music singer. She had been talked into moving to the country music capital of the universe by an agent who had heard her sing at an open-mic night. No one had ever compared Heather's voice to her idol Patsy Cline; truth be known, no one had ever compared it to the melodious singing voice of a snapping turtle, but nothing could deter her from trying. To say Heather and Charles's move to Nashville was a disaster would be a gross understatement. The highlights of the trip included Heather being arrested for killing her agent, her attempting to kill herself, and me nearly being murdered. I'll save the details for another time, but suffice to say, only two good things came from their move: Charles's cell phone purchase and Heather deciding they should move back home to Folly where she could pursue singing in front of far less discerning audiences. I hit redial and gave Charles one more chance to get the latest news. No luck. You can lead Charles to a phone, but you can't make him answer.

I tried again the next morning with better luck. Charles answered, and I began telling him what I had learned about the body in the park.

"Whoa!" he interrupted. "When did you find out?"

"Last night."

"Last night! That was hours ago. And you waited all those many hours to tell me? Why didn't you call me?"

I rest my case!

"Charles, I tried. I called twice but you didn't have your phone on."

"Excuses, excuses. Hmm, maybe I was sort of with Heather. We were…"

"More than I need to know. The point is I tried."

"Okay," Charles said. "Apology accepted. What'd you learn?"

I must have missed the apology; regardless, arguing with him would be like arguing with a jellybean. I told him the details Cindy had shared and who Lauren's parents were.

He hesitated and said, "You're kidding."

I assured him I wasn't.

"I didn't know he had a daughter."

"I didn't either," I said, "but I also don't know much of

anything about him other than he was a terrible detective, he can't stand me, and he lives next door."

"When are we going to go pay our respects?"

"Never, would be my first choice," I said.

"He's your neighbor. Because he hates you is no reason not to tell him, especially his wife, that you're sorry about their loss."

Charles was right, at least this time, and I told him we should probably wait until this afternoon or tomorrow. Charles said he had to make some deliveries for the surf shop and wouldn't be available until late afternoon. I thought the later the better and suggested tomorrow. He asked what time this afternoon would work. I sighed and said around six.

"I'll be at your house at five."

Charles hasn't owned a watch since I've known him, but time was one of his many quirks. He considers on time to be thirty minutes earlier than most mortals do and seldom fails to point out how late people were if they showed up on time. When he said he would be at the house at five, I assumed he thought it would take us a whopping half hour to walk from my house next door so we could arrive by five-thirty instead of six o'clock like I had suggested. Charles was Charles, love him or leave him. Until moving to Folly, I had been under the misunderstanding that appointed times equaled appointed times. I had adjusted to Charles time.

As sure as clockwork, I stepped out my front door at five o'clock and was greeted by Charles. It was in the upper eighties, but he wore a long-sleeve, navy blue T-shirt with a gold NYPD logo over the breast pocket. His usual attire included a long-sleeve college T-shirt or sweatshirt with a logo of the college mascot adorning the front. He didn't say it, but the NYPD shirt was his way of showing respect to Brad Burton, the former cop.

For reasons I had not been able to determine, the shirts were always long-sleeved, and he carried a handmade, wooden cane. Charles, at five-foot eight, was a couple of inches shorter than me and a few pounds lighter. He had shaven for today's sympathy visit, but still had stubble on his chin and with his unruly gray hair, could have been mistaken for a street person. Today he looked his best.

"Well, I see you're looking boring as usual," he said and pointed his ever-present cane at me.

My green polo shirt was adorned with nothing, and I had on light-weight tan slacks, and boat shoes. Most of my work life had required a coat and tie, and I seldom wore a message on my chest. Charles considered it boring, and to him it was, but it was me. The one thing that did surprise me about Charles was that he was carrying a clear vase with several flowers in it. They looked suspiciously like blooms from a landscaped area in the yard next to Charles's apartment.

"You didn't have to bring me flowers," I said.

"Ha, ha. They're for the Burtons."

As if I didn't know that. Regardless of their origin, it was a thoughtful gesture, but I wasn't about to acknowledge it.

"Want a beer?" I asked since I was in no hurry to visit my nemesis.

Charles looked at his watch-less wrist. "Guess we have time."

"Do they know we're coming?"

"No."

I chose not to comment further about having time and waved him in. He set the flowers on the front porch and followed me to the kitchen, grabbed a Bud Light from the refrigerator, took a large sip, and plopped down in one of the chairs at my kitchen table.

"Hear anything about Lauren's death?" I asked and poured a small glass of Chardonnay.

In a community of numerous rumor collectors, Charles was among the best. If he put half as many hours in something that paid as he does cajoling information—both fact and fiction—out of others, he would be one of the city's wealthiest citizens.

"Heather said she heard from one of the hairdressers at the salon that Lauren was dating someone over here."

In addition to being an aspiring singer, Heather was a psychic, or so she said, and made a living as a massage therapist at Milli's Salon.

I took a sip of wine and asked, "What's interesting about that?"

"The hairdresser has known Lauren for several years and while she's dated several guys, this was the first serious one."

"Who is he?"

"The hairdresser didn't know."

"Hear anything about her death?"

Charles looked at his wrist. "That's one of the reasons we're going next door."

Charles prided himself on being a private detective. That's using the terms loosely since he had zero training in the field and wouldn't qualify as a private detective in South Carolina, or any other state that had a semblance of qualifications for the profession. His rationale for being qualified was that he had watched countless police shows on TV and had read countless books involving private eyes. Charles was a voracious reader and owned more books than many small-town libraries. His imaginary profession had been bolstered over the last few years because he and I had stumbled, bumbled, and fell into several murders and through pure luck and a little skill, had helped the police catch some killers. Which brought me back to Brad

Burton and why he had such strong negative feelings about me, and probably Charles.

I nodded. "And I thought it was to express our sympathy to Lauren's parents."

"That too," Charles took a sip of beer, clinked his can down on the table, and pointed his cane toward the front door. "We're late."

I shook my head and followed him out.

CHAPTER FOUR

The Burtons had lived in their home for a brief period, but during that time they improved the exterior, both house and the landscape. Hazel spent hours planting flowers, rearranging landscape beds, and supervising a landscape company as it cut the grass on a regular basis. I had never seen Brad in the yard other than when he was showing a painting crew what he wanted done to the exterior. And, I never saw anyone visit. I would have sworn they didn't have any children, or at least none who lived nearby.

It only took us a couple of minutes to make the trip from my cottage to the Burtons' newly painted, attractive ranch house. It was larger than my cottage, and I had wondered how the Burtons could have afforded it on a detective's retirement. Charles knew my feelings about Brad and on the walk over suggested that the retired detective had mellowed since turning in his badge. Charles was an eternal optimist but was often eternally wrong. As we stepped on their recently painted concrete front porch, I hoped he was right, but didn't think there was a chance.

I took a deep breath, motioned for Charles to join me on the porch, knocked, and prayed Brad wasn't home.

Hazel opened the door and smiled. Her smile appeared sincere, but her bloodshot eyes told a different story. She was a few years younger than her husband, but the shock of the last twenty-four hours had aged her. She wore a black blouse and a dark gray skirt.

"Hi, Chris," She didn't appear to know what to do next. She added, "Umm, come in."

I reached out and gave her a hug. "I'm so sorry about Lauren."

She mumbled, "Thanks."

"Do you know my friend Charles Fowler?"

Charles stepped to my side and held out the vase.

Hazel glanced at the flowers and up at Charles. "Umm, we've not met. I have seen you around town.

Charles handed Hazel the flowers and looked like he didn't know if he should try to hug her or shake her hand. It was one of the few times I'd seen my friend indecisive. He said hello and expressed his sympathy.

Hazel smiled. "Gosh, I'm being rude. Please come in. Can I offer you something to drink, or perhaps something to eat? God knows we have more food in here than we could ever use. People are so sweet."

That was a sentiment I doubted her husband had ever uttered. I declined and said we didn't want to interrupt anything and wanted to say how sorry we were.

Charles looked at me and at Hazel. "A glass of something cold would be nice."

I gave him a dirty look as Hazel headed to the kitchen. I realized I had already forgotten his second reason for wanting to visit. As we waited for Hazel to return I looked around. The floors were a highly-polished, light colored hardwood and there were two colorful nautical-patterned area rugs covering much of the floor. The furniture was even a shade or two lighter than the floors. Two whitewashed chairs had bright blue and green cushions and a large side table had two large, pink and white conch shells in the center. The furnishings looked more like a high-end condo package rather than the furniture in a retired couple's house. A 56-inch flat-screen television sat on a chrome stand against the far wall. It was oversized for the room. Everything was neat, cheery, and nothing reminiscent of the rumpled, poorly attired detective I had come to dislike. In addition to the two conch shells, there were two photos in silver frames on the table. One was of a smiling couple with a young girl probably no more than six years old, the other of the same girl playing on a swing. I looked around and didn't see other pictures.

I heard Hazel saying something, and Brad responding in a louder voice. Hazel interrupted him and a moment later appeared in the doorway. "Chris, Charles, come on in. Brad would like to say hi."

I knew things were going too well. Charles said, "Sure," smiled and followed Hazel to the kitchen. I followed.

The blinds were closed and although the sun was shining, only filtered rays penetrated the room. If it wasn't for an overhead light, the room would have been dark. I was able to see new stainless appliances. On the granite counter there were three small cakes, a basket of fruit, two plastic bowls covered with aluminum foil, and a bundle of flowers in the sink. Hazel had been right about the kindness of people. A coffee pot was on the back of the counter and the aroma of day-old coffee lingered.

Hazel saw me staring at the flowers. "Several of Brad's former colleagues have already visited and brought the flowers and food. Are you sure you don't want something to eat?"

The kitchen was tiny for the size of the house and Brad was seated at a small, glass-top table within inches of us. He hadn't looked up or spoken.

We again declined food as Hazel handed Charles a Coke and offered me one. I said yes, mainly so I wouldn't appear rude.

I felt strange being this close to the retired detective without acknowledging his existence, and said, "Hi, Brad."

He gripped a coffee mug like it was trying to escape. He had always looked old to me but appeared much older today. His shoulders slumped, his hair, always unruly, was a mess, and his white dress shirt was untucked, wrinkled, and raveled at the cuffs. I felt sorry for him, until he spoke.

He pointed his mug at me. "What the hell are you doing here?"

Hazel interrupted, "Now sweetie." She put her hand on his shoulder. "Chris and Charles were kind enough to stop by to express condolences. And look, they brought flowers." She held the vase in front of her husband who was still seated.

"Crap, Hazel, just what we need, more damn flowers. Our daughter's gone, and we get flowers."

Hazel squeezed Brad's shoulder, I wanted to bolt out of the house, and Charles said, "You have a lovely house Mr. and Mrs. Burton."

Hazel smiled, and Brad looked at Charles like he wanted to put a bullet in his head.

"Brad," I said, "we're neighbors and when I heard the young lady who ... umm, was found dead was your daughter, I was heartbroken. Charles and I wanted to say how sorry we were."

Brad tightened his grip on the mug and twisted around to stare at me. "You mean the woman who offed herself with a drug overdose. You probably think it's funny. The old cop who spent his life putting bad people in jail has ... umm, had a damn kid who kills herself doing something her law-and-order dad hated, despised." He looked down at the table. "The kid who's been in and out of drug rehab facilities. The kid who ... oh shit, please get the hell out of here. Leave me alone."

Hazel let go of Brad's shoulder. She moved toward the door and motioned for Charles and me to follow. I wanted to say something else to the grieving father but knew this wasn't the time. We followed Hazel to the living room.

She shook her head. "Gentlemen, I apologize for my husband. Brad's grieving, or the best he can do. He's torn up. He's never handled emotions well. And when it comes ... came to Lauren, he ... well, you saw how he is."

"We understand," Charles said.

Hazel looked toward the kitchen. "The minute Brad retired, we sold our house in North Charleston and moved to Folly because Lauren lived here. Brad thought if we were closer we may be able to help her. She'd just got out of a horrible marriage from Sebastian Craft and was a mess." She looked at the ground and then up at me. "At first we thought we were helping. With the drugs, and everything. We thought we were helping." She faked a smile. "Anyway, Brad didn't mean anything personal in there."

I doubted that, but said, "That's okay, Hazel. We understand. Thanks for the drinks and again, we are so sorry. Let me know if there is anything you need."

She said she would and saw us out.

On the way to the house, Charles said, "Well, that went well."

That wouldn't have been my take, but I didn't say anything. Charles said he had a date with Heather and I was glad to hear it was at a barbecue restaurant on Folly Road about five miles from the island. Until Charles and Heather moved to Nashville earlier this year, neither had a vehicle that used anything other than pedal power. Before they moved, Charles bought a used Toyota Venza and now that they had returned to the island they should have never left, he had rediscovered the world of restaurants, shops, and sights off island; locations to which I had previously been his primary chauffeur. I encouraged him to explore without me. I was glad he didn't ask if I wanted to go since I had planned to meet Barb when she got off work and knew she would be exhausted and wouldn't want to go anywhere off island. Before he left, he told me I'd better call if I learned anything about Lauren's death. He held up his cell phone as if I wouldn't know how to let him know.

CHAPTER FIVE

I'd met Barbara Deanelli six months ago under less than ideal circumstances. I happened to stumble on a body splayed out in the alley near the back door to Barb's Books. Things tumbled downhill from there. First, Barb moved her used bookstore into the space I had rented for several years while trying to make a go of Landrum Gallery, a shop featuring my photographs. As hard as I found it to comprehend, the fine citizens of Folly and the thousands of vacationers the island attracted each year failed to appreciate the fine artistic images that I had for sale. Oh sure, many said they liked the photos and some bought a few, but overall, they decided they would rather spend their hard-earned money on luxuries like rent, gas, electric, taxes, cell phones, and the latest iWhatever. Go figure.

Even though I had closed the business before Barb came to town, I resented her from before we'd even talked. And when we met I found her aloof and appearing, for lack of a better term, snooty. Add to that the fact many suspected her to be the murderer. As is the case with many things on Folly, appearances don't tell the whole story. After several conversations leaning toward the cold side, either she had begun to warm toward me, owing to my charm, I hoped; more likely, it was because I'd saved her life and managed to catch the person who was willing to stop at nothing to kill her. Regardless, we started seeing each other on a semi-regular basis. We enjoyed each other's company, and if I was honest with myself, it was great to be able to enjoy time with someone other than Charles.

I met Barb for supper at the Folly Beach Crab Shack, one of several popular restaurants on Center Street, the island's six-block long primary commercial district. Charles's time obsession had rubbed off on me. I arrived at the colorfully painted Crab Shack fifteen minutes before Barb said she could get there. I was seated at the last vacant table on the deck overlooking the street and the variety of pedestrians taking in the sights and sounds of the island.

Barb spotted me as she turned the corner to the restaurant's entrance and headed my way. She wore tan shorts and one of her trademark red blouses. She weaved her way through the restaurant and out the door to the patio. Her hazel eyes gleamed as she pointed to the container of peanuts I put in front of her chair. I envied her metabolism. It seemed like she could eat all she wanted and remain thin. She was my height at five-foot-ten and looked younger than her sixty-four years. Her short black hair was also in contrast to my rapidly balding, blond turning gray head.

I stood and pecked her on the cheek; she grabbed a peanut and looked around for someone to order a drink. Elizabeth, one of the restaurant's personable employees, was nearby and Barb ordered a beer.

"Rough day in the book selling business?" I asked as Barb cracked open the peanut shell.

"You know how much I can't stand romance novels."

I nodded.

"About 11,000 customers stomped in today and 'just had to have' something by Danielle Steel, Barbara Taylor Bradford, Nora Roberts, or blah, blah, blah. My head started thumping by three o'clock."

I laughed. "You're complaining to the wrong person about 11,000 customers. I would have been thrilled if eleven customers had ever graced the door in one day during the time your building housed Landrum Gallery."

She reached across the table and petted my hand. "That's probably because you didn't have photos of Danielle Steel."

"True," I said as the waitress set a bottle of Budweiser in front of Barb. It didn't stay on the table long.

"Enough about my day. What's happening in your world?"

"Glad you asked," I said. "Did you hear about the body they found near the county park?"

"Between requests for Judith McNaught and Julia Quinn gooey romances, someone mentioned it. Something about a drug overdose." She flipped a peanut shell in a blue pail in the center of the table. "Why?"

I explained about who she was and who her father was.

"You've mentioned him. You're not his biggest fan, right?"

"That's an understatement," I said, and proceeded to share some of my history with the retired detective.

Barb was an attorney but had given up a lucrative practice in Pennsylvania and a husband that went with it when he was arrested for bribing state officials. She didn't know anything about his illegal activities and was exonerated of any wrongdoing but felt the need to leave that world behind and moved to Folly. She used the listening and questioning skills she had learned in law school and had honed through her practice. She interrupted a couple of times with questions, but listened, something I wasn't used to from my other friends.

I shared much of today's conversation with Brad.

"Not the kind of reception you would have liked, I suppose."

"Hazel was as sweet as could be, considering the circumstances. Brad was an ass. I thought since he was retired and my next-door neighbor, he'd have mellowed."

Barb grabbed another peanut, deposited the shell in the bucket, and started to pop the peanut in her mouth, but hesitated and pointed the nut at me. "Did you ever think he was angry at the world and not only at you? People close to suicide or drug overdose victims often feel guilty. They think there must have been something they could have done to prevent it. He could also be embarrassed about what happened. He'd been a cop, yet he couldn't prevent whatever happened to his daughter."

"I suppose that's ..."

Barb interrupted. "One more thing. While he lashed out at you, it may not have been personal. You were a handy target for his emotions."

"Barb, those are good points, and I would like to give him the benefit of the doubt, but with our fractured, and often hostile, history, it's hard to do."

Barb smiled. "Give the man a chance. You never know."

I returned her smile. "Okay."

"Now with that out of the way, are we going to order food or are you going to sit there and watch me shrivel up and blow away?"

There was little chance of that happening, especially if there was an unlimited supply of peanuts, but I got the waitress's attention and we each ordered a fried fish basket and another drink.

I realized my stomach was still in knots from thinking about my history with Brad Burton and how my recent conversation with him had dredged up the memories I had mostly put out of my mind. Time to change the subject.

"Heard from Dude lately?" I asked.

Jim "Dude" Sloan was Barb's younger stepbrother, and owned the surf shop, one of Folly's stores catering to the significant population of surfers and surfer wannabes. He was a long-time resident of Folly and had encouraged Barb to move here after her divorce.

"He called a couple of nights ago. Said he was wondering if I was still doing okay, of course he didn't use those words. I think his quote was, "Fractional-sis be OK?""

Dude was as opposite from Barb as a magnolia tree was to poison ivy. Both were living things, but that was about it. Dude had never met a sentence he couldn't mangle. He treated words as if they were gold and shared as few of them as he could. Charles had sworn—partly in jest—that Dude had come to Earth from another planet, and I think he was disappointed when Barb confirmed Dude, in fact, was from Earth, more accurately Altoona, Pennsylvania.

"Did you tell him that you be good?"

She rolled her eyes—a motion of endearment, or so I wanted to believe. "Sort of."

"He say anything else?"

"After I said I was fine, he said something in surfer talk that I think meant good and hung up."

Our food arrived, preceded by the strong aroma of frying fish. Barb had taken a bite before I reached for my fork. Eleven-thousand customers heightened her appetite.

"I know you don't want to talk more about Brad and the death of his daughter," Barb said between bites, "but let me ask you one more question. Is there a possibility the death could have been more than an accidental overdose or suicide?"

I was surprised by her question. "Why do you ask?"

"No reason. From my experience, most deaths like this one are treated as if there could be more than the obvious. I know you have connections with the police and would probably know how they were looking at it."

"Cindy, Chief LaMond, told me it looked like an overdose, but wouldn't know more until she had the coroner's report. I'll let you know when I hear anything."

Barb cocked her head. "You don't talk like you're convinced it was accidental."

I gave a slight nod. "It probably was, considering her history with drugs. Besides, the police will figure it out. It's none of my business."

She looked up from her plate. "Um hum."

Honest, I thought.

I walked Barb to her condo in the Oceanfront Villas complex and slowly walked home. I stepped in my living room when my cell rang. I was surprised to see Brian Newman's name on the screen.

"Good evening, Brian."

"I'm beginning to see why you hate caller ID," he said.

I started with something polite and appropriate, not like most of my friends who feel they must start phone conversations with … oh well, never mind. "To what do I owe the pleasure of hearing your voice?"

"I wish more of your fellow citizens had your attitude. You know how many bitchy, complaining, irritated calls I receive?'

"Mr. Mayor, you want me to guess?"

"No, but it's a bunch. When I was police chief, I had a staff to hand off most of the complaints to. As mayor, the buck stops here."

"Public service," I said, still not knowing why the mayor had called. But I also knew him well enough to not push.

"Listen," he said, "I hate to call so late. It's almost your bed time but wanted to know if you could meet me in the morning for breakfast."

"Sure," I said. "Where and when?"

"The Dog, 7:00 o'clock."

"I'll be there."

He said thanks and was gone. And I still had no idea why he had called. What I did know was that it was important.

CHAPTER SIX

The Lost Dog Cafe is a block off Center Street and most days it was the epicenter of early-morning activity on Folly Beach. It was cool for August, so the mayor was inside. His hands were wrapped around a coffee mug as he was reading today's newspaper. Amber, my favorite waitress, had her back to me and was leaning over Brian's shoulder and looking at the page he was holding. I had known Amber since my first week on the island and we dated for a time. After we stopped dating, she remained a good friend and one of the best sources of information—fact and fiction—about most anything Folly.

I patted her on the shoulder and she jerked back.

"Sorry I startled you," I said.

"Chris, you gave my old heart a scare."

Old wasn't a word I would use with Amber. She was approaching fifty but still looked in her early forties. The only person I'd ever heard referring to her as old was Jason, her nineteen-year-old son; but to him, everyone over forty was about ready to kick the bucket.

"A bit jumpy this morning?"

"Brian was showing me this story about that guy who killed three members of his own family. Can you believe that?"

"Sorry. Yes, it was terrible."

"Hmm!" interrupted Brian. "Umm, Chris, I'm here too. Remember me, I'm the person who asked you to breakfast."

"Sure," I said and put my arm around Amber's waist. "But, she's much better looking."

"You're still my favorite mayor," Amber said as she leaned over and kissed the top of Brian's head. "I'll leave you two to your confab. Chris, coffee?"

I said, "Duh!"

Amber headed to the kitchen and past the nearly countless dog photos that dotted the walls of the restaurant like spots on a Dalmatian. Brian motioned for me to sit at the other side of the table. The tall, trim, and confident mayor leaned back in the chair and looked around to see who was nearby. With short black, but graying, hair, he oozed military which made sense since he had been in the armed forces before retiring after thirty years.

"Thanks for joining me."

"Glad you called."

"I suppose you're wondering why I asked you here."

I shrugged. "It did enter my mind."

Brian looked around again. No one appeared to be paying attention to us. "Chris, I'm going to run for reelection."

That was no surprise. He was in his early seventies but had unwavering enthusiasm for his job and the island, and although he was thrust into the position when his predecessor had slinked out of state after some untowardly information was revealed, the role fit him like a wetsuit. I was however surprised by how early he was making the decision.

"That's great but isn't the election next April, what, almost eight months from now?"

Amber arrived with my coffee and asked if I was ready to order. I ordered French toast, my favorite Dog breakfast item, and Amber shook her head but said she'd get it started. She had been on a one-person crusade to get me to eat better but had conceded defeat.

Brian watched her go, and said, "I know that's a long time from now, but rumors are that there will be at least one well-financed opponent, and maybe a couple more. If I want to stay on the job, I need to get an early start."

"Who's running against you?"

"Do you know Joel Hurt?"

"The landscape guys?"

Brian nodded.

"I've seen him a couple of times at Bert's and it seems like Hurt's Landscape trucks are always running around town."

Brian took a sip of coffee and said, "He has more than a landscape service. He owns the three Lowcountry Garden Centers, the one on Folly Road near the cutover to Charleston, one past Mt. Pleasant on the way to Georgetown, and one in North Charleston. He also owns a large nursery."

"I didn't know the garden centers were his."

"Not many do."

"Sounds like he's successful."

"Very. Not only will he throw a lot of his personal wealth to the campaign, but he'll have the support of several well heeled locals who want to run off our more, let me say, bohemian residents, and especially the college students who flock to the beach on weekends and during the summer. *Sanitize the island* is a phrase I've heard some of his supporters are whispering about."

"Take the folly out of Folly."

Brian nodded, and Amber arrived with my unhealthy breakfast. I thanked her, and she rolled her eyes when she said, "Enjoy."

"Chris, I know Folly's not perfect. We all know in season there are many weekends, and now an increasing number of weekdays, when more and more people swarm to the beach than there's room for their vehicles. I'm not blind to the fact that inconsiderate day-trippers flagrantly violate the law against drinking on the beach, throw their trash in yards, and don't hesitate to share their loud opinions of most anything. Hell, when I was police chief, I dealt with it every day."

"True."

"I'm not defending anyone who commits a lawless act or infringes on the personal space or property of others, but I don't want our small slice of heaven to become a Kiawah Island or a place where a visitor needs a passport and a good conduct medal to be allowed to enter. Our island has a long history of being tolerant of people of all shapes, sizes, colors, and views on life. We have always been inclusive, and I don't want that to end."

It sounded like a campaign speech and still didn't tell me what he wanted me to do, so I said, "I agree."

Brian took another sip of coffee and I took a bite of French toast. I waited for him to say something, but when he didn't, I said, "Brian, you're respected, have done an excellent job as mayor, and are popular. Does Joel have a chance?"

"Many will call him a dark horse candidate, but he scares me. He and his supporters have the money to make a difference. You know the local races usually don't involve mega-bucks." He looked down at his mug and chuckled. "In past elections, some of the council candidates have considered it obscene if they had to spend more than pocket change and they stuck a few God-awful looking yard signs in some yards, and that was it."

"Don't remind me of that yard clutter."

"This is going to be different. Rumors are Joel is holding hush-hush meetings with potential supporters and getting commitments from them to use their influence to get as many people as they can to contribute to his campaign, and these people have money. Understand, I don't have anything against Joel Hurt. In fact, I think he's a nice guy and from what I can see, he's sincere. I think we could be friends even though we have drastically different ideas about what's good for Folly. Unfortunately, some of his supporters and donors have more drastic, and I believe harmful, ideas about what Folly should become."

Brian tilted his head and stared at me like he wanted me to say something.

"So, what can I do?"

"There's one more thing," Brian said, sidestepping my question. "I'm not the only one with a target on his back. They're going after Marc and Houston."

Marc Salmon and Houston Bass were two long-term council members. They were on the council when I moved to Folly. I didn't know Houston well, but was more familiar with Marc. The two met daily in the Dog, and I was a little surprised they weren't here now. Marc tried to tell those who happened to ask that he met Houston to discuss city business, but from what I could tell, their main goal was to gather as much gossip as possible. Marc would pass on facts, but gossip was his forte.

"Why them?"

"The misconception that they vote for anything I tell them to."

"Who'll be running against them?"

"No idea, but you can be assured whomever it is will have money behind them."

"Great."

The Dog was full, and the sounds of happy diners seemed louder than usual. Brian looked around and again, no one appeared to be paying attention to us.

"Now to your question. One of my biggest flaws as a candidate is asking for money." He laughed. "I suck at it. I know it's important, but so far, I haven't had to go far down that road. That's changing and is the reason I'm starting my campaign early."

I wasn't wealthy. In fact, my failed photo gallery drained a sizable chunk of my life savings, but unless I live to reach triple digits, I should have enough money to live if not comfortably, at least adequately. Brian knew this, so I wondered what could be coming next.

"Bottom line, Chris, is I need to raise far more than I ever have needed to win reelection. I'd like your help."

"Brian, I'll contribute what I can."

"Thanks, you don't know how much I appreciate that, but I'd like to ask more."

"What?"

"To host a couple of fundraisers."

I started to laugh, but saw he was serious. Before retiring and moving to Folly, I had attended a few political fundraisers. The events were usually held at the homes of some of the wealthiest people in my hometown. Most of those in attendance were recognizable and were some of the wealthiest leaders in the community. I was invited because I worked for one of the city's largest employers and was expected to make contributions to candidates the company felt could help their business. I had a good salary and could contribute without cutting too far in my savings. But even then, my contributions were limited to the lower end of the amounts expected.

"Brian, you know most of my friends well enough to know they're not rolling in dough."

He laughed, "You mean Charles, Cal, and Mel don't have gold bars buried in their back yards?"

"Brian, they don't even have back yards."

"True, but you forgot to mention your successful real estate buddy Bob Howard. And how about Barb, that lovely lady who for some strange reason has decided to date you? Then, despite outward appearances, Dude, your other good friend who has more money than probably all the rest of us combined."

He had a good point, although I had never looked at it like that. A few of my friends could probably make significant contributions. Brian had also never asked me for anything and if I could do something, however minor, to help, I would.

"Okay," I said. "I'm in. Let's talk about it."

And we did. Brian had already given it a lot of thought and we decided two distinctly different events would be best: one on Folly with my closest friends, and one in Charleston, and hopefully at Bob Howard's house where some of the wealthier donors could be invited. All I had to do was to convince Bob. Brian agreed it would be no simple task but appreciated that I would try.

Brian relaxed after he made it through the part of running for office that he was most uncomfortable with, so I took the opportunity to get into another difficult topic. "Now that that's out of the way, have you learned anything new about the death of Brad Burton's daughter?"

His smile turned to a frown. "No, why?"

"Curious. Charles and I visited the Burtons and it was still on my mind."

His eyes narrowed. "Everything points to an unfortunate drug overdose. Tragic, but it happens. Is there some reason you think it may be something more?"

"No, like I said, I was curious."

"Yeah, right. You're not planning on sticking your nose where it doesn't belong?"

"Of course not. There's no reason for me to get involved, there's nothing to get involved with."

Brian took the final sip of coffee and shook his head. "Chris, you need to get some business cards that say: *I'm not going to get involved.* On the other side: *Kidding.*"

CHAPTER SEVEN

I spent most of the time on the six-block walk from the Dog to my house trying to figure out how Brian had convinced me to organize not one but two fundraisers for his campaign coffers. The answer simply came down to friendship. Many island residents had befriended me, and I had reciprocated. Finally, I came to the realization there weren't many things more important than true friendship. Granted, it had nearly gotten me killed on more than one occasion, but my deep bonds with a handful of people were worth it. My thoughts were transitioning from the theoretical to the tasks necessary to pull together the fundraisers when I bumped into Hazel Burton on the sidewalk in front of Mr. John's Beach Store.

"Sorry, Hazel," I said and stepped aside.

She looked better than the last time I saw her, but her eyes were still bloodshot and her cheeks had a slight red tone from crying.

"That's okay, Chris. I was walking and not paying attention to where I was going."

I smiled. "That makes two of us."

"Thanks again for stopping by the house."

"Sorry it was under such terrible circumstances."

"Are you in a hurry," she said.

"No, just had breakfast and was heading home."

She looked in the direction I was going and turned back to me. "There's something I wanted to tell you. Care to walk?"

Since she put it that way, even if there was somewhere I needed to be, I would have gone with her.

I moved in step beside her, wondered where she was going, but didn't say anything. She had a need to talk and that was okay with me. I thought she was going to the Dog, but instead she turned into the small park beside the combination library and community center and led me to a bench overlooking a nicely landscaped area. The bench was shaded so the temperature was comfortable. I waited.

After an awkward silence that felt like it had lasted for hours, she looked at the Lost Dog Cafe located on the adjacent property, and said, "Nice place. Brad and I like eating there."

I agreed and said it was where I had had breakfast. I didn't think she brought me over here to say that, so I waited for her to continue.

"How long have you lived here?" she asked at the end of the long pause.

"Almost nine years."

"Oh yeah," she said, "I remember Brad telling me about meeting you. Out at the end of the island overlooking the lighthouse, wasn't it?"

I nodded. "A bad day. I stumbled on a man who'd been shot. Detective Burton, umm, Brad, and Detective Lawson were investigating."

Hazel looked at me and grinned. "Brad thought you were the killer."

I told her more about my unpleasant encounter with her husband and tried to make light of a traumatic and sad occurrence. She listened but seemed distracted. I ended the story as quickly as possible and hoped she'd get to her reason for us being here.

Hazel looked at the ground. "I'm not going to tell Brad I talked to you."

I nodded but didn't ask why.

"To be honest, Chris, my husband doesn't take too kindly to you."

Duh, I thought.

She chuckled, "He thinks you're a nosy, busybody who can't help but stick your nose into anything bad that happens."

I smiled. "Looking from his perspective, I see where he's right. I have been way too involved in several situations that should have been handled by the police, but most of the time, I'd been sucked in by friends, and to be honest, the police weren't always doing their best to solve the crimes."

"That's what Brad said."

I was surprised her husband would admit the police weren't being effective.

I started to say something about it, but she held her hand up and motioned for me to stop. "When Lauren was a little girl up through much of her teens, Brad was always working. He was trying to prove he could be a good cop and I suppose it paid off since he was promoted to detective. He missed most of her school activities. She was a cheerleader and acted in several school plays, but Brad only made it to one play, and seldom got to see her cheer." Hazel blinked a couple of times and looked at the ground. "He feels guilty about not being there …. umm, he really does."

"A lot of men go through the same thing," I said. "I can't imagine what a demanding job being a cop can be. And the family almost always suffers."

"Lauren got hooked on pills while she was in high school. I was married to a cop, but I was sheltered from the serious stuff that goes on in the world. Chris, I didn't know anything about her drug abuse until the school principal called me to come get her. She had been in a math class and started acting strange. She gave me a story about someone giving her one pill to take and that she didn't know what it was. Said she'd never done anything like it before. Brad was working a double homicide and didn't get home that night. Stupid me, I bought her story and didn't tell Brad the next day."

"You wanted to believe her," I said.

"Mistake number one," Hazel said. "And that was only the beginning. Her use—abuse—got so bad we had to place her in an outpatient rehab program. We didn't want to disrupt her life more than we had to. That was mistake number two. She was getting therapy, but she was still in a toxic environment with her friends. Temptations were too strong. Poor Brad kept kicking himself. Kept saying he was in the business of catching the bad guys and trying to make life safer for everyone, and in his own house he had a daughter who was using and probably laughing at him behind his back. It tore him up. It hurt his home life; screwed up his work life. I'm embarrassed to say it almost broke up our marriage."

I remembered Chief LaMond had said Lauren had been in and out of rehab facilities, so I knew the answer to my next question but wanted to hear it from Hazel.

"What happened then?"

Hazel wiggled her hand back and forth. "We thought things were getting better. I suppose they were, but it didn't last. She graduated from high school and was trying to take classes at the community college. She had a waitressing job and managed to rent a small apartment. A patrol officer pulled her over in the middle of the night. Her car was weaving all over the road, and … Christ, Brad would kill me if he knew I was telling you this. The cop was certain Lauren was under the influence of something, but instead of hauling her in, he called Brad who dragged himself out of bed and picked her up where the patrol officer was waiting. Brad brought her home and we got her car the next day. By now she wasn't even trying to lie about what was going on. We got her committed to a residential facility through a contact Brad had with the director."

"Did it help?"

"For a while. She stayed with us a few weeks after they felt she was in good enough shape to be out on her own. She said the people who were a bad influence on her were in Charleston and she persuaded us she needed to get a little farther away and had met some women who rented a house over here. It wasn't six months later that the cycle began all over again. That's when Brad decided to retire, and we bought the house next to yours, so we could be closer to her. To make the story a little shorter, she went back in rehab, stayed until they felt she was better, and moved back in with the girls over here." Hazel hesitated and stared into space. A tear rolled down her face. "We thought she'd kicked it. We moved here, were able to see her every few days, and she seemed better than she had in high school before it all began. Chris, we thought she'd kicked it."

"I'm sorry."

She wiped the tear away and tried to smile. "Sorry to dump this on you. All I wanted to do was apologize about the way Brad treated you when you came to visit. The thing is, he feels responsible, he feels guilty, he's angry with himself, and took it out on you. It wasn't anything personal. I want you to know that."

I understood how Brad must be feeling and didn't doubt it was taking a toll on him, but I thought she was wrong about me. It was personal, but I didn't see any benefit of getting into it.

"I understand and again, I'm terribly sorry about what both of you are having to deal with."

She reached over and gently touched my arm. "Thank you. You're easy to talk to; I didn't mean to spill this on you. Thank you for listening."

"No need to thank me. Please let me know if there's anything I can do."

"I will."

"Would you like me to walk you home?"

"Thanks, but no. I'm going to walk around some more before I head home. There is one thing you could do. Please don't let Brad know we had this talk."

You can bet on that, I thought, and said I wouldn't.

CHAPTER EIGHT

I hadn't given much thought to the Burtons or their daughter's untimely death since my conversation with Hazel three days ago. The routine chores of life had taken much of my time. I had written my check for homeowners' insurance and went through my annual rant about how it was three times more than I had ever paid in Kentucky. I spent an additional hour praising myself for the wise decision to move to the ocean, or as some would say, my rationalization for the excessive cost of insurance. I also remembered how thankful I had been to have insurance when a hurricane had nearly ripped my home off its foundation a few years ago. Then there was grocery shopping, an exhausting event that I do at least once a month, whether I needed to or not. That ate up a couple more hours. Finally cleaning the inside of my cottage, something I don't do as often as I go grocery shopping, took up another half day. The total of hours I spent on these activities didn't add up to three days, but it seemed like it. If I admitted it to myself, reaching the latter stages of my sixties added more hours of rest and naps to fill the time I had to do other things during earlier years. Many of those hours had been taken up with my career, so regardless how I look at it, I'd chosen retirement and aging, naps, and exhaustion came with it.

I realized after I had wasted three days with the mundane chores of life, that the autopsy results from Lauren Burton should be available, and I hadn't heard from Chief LaMond. I put my broom in the closet, told it I'd see it again in a month or so, and punched Cindy's number in my phone.

"Thought you were dead," the chief said as way of a pleasant greeting.

"Don't think so."

'It's been three days since you've pestered me about Lauren Craft's death. You already cost me the ten bucks I won from Larry. I went double or nothing with him that you would've been on my case two days ago. You owe me big time."

I smiled thinking how great it was to have friends like Cindy. "Okay, I'll buy you a cup of coffee the next time I see you. It should—"

"Cup of coffee?" she interrupted. "You mean a meal."

"Okay, so have you—"

"With dessert."

"Okay, okay."

"Good. Now if you're interested, I have the autopsy results."

I waited for her to continue.

"Aren't you going to ask what they are?"

"Didn't think I had to."

"You better be glad I'm in a good mood, Mr. Nosy Citizen. You can thank Larry for that, and no, it's none of your danged business why." She chuckled. "You do know nowhere in my job description does it say I have to give confidential information to you?"

"An obvious oversight."

She sighed. "You want to hear what I know or pretend that you're back being an overpaid HR bigwig writing job descriptions?"

"I'd love to hear what you learned, Chief LaMond."

"That's better." I heard papers rustling and Cindy continued, "Ms. Craft has joined Janis Joplin, River Phoenix, John Belushi, and Philip Seymour Hoffman with a common mode of demise, an overdose of heroin. She also had enough alcohol in her blood stream to pickle a bull elephant."

"No surprise there," I said, more to myself than to Cindy.

"No, but while that's the official cause of death, it still doesn't answer how or why."

"Doesn't a needle found on the floorboard answer how?"

"Sort of," Cindy said. "The OD was administered with that needle, but did she squeeze it into her vein willingly? Was it an accident or did she know what she was doing? Was she so drunk she only vaguely knew what was going on."

"Suicide?"

"Possibly."

"What's that mean?"

Cindy said, "Could someone else have injected her or made her inject herself?"

I was confused. "Were her prints on the needle?"

"Good question. Yes."

I was still confused. "Why would there be any question about her doing it?"

"A couple of things. Want to guess what, Mr. Faux Detective?"

"That's Charles, not me."

"If you say so. Guess anyway."

"Where her car was found isn't near where she lived. Do we know if she drove to where she was found?" I asked.

"Excellent question. We think she did."

"Were her prints on the steering wheel or the door handle?"

"Even better questions. The answers are yes and yes."

I was beginning to feel like I was on a quiz show and about to lose a zillion dollars because I didn't know the right questions to ask. What was I missing? There had to be something or Cindy wouldn't be playing 20 questions.

"Were there prints on the passenger side door?"

"Bingo!" the chief said.

"No prints."

"Clean as, as … umm, something really clean."

"So, no prints?"

"There were some smudges, but no clear prints, no dirt, hell, no bird crap, no nothing," she said.

"Was the rest of the car clean?"

"Not dirty, probably had been washed recently, but there was dust on it." Cindy paused. "You can't park where it was in the sandy berm without some grimy ocean crap landing on it."

"So, you think it was wiped clean which would mean someone may have been with her when she died and skedaddled before she was found?"

"No way to prove that. It's possible the EMTs rubbed their hands on it when entering the car."

"If they did, would it have been as clean as you found it?" I asked.

"Don't think so, but it's possible since they wore those cute blue gloves. It's also possible someone may have stumbled on the car, looked inside, saw the highly deceased Ms. Craft, panicked and wiped the handle clean, before hightailing it so he, or to be politically correct, she could avoid being questioned. That seems unlikely to me."

"Are you thinking she was killed and someone wanted it to look like an overdose?"

"That's a possibility, but it could also mean someone was shooting up with her and when she accidentally overdosed didn't want to get caught. We coppers look askance at our fine citizens shooting heroin along a city street, especially if they're found sitting beside one of our former fine citizens."

"True. You said there were two things that raised questions."

"The other thing might not mean anything, but it strikes me as odd. Lauren had apparently been in and out of rehab facilities several times, all for heroin use."

"So, her death shouldn't be a surprise."

"I agree, but the medical examiner said the fatal needle mark was the only recent mark on her. It'd been a long time since she'd used, or at least injected."

"Couldn't she still have misjudged the strength and taken a fatal dose?"

"Yes, but from my experience with addicts, they have to be mighty high to make that mistake. All I'm saying, Chris, is that it seems strange."

"What happens next?"

"It's in the hands of the Sheriff's Office. They'll be conducting an investigation, if there is one."

Folly Beach is in Charleston County, and the Charleston County Sheriff's Office is charged with investigating major crimes on the island. Cindy's staff is limited in size and experience in dealing with most deaths but handles most other infractions and the daunting task of traffic, particularly during vacation season.

"Do they agree it seems strange?"

"They're giving lip service to it, but their plate is full, and I wonder how much actual investigating they'll be doing. It's still an open case and Detective Ken Adair is working it."

I knew Detective Adair from another death I got stuck in the middle of. He considered my friend Mel Evans as the prime suspect in a murder, but Charles and I stuck our noses in the case enough to prove Mel wasn't guilty. I almost got killed in the process, but that's another story. Other than that error in the detective's judgment, he appeared to be a good cop. But, I also knew his workload, as it was for all detectives with the office, was overwhelming.

"So, what are you doing?" I asked.

"Keeping my eyes open, talking to everyone who knew her here, and praying."

CHAPTER NINE

I also hadn't heard from Charles the last three days. Since he has a mode of transportation that didn't depend on pedal power, he had spent hours exploring the many sights of interest in and around Charleston. I know because he felt the need to tell me about every place he visited, including its location, historical significance, and mound of trivia surrounding it.

He answered on the third ring.

"Well, well," he said. "Have you returned from the dead?"

"You been talking to Cindy?"

"No. Why?"

"Never mind. Available for lunch?"

"Depends."

"On what?" I said and realized I had nearly forgotten why I'd called.

"Where you're buying."

"Yogurt, Kangaroo Express."

"Shucks, Chris, my calendar's crammed full."

"Fish sandwich, the Grill."

"Whoa, look here, a spot just opened up. Noon. Bye."

That meant eleven-thirty and I surprised myself when I arrived at the Grill and Island Bar five minutes before Charles-time. The Grill was on Center Street and was one of the small island's largest restaurants. I was a regular at its Thursday evening performances by the Folly Beach Bluegrass Society, a collection of talented bluegrass musicians who converge on the restaurant to share their love for traditional bluegrass music with enthusiastic audiences. There was no live entertainment today, but the smell of fried flounder greeted me and made me realize I hadn't eaten.

I was seated on the patio overlooking Folly's main drag when Charles rounded the corner from his apartment three blocks away. He wore a gold, long-sleeve T-shirt with the outline of a buffalo and UC in the center.

"See you're on time for a change," he said, making me wonder about the wisdom of inviting him to lunch in the first place. He continued, "It's Ralphie, University of Colorado's mascot. Most think it looks like a dude buffalo but it's a chick."

"Fascinating," I said.

"Thought you'd think so. I love learning new stuff," he said, not catching or simply ignoring my sarcasm. "John Quincy Adams said, 'Old minds are like horses; you must exercise them if you wish to keep them in working order.'"

Another of Charles's quirks was quoting U.S. Presidents, or he claimed they're actual quotes. Of all my priorities, verifying the source would be at the bottom of my list next to doing the backstroke in boiling motor oil.

"Good to see you, Charles," I said, trying to interject civility into the conversation.

"Guess where I was this morning?" he asked as he threw his

Tilley hat on the bench seat beside him and carefully placed his cane on the concrete floor.

"Lisbon, North Dakota."

Charles tilted his head and gave a slight nod. "Close. Went to check out Charles Towne Landing. Neat place."

I didn't want to tell him that even though I'd lived here for years I'd never been to the historic landing.

"Did Heather go with you?"

"She had to work, but that's okay. She's not much into history stuff. She says all of it's old. Can you believe that?"

I could, since I wasn't into it either, but again, I didn't want to remind him. A waiter appeared before I had time to respond. We each ordered grilled tuna sandwiches, Charles ordered a Budweiser and I chose the house chardonnay.

Charles watched the waiter leave and pointed his index finger at me. "So, why the lunch invite?"

I smiled. "Maybe I've missed you the last few days."

Charles shook his head. "Of course, you have, but that's not why we're here."

"You're right."

"Of course," he interrupted.

"I talked to Cindy this morning and wanted to let you know what she'd found about the death."

"What's stopping you?"

Nothing, so I shared the information. My sharing was only interrupted about seventeen times. Charles had to know every detail, most I didn't know, but that didn't stop him from asking.

After I'd finally finished, and the waiter had delivered our lunch, Charles took a bite and mumbled through a mouthful of food, "What do you think?"

"Everything points to an accidental overdose. She was drunk and didn't know she was shooting too much heroin. She had a long history of drug abuse, and other than the passenger door handle being clean, nothing points to anything other than an overdose."

Charles watched two SUVs slowly roll past us on Center Street, gazed at the three other tables of diners on the patio, and turned to me.

"No offense, but that's a crock of bull hockey."

Charles may lack many things but opinions were not among them. "Why?"

"Didn't you hear Cindy? She said poor Ms. Craft's death was murder."

"Charles, I must have missed that. Refresh my memory, what exactly did she say that meant murder?"

"I have to explain everything, don't I?"

I shrugged.

"First, she said Lauren had kicked the drug habit, so an overdose of something she wasn't doing would be impossible. Then she said someone wiped fingerprints off the passenger door and was trying not to leave any evidence of being there. And, the most important thing was when she said she was praying. Don't you see, she's praying for us to get involved and help her solve the terrible murder." He slammed his hand on the table. "So there."

That may have been how Charles loosely translated what I said, but I'd learned over the years, his reality often doesn't mesh with the real world. I also learned that arguing with him was as big a waste of time as trying to teach a turtle to type.

"I don't think that's exactly how she meant what she said."

He grinned and shook his head. "Chris, oh Chris, when am I going to teach you how to read between the lines. Of course, that's what she meant. And the cherry on top of the hot-fudge sundae was when she said it was still an open case and Detective

Adair was working it. They don't have detectives working things that aren't crimes. I rest my case."

"It's something to think about," I said as insincerely as possible and knew it was time to change the subject. "Brian Newman met with me the other day."

I knew Charles wouldn't leave his opinions about the death on the table, but his insatiable desire to know what was going on would delay more murder talk until he learned what there was to know about my talk with the mayor.

"Without me?" he said, like me meeting with the mayor without my sidekick was one of the most ridiculous things he'd heard.

I nodded.

"Let's hear it."

I shared that Brian was concerned about a heated race for the office and there were big money citizens lining up behind the potential opponent. I was surprised when Charles asked who the opponent was. With his ear to the gossip of the community, it seemed unlikely he wouldn't have already known.

"Joel Hurt. You know him?"

"You're kidding. Joel, the landscape, garden center guy?"

Charles was already shaking his head when I said yes.

"Crap," Charles said.

"I know. I hate anyone running against Brian."

Charles shook his head faster and said, "That's not what the crap was about."

I shrugged.

"Guess who Joel Hurt was dating?"

From the look on Charles's face, it wasn't much of a leap when I said, "Lauren Craft."

"Yep."

"How do you know?"

"Heather heard about Lauren's death when she was giving a massage to Mrs. Teeter. Heather said that Old-Bitty Teeter—Heather's not one of her fans—rambled on about how sad it was about Lauren being a druggie and how rough her death must be on her wonderful, handsome, charming boyfriend, Joel Hurt."

"Did Old Bitt … Mrs. Teeter say how she knew Lauren?"

"Teeter cleans beach houses for some of the frou-frou folks with more money than interest in cleaning their big houses. Heather says she's the snootiest cleaning lady she's ever known. Anyway, Teeter heard Lauren was friends with some of the kids of the frou-frous and their parents were always talking about how the younger generation was going to hell in a helium balloon—drugs, drink, and sniffing around things where they shouldn't be."

I nodded. "Heather got all that from one massage?"

Charles smiled. "She's learning information gathering techniques from me. A quick study, I must say."

"How to be nosy?"

"Some less-enlightened folks might say that."

"Did Heather know Lauren?"

"Said she never met her."

"Do you know Joel?" I asked.

"Said hey a few times but never got beyond that. He seems a little standoffish. I see his trucks around town and stopped at his garden center a couple of weeks ago."

Charles lived in a small apartment with no landscaping, and I don't recall him ever mentioning growing anything other than a scruffy beard. "Why?"

"Was driving by and saw a big orange sign out front saying SALE. Thought he might have some cheap books on gardening. There's a big dead patch in my book collection in the gardening area."

I smiled at the thought of Charles buying anything related to gardening. "Have any?"

"Not a one, well they had some, but they weren't on sale and the ones they had cost as much as my cell phone monthly payment; you know, the cell phone you made me buy and's breaking me with the bill."

I suspect Charles could roll out a president's quote saying something like *history is determined by who is telling it*, but since I couldn't care less about what old, probably dead, presidents had said, I would remind him I had never insisted he enter the current century and buy a cell phone. He and Heather had decided they would need one when they moved to Nashville. I ignored his comment.

"Was Joel in the store?"

"Didn't see him. So, what does Brian want us to do?"

I didn't recall Brian saying anything about *us* but told Charles that the mayor had asked if I could hold two fundraisers. Charles asked the same question I had posed to Brian about who I knew who had any money and I gave him the same answer Brian had given me.

"Well, what're we waiting for? Let's get raisin' dough to keep Brian governin'."

I wanted to ask Charles if we should start raising money before or after he caught the person who had murdered a person no one thought had even been murdered. Before I could, Charles's phone began an instrumental version of "Crazy," Heather's favorite song.

"Yes, sweetie pie," he answered and after listening for a few seconds, said, "Of course I'm on my way. Just around the corner."

He hit the end call icon, took a deep breath, and looked around the patio for the waitress.

"You gotta go?"

He rolled his eyes. "How could I have forgotten about the big toilet paper sale at Walmart?"

"The one you promised to take Heather to?"

He shook his head, grabbed his Tilley and cane. I said I'd get the check, something I would have had to do anyway. He thanked me and rushed out. I was thankful Charles had found someone he could rush to a toilet paper sale with and that he had finally bought a car, so I wouldn't have to take him.

CHAPTER TEN

I didn't have a sale to get to, toilet paper or otherwise, so when the waiter returned to clear the table, I ordered another glass of chardonnay and leaned back in the booth and thought about Charles's opinion that Lauren had been murdered, all from what I'd said about Cindy's comments that he —we—were supposed to help the police catch an alleged killer. I pondered how big a coincidence it was that Brian's opponent had been dating Lauren. My phone rang before I was able to make sense of any of it. A glance at the screen indicated that it was Bob Howard.

"Hello, Mr. Howard."

"Humph, don't be all cheery with me, caught the killer yet?"

"Bob, no one said anyone was—"

"Never mind," he interrupted. "That's not why I'm calling. Are you going to buy me supper?"

It would have been useless to ask why, besides, whether he would admit it or not, Bob wouldn't have called unless it was for something important.

"When and where?"

"Six o'clock, Rita's."

"See you there."

He had already hung up.

Three hours later, I was sitting at a table on Rita's patio. It was hot and muggy, but I would rather be outside enjoying the late summer breeze blowing off the ocean than inside. Rita's sat on a prime piece of property and since I'd lived here, had been three different restaurants, and was previously the site of a bowling alley. It was at the corner of Center Street and Arctic Avenue, catty-corner from Tides, the nine-story oceanfront hotel; directly across Arctic from the iconic Folly Pier; while directly across Center Street from the Sand Dollar, a popular members-only bar.

Bob didn't share Charles's penchant for promptness, for that matter, he didn't have any of Charles's proclivities, so he saw nothing wrong when he barreled onto the patio fifteen minutes late. My realtor friend was as oversized as his profane vocabulary. He stood six-foot tall but carried the weight of a seven-footer. He wore a four-day old beard, a flowery Hawaiian shirt covering his ample stomach, and bright green shorts that looked as stylish on him as a lampshade on a pig. He turned sideways to get past two tables on the way to me, bumped the chair of a man sitting at one of the tables, and mumbled something to the man that, depending on Bob's mood, could have either been, "Sorry, my fault" or "Get the hell out of my way." I lowered my head as if not to notice the interaction.

"Well, well," Bob said as he reached the table. "See nobody's killed you yet."

I didn't think I needed to confirm his observation, so I pointed to the empty chair on the other side of the table.

He plopped down, pointed to my glass of wine, and said, "Where's my beer?"

I held up my wine and said, "If I'd ordered your beer when you said you'd be here, it'd be hot by now."

"I suppose that's your damned subtle way of saying I'm late."

I smiled. "If the shoe fits."

"Crap, Chris, if I'd wanted a lecture on being tardy, I would've brought Betty."

Betty was Bob's wife of nearly forty years, and in my opinion, should be a candidate for sainthood for putting up with Bob

"What brings you to my island?" I asked.

"Maybe I wanted to have supper with my good friend."

I stared at him.

"Okay, that and I'm meeting a couple to show an overpriced house on the ocean that's about the size of the Pentagon. There'd only be two of them living in it so they need that big of a house as much as I need shingles."

"Don't suppose you'll share your astute observation when you show it to them."

"Hell no. It'll be the perfect damned casa for them. There'll be room for each to have their private space, and with seven bedrooms, and enough bathrooms for a senior citizens' center, the resale value will be off the charts. The perfect house." He paused and bellowed at a waiter who was at a nearby table, "Beer!"

The waiter, who wasn't assigned to our table, smiled his best faux smile, and scurried away.

Bob wiped perspiration off his forehead. "So, enough about me—for now. Who killed your neighbors' kid?"

"You know everything I know about what happened."

"I bet your street-person buddy thinks it's murder," Bob said as our waitress set a bottle of Coors in front of him.

"Yes, Charles does," I said, while Bob attacked his beer. "The cops are still looking at it, but they're not sure if it was anything other than an accidental overdose. I don't know more than that."

Bob's beer bottle was half empty when he said, "But I damned well bet you will find out more."

The waitress returned before I could deny it. Bob fanned his face with the menu and said, "Don't confuse me with your over-priced specials, get me the biggest damned steak you have back there." He pointed the menu at the kitchen.

I pictured a big hit to my checkbook and ordered a burger and fries. Bob told her to add two orders of fries with his steak.

"Takes a lot of fuel to keep this fine-tuned machine running at its peak. Especially to con—umm sell—tonight's overpriced mansion to the sweet young, more money than sense, couple." He fanned his face again. "Speaking of fine-tuned machine, there's another reason I wanted to talk to you."

I motioned for him to continue.

"It's about Al."

Al Washington owned a small, tired, bar in Charleston. Bob and Al were as different as black and white, a fitting analogy since Al was African American and Bob was as white as snow, but not anywhere near as pure. Regardless of their cultural and upbringing differences, the two bonded years ago and had been friends forever. Bob once confided he considered Al a true hero, both of the Korean conflict where he had saved seven soldiers from certain death and because Al and his now deceased wife adopted nine children, giving them love, and a solid upbringing.

"What about him?"

"He's been having health problems."

Al was eighty and spent most every day, and late until the evening, at his bar. Except for a part-time cook, it was a one-man show. I wasn't surprised.

"What's wrong?"

"You know he's had damned heart problems for years and his arthritis in his knees has him moving about the speed of a slug on Ambien."

I was aware and nodded.

"The last time I was in there, I was surprised to see Tanesa talking to him. Think it was the first time I'd seen her in her dad's bar. I asked her what a lovely ER doc was doing in a dump like Al's. I think she's got a crush on me, all my charm, good looks, and wit. Think she sees our forty-year age difference as sexy."

I rolled my eyes. Bob stepped out of his fantasy world, and continued, "Anyway, she walked me to my table while her dad went back to the grill to get a burger for someone. She said she was worried about him. Said because of his heart condition, the countless hours he's in the bar, and his age, that he's the perfect candidate for either another heart attack or blood clots that could scamper from his legs, up his veins, to his heart or lungs, or something like that. She said all of it in doc-speak, too complex for this old dullard to understand. The part I did catch was when she interjected dead into the description."

Bob was anything but a dullard. After knowing him for nearly four years, I had learned he held an economics degree from Duke University, in addition to being a highly successful realtor. An even bigger surprise after noticing his outward appearance and listening to him, he had a heart that was bigger than many ministers and would do anything to help people in need.

"Sorry to hear that," I said.

"You're not kidding," Bob said and shook his head. "If he's dead, where will I get the best cheeseburgers in the world?"

I slowly shook my head. "That's touching Bob, so caring."

"You know I'm kidding. I'd do anything for Al."

I did know and told him so.

"That brings me to what I wanted to talk to you about. Al won't admit he has a problem. He needs to hire help but can't afford it. He's still paying on some student loans a couple of the kids have. He's getting later and later paying his damned rent. So, guess what?"

I told him I had no idea what.

"Your highly-successful realtor buddy is riding to Al's rescue on his white elephant, or whatever animal is large enough to carry this fine-tuned body. I'm buying the bar."

I'm glad I didn't try to guess. "You're what?"

"Crap, have you turned deaf in your senior, senile years. I said I'm buying Al's."

I started to laugh, but saw that Bob was serious. "Really?"

Our supper arrived, and Bob grabbed a steak knife and sliced into the beef. I slowly took a bite of burger and pondered what he had said.

Bob took a bite and looked around the restaurant, before turning his attention to me. "Chris, I'm seventy-six years old. I owned my own commercial real estate firm for a quarter of a century and have had Island Realty fifteen years. Real estate has been good to me, but I'm getting damned burned out with it. I think I used up my quota of customer smiles a while back, and if you ever repeat this, I'll deny it and break your big toe, but I feel bad about convincing folks to buy houses they can barely afford. They seem to think they need to buy the most house that some greedy bank will finance. They never think life changes and expenses go up, but their incomes usually don't go up as much. That's not necessarily a bad thing for realtors." Bob smiled. "Hell, we get to sell the house again." His smile faded. "But that's not right." He took another bite.

"You're retiring?"

"Isn't that what I said?"

Not exactly, I thought. "I understand about you retiring, but buying Al's?"

"Betty said I could do whatever I wanted to do, but she doesn't want me around the house. Something about me being a pain in the ass, and if she had to put up with me more than she already does, she'd either kill me or move to Switzerland."

"That I can understand."

"Al needs me."

"No offense, Bob, but what do you know about running a bar and restaurant?"

Bob pointed at his stomach. "Do I look like I should be running a fitness center? I'm the perfect shape for a bar and burger joint owner. Besides, all I need to do is hire a cheap cook and use my charm to bring in the customers."

And I thought Charles's logic lacked something. Now a more delicate topic. Bob had never been known for his political correctness, and with roughly ninety-nine percent of Al's customers being African American, I could see problems abound.

"Do you see a problem with you buying a bar serving mostly black customers?"

Bob sighed and shook his head. "Shit, Chris, I've seen some of the same customers in Al's for years. Some even talk to me; okay, they mostly mumble about me, but they know I don't like blacks. They also know I don't like whites, browns, reds, and even those starchy white-faced Scandinavians. I'm an equal opportunity disliker. Hell, I can count on one big toe the people I like." He grinned. "His customers will love me."

"What's Al think about it?"

"Are you going to let me finish my food or keep asking stupid questions?"

"I've never known you not to finish your food, and everyone else's around you, besides you brought it up."

"Al tried to protest, but it was feebler than his feeble body. He started with *no way,* but that became, *are you sure,* and ended with *thank you.* He's deeper in debt than he'd let on." Bob looked down at the table and in a deep voice—low for Bob—said, "He started crying and put his thin arms around me. Chris, I love that man."

I suspected Bob would regret showing me his kinder, gentler side, so I didn't say anything except, "That's great. I know you mean a lot to him, and he has to be relieved."

"Yeah, well shit, now you know it. So, what's going on in your life?"

"Hold on, you can't leave it there. When are you taking over?" What I meant to say was who would give him a crash course in restaurant/bar management and where would he get a suit of armor big enough to protect him from being attacked by customers he would insult, irritate, and drive to violence.

Bob said, "Sort of already have."

"Sort of?"

"Do I have to spell out every damn thing to you?"

"Yep."

"And everybody says you're so smart. Okay, listen well, I asked Al to give me a list of his debts, the longest past due first. He did, and I wrote him a check to cover everything. Chris, please keep this confidential, but he had some bills that were a year old. The landlord had already begun eviction procedures." Bob shook his head. "It's no wonder why the poor man is in such bad health. Anyway, I have my lawyer working on all the damned paperwork to make the purchase official. When he finishes milking me for as many billable hours as he can, I'll write Al another big ole check and voila, the business will be legally mine, lock, stock, and all those damned worthless tables, chairs, and a stinking grease-filled kitchen that must've served soldiers in the Revolutionary War."

The only reason Bob was buying the business was to save Al, an extraordinarily generous gesture, but one Bob would never admit to.

"What's Al going to do?"

"First, the broken-down, ancient, geezer's going to the hospital and get a bunch of God-awful expensive tests run to see if he's about ready to croak. If he makes it though that poking and prodding, he said he'd stop by the bar each day and check on how I'm doing. He didn't say it, but that means making sure none of his regulars have threatened me with bodily harm. He said he could sit by the door and do the Walmart greeter thing."

It was a clever idea and I told Bob so.

"Guess I can waste a chair for him to plop his bony ass down on."

That was Bob-speak for *I'd love to have him around. He's a great guy, and I'll need all the help I can get.*

"Good idea," I said.

"That's enough damn talk about that old man and his—umm, my—bar. What's going on with you?"

That was probably the first time he'd ever asked about me, so I knew he was embarrassed about what he had shared about Al and the bar.

"Glad you asked," I said as he stuffed a large bite of steak in his mouth and waved for the waitress to get another bottle of beer. "The election for Folly's mayor is in April."

"That's a half year away, and why the flying flip would I care?"

Bob was back to normal. I proceeded to tell him about Brian's opponent and why Brian needed to raise more money than usual to have a chance at winning.

"So, back to my flying-flip question. Why would I care?"

Bob liked Brian and in the last election had supported him with the maximum individual donation allowed. "Because Brian would like you to host a fundraiser?"

I gripped the side of the table and readied myself for a flurry of expletives.

Bob took a sip of his new beer, stared at me, and nodded, "Okay. Where and when?"

I pictured a gaggle of aliens taking over Bob's body and sucking out all his hate brain cells. I was shocked, but slowly regained my composure as he took another bite.

"Your house and as soon as possible."

"Okay," he repeated.

We discussed some details and he started naming realtor friends he could invite and some of his best customers over the years and joked he could have his new gourmet restaurant cater the event. I assumed he was joking. He said, "Anything else? I've got to meet the rich suckers."

"One more thing," I said. "I don't think it's related to the mayoral race, but I heard Joel Hurt had been dating Lauren Craft."

Bob raised his eyebrow. "The dirt-digging, landscape guy turned mayoral candidate, and your best-bud, Brad Burton's dead daughter. And you, the person who doesn't believe in coincidences, don't think that's related?"

"I don't see how."

"Hmm."

Bob pushed away from the table and on his way to the door

told the waitress I was getting his check and to be sure and add a humongous tip.

That was more like the Bob I knew, I thought, and looked out the window. Could Bob be right in thinking Lauren's death may have something to do with Joel?

CHAPTER ELEVEN

I stopped at Burt's on the way home to grab something for breakfast. It was one of the store's prime beer-buying hours and several customers were milling around. Three men I had seen in the store many times were in deep conversation in front of the beer cooler. An elderly woman I only knew as Mary was at the counter holding the collar of her large collie and talking to Eric. I smiled when the dog jumped and placed its front paws on the counter hoping Eric would give it a treat.

I weaved my way to the side of the store, grabbed a cinnamon Danish and turned to head to the cash register when I nearly ran into Brad Burton. I barely recognized him. I thought he'd looked bad when Charles and I visited his house to offer my condolences, but compared to now, he'd looked like a television star that day. His brown eyes were sunken, and he had on the same wrinkled white dress shirt he'd worn during our visit but with added food stains on the front. He was carrying a loaf of bread and his hand trembled and I was concerned he would drop the bread.

"Landrum," he said and gave a slight nod.

"Burton," I responded and gave a weak smile.

"I see you're shopping," he said and nodded toward the Danish.

I started to make one of my patented smart-aleck comments like, "I see why you were a detective," but first, I had learned years ago he didn't appear to have a sense of humor, and second, I was feeling something I had never thought possible: sympathy. I limited my response to, "Breakfast."

Our awkward conversation was interrupted by Chester Carr who patted Brad on the back and said, "Brad, I was sorry to hear about your loss."

I had known Chester for several years and got to know him much better a couple of years ago when he had dated Charles's aunt who had spent her last few months on Folly before succumbing to cancer.

Brad turned to the newcomer and thanked him for his concern. I took the opportunity to move away from Brad. Chester stopped me. "Hey Chris, see you and Brad here are becoming friends. Glad to see it, you being neighbors and all."

"Good to see you, Chester. I was sharing my condolences with Brad. How are you?"

Chester smiled, said, "Good," and looked at the carton of milk he was holding. "Better be going. Need to get this home." He glanced back at Brad, said he was again sorry for his loss, and headed to the cash register, leaving Brad and me staring at each other in awkward silence.

I was saved by Eric who apparently had to go to the shelf behind us to find something for a customer. He handed the small jar of pickles to the appreciative woman and turned to Brad and me.

"How are my favorite detectives?"

Clearly, Eric hadn't heard as much about Burton and my ongoing disagreements as had Chester.

I was surprised when Brad chuckled rather than going into a rant about how terrible I was. He patted Eric's shoulder and said, "You've got that wrong. I'm a has-been detective." He tilted his head toward me. "And he never was one."

Eric stroked his long beard. I smiled and said, "Brad's right about me, but he may be retired but was a top-notch detective for years."

Brad gave me a sideways glance, probably because he knew I was lying about what I thought of his skills. I would have looked at me that way too and was surprised I had said it.

"Anyway," Eric said, "it's nice to see you neighbors gabbing, and Brad, I'm terribly sorry about Lauren. She seemed to be a nice gal."

Brad nodded and Eric said he had to run. "Got to help keep our fine citizens lubricated."

Brad remained at my side and twisted the tie on the bread wrapper.

What do I say now? No words were necessary. Brad looked at the concrete floor and muttered, "I did appreciate you and your friend stopping by the house. I know I treated you badly when you were there. I'm sorry."

"I understand. It must have been terrible on you and Hazel. If there is anything I can do, please don't hesitate to ask."

He looked at me. "That's kind. You have no idea how horrible this has been on Hazel."

I didn't know about him, but it felt strange for the two of us to be carrying on a civil conversation in the middle of the busy store after years of such an acrimonious relationship. It seemed like he wanted to talk, so I said, "You walking home?"

He looked toward the register and said he was. I followed

him to pay and walked beside him as he went out into the humid night air.

"We moved here to be closer to Lauren and somehow try to help her," Brad said as we reached my yard.

Hazel had told me that, but since she'd requested I not let Brad know she had talked to me, I didn't let on I'd already heard it.

"I'm sorry you weren't able to help." I pointed to my front step. "Want to sit?"

He glanced next door to his house and at my step. "Okay."

We sat on the concrete step and shared another awkward silence.

Brad took a deep breath and said, "I was never there for her when she was a kid. Don't try to deny it because I know you think I was a horrible detective." He paused, and I quickly decided silence was my best response. "When Lauren was little, I was a great cop. Before I got promoted to detective, I ran rings around the other beat cops. I wasn't the smartest guy on the force, but I wanted to make a difference and the only way I knew how was to put in as many hours as possible." He hesitated and smiled. "Some of the guys swore I was bucking to be police chief. I wasn't, but I did want to be the best I could be. What I became was the worst dad in the world. I can count on one hand the total number of concerts, plays, games, activities, and whatever my little girl participated in that I attended. And Chris, she was in everything. She played the violin in the school orchestra, acted in every play, was cheerleader for both football and basketball, and still found time to get straight A's in class. Her mom was there for everything; I let the damned job dominate my life."

I knew that wasn't unusual at the time when Brad was raising a family, but I also didn't think Brad needed me to tell him so.

"I'm sure she knew you loved her."

He looked over at me. "I'm not."

I waited for him to continue.

Brad stared as two trucks sped past the house, and he said to me, "During her junior year of high school, she got mixed up with the wrong crowd. Alcohol and pot. I didn't learn about it until months later. Me, the big-time cop who was always out catching criminals, and helping others, couldn't even see that my own kid…. If I had spent more time looking out for my little girl instead of being gone and worrying about everyone else, things … things could have been different. Chris, she would still be with us."

"Brad, you don't know that. Over the years, I've known several parents who were perfect with their kids, did everything with them, doted over them, and did whatever possible to keep them away from bad influences. Despite those efforts, some of their kids ended up being the kind of people you spent years catching."

"I know that, but I still failed her. You know what's so strange? The last year I thought she'd turned her life around." He glanced at his house again. "We had her over to eat several times. She seemed fine. She had a job. She was dating a successful, well-liked guy. Sure, she still had bouts of depression, but nothing like how it had been when she was a regular at rehab." I followed Brad's gaze as he looked down at his hand. It was shaking, and he grabbed his knee to stop the shake. "I know the ME is still futzing around with the cause of death, but I know it was an overdose. It had to be."

"Brad, you said she still had bouts of depression. Is it possible she had, umm, intentionally overdosed?"

He let go of his knee and his hand balled into a fist. "Suicide?"

I nodded.

He unclasped his fist and sighed. "If I saw it once, I saw it a thousand times. When I was a cop, some guy would be found in his room hanging from the ceiling, or someone in a bathtub with her wrists slit. Obvious suicides, but the family swore it couldn't be. They'd say maybe it was an accident, or someone murdered the poor soul to make it look like suicide. Basically, the relatives couldn't handle the guilt associated with their loved ones killing themselves. I've thought about it every waking moment since it happened, could I be doing the same thing and wanting it to be accidental for the same reason." He paused and shook his head. "Chris, it was a damned, horrible accident. She'd been off heroin for a while and somehow overdosed when she got back into it. It was; it had to be."

Perhaps it was, but I couldn't shake how strange it was that there were no prints on the passenger side door. I was feeling uncomfortable with Brad's deteriorating mood and wanted to change the subject.

"Brad, you mentioned she had been dating someone. Was it Joel Hurt?"

His head jerked toward me. "How'd you know?"

"I heard it somewhere around town. Have you talked with him since, umm, her passing?"

"He stopped by the house to bring us food and a plant. I don't know him well, but from what Lauren says, said, he was a nice guy and seemed good for her. Hazel likes him. Why?"

"Nothing. I heard he was going to run for mayor."

Brad seemed surprised. "Against Brian Newman?"

"Yes."

"That's news to me. Brian's a good mayor. For someone who had been a cop most of his life, he's maybe a tad too soft against vagrants and some of the other bums who hang around Folly. Brian's popular so I don't see how anyone could beat him." Brad looked at his watch. "Better get home. Hazel will start worrying. She knows I'm not handling this too good and is afraid of what I might do."

He thanked me for listening, stood, and headed home without turning back.

CHAPTER TWELVE

Since the first day I'd met Brad Burton some eight years ago on that hot, sandy path to the beach overlooking the Morris Island Lighthouse, he'd been a pain in my side, and I suppose, I to his. I still think he'd only been going through the motions his later years as a detective, but I suppose he was honest about how he'd done his job at first. When he had moved next door, I doubted we'd ever have a pleasant conversation, and for his first year there, my doubts had been confirmed. Now I didn't know what to think. Sure, I knew he was torn up about the death of their only child, and could understand how that might alter his behavior; but I couldn't get over how much he felt comfortable confiding during our strange conversation on the porch.

I awakened the next morning thinking about it; not only thinking about how funny it felt to have had a real, and emotional, conversation with Brad, but how I couldn't shake my uneasiness about the missing prints on the car door. I had reached

for my phone to call Chief LaMond to see if there was anything
new with the case when the phone rang.

"Chris," came a vaguely familiar voice through the speaker,
"this is Wayne Swan."

Wayne was a successful contractor specializing in home
remodels. It's rare to drive more than a few blocks on Folly
without seeing one of his job signs. He had a reputation for
quality work, on time, and at reasonable prices—all rare qualities
in today's construction industry.

I had known him five years, since he was one of my regular
—unfortunately, one of only a few regular—customers when I
had owned my photo gallery. I couldn't keep the shop open with
only a few, a very few, regular customers, and truth be told, not
that many irregular ones as well, and was forced to close it a year
ago. In addition to buying prints, he had an interest in photography and would stop in to talk cameras. I enjoyed our conversations. He also invited me to a couple preview parties he held
upon completion of major projects. He'd paid for the events
which were hosted by the happy homeowners who were anxious
to show off their remodeled spaces.

"Morning, Wayne. Inviting me to a party—I hope?"

He chuckled. "Not this time. Have you heard Joel Hurt is
planning to run for mayor?"

"Think I heard something about it," I said. I avoided telling
him I hated the idea.

"Good. He's asked me to be his campaign manager and I've
got a favor to ask."

"Congratulations, I suppose."

Wayne's chuckle turned into a laugh. "Condolences would be
more appropriate. Kidding aside, I'd like you to meet with Joel."

"Wayne, if you don't already know, I'm a good friend of

Brian Newman and will be supporting him in the election. Why would Joel want to meet with me?"

"Yes, I know about your connections with the mayor, but Joel said he didn't know you other than in passing, and since you're a well-respected member of the community, he wanted to at least share his vision with you." He laughed, again. "We're not asking you to wear a *Hurt for Mayor* button or stick a sign in your yard, just to give my candidate a chance to share his ideas. How about it?"

I was still absorbing that someone thought I was a *well-respected member of the community*. "Let me think about it and get back with you."

Wayne hesitated, and said, "I go way back with him, Chris. I think you'll like Joel. He's a great guy with some progressive ideas for *your* island."

"Got a question, Wayne. Do campaign managers ever say anything negative about their candidates?"

"Hmm, give me a sec." Another chuckle. "Got it, Joel chews his fingernails."

"I won't tell anyone."

"Good. And get back to me soon. Joel wants to talk to as many community leaders as he can before officially announcing."

I said I would, hung up, and thought *community leaders!*

What was Joel's real reason for wanting to meet with me? I had been on Folly for several years and had been thrust into notoriety because of a few horrific events, but I didn't for a second believe the *community leader* and *well-respected member of the commu-*

nity baloney. And if he thought he could win me over, there wasn't a chance in Vegas for me making a significant donation to his campaign. And, if I did meet with him, would it look like I was being disloyal to Brian?

Instead of spending time pondering these unanswerable questions, I called Charles.

"Caught the killer yet?" Charles said, instead of a common courtesy.

I told him there wasn't a killer so I couldn't have caught him.

"If you say so. Anyway, guess where I am?"

"Getting a facial."

"Yuck. Try again, never mind, I'm at Office Depot looking at computers."

Charles had never owned a computer, not surprising knowing that he didn't have a cell phone or an answering machine until a few months ago. When I had the gallery, he considered the computer there as his.

"Why?"

"The times they are a changin'. I might need to look something up, and besides, Heather says she can use it to watch videos of her favorite singers. Think about it. If she's using my computer, she'll need to be at my apartment. If she's at my apartment we can—"

"Got it," I interrupted. "Want to know why I called?"

"Thought you wanted to know where I was, what I was doing, and what Heather and I would be doing while she was at my apartment."

"That too, but figured you'd be interested in knowing who I got off the phone with." I told him about my conversation with Wayne. Charles was being unusually attentive, and not interrupting, until I told him what Wayne had said about me being a community leader.

Charles laughed so loud that I held the phone away from my ear. "He said you were what?"

I repeated it, and Charles said he'd heard me the first time, but couldn't imagine anyone uttering those words when referring to me. I assured him Wayne had.

"A politician couldn't find the truth if it squawked in his ear and bit him on the nose."

"Did a president say that?"

"Why?"

"No reason other than you're always quoting presidents."

"Nope, this time it'd be little ole me being profound. So, when are you going to meet him?"

"Don't know that I am. I think it'd look bad since I'm supporting Brian."

"Wrong," said Charles. "Of course, you are. You have to."

"Why?"

"Data gathering, spying, reconnoitering, surveilling; come on Chris, get with the program. Look how helpful this will be to Brian. Oh yeah, make him buy you a meal, order two desserts, and bring me one."

I wouldn't have gone as far with the purposes, but I saw how it may be helpful in knowing what Joel disliked about the job Brian was doing. And, in the back of my mind, I was thinking about Lauren. Perhaps Joel could share insight into her mental state.

"You win, I'll meet with him."

Charles made a clicking sound with his mouth. "Wise man. Keep listening to me and there's hope, albeit slight, that you could grow into a community leader."

I called Wayne Swan and told him I was willing to meet with Joel. Thirty minutes later, Wayne called and said Joel was available and wanted to know if I could I meet him tomorrow evening at BLU, the upscale restaurant in the Tides Hotel. I told him I thought I could fit it in my busy schedule and we agreed on a time. I spent the next day running some routine errands and continued to wonder what Joel really wanted.

CHAPTER THIRTEEN

W ayne was waiting for me as I walked through the automatic doors at the Tides ten minutes before I was to meet with Joel. He looked the part of a professional campaign manager with his navy blazer, blue button-down shirt, and gray slacks. I looked the part of a retired executive with my faded red golf shirt and wrinkled khakis. He and I were about the same height but unlike my blond and graying hair, he had dark hair with a bald spot on the back of his head. My bald spot had spread over most of my scalp. Wayne was also two decades younger than me.

Wayne reached out and grabbed my hand like he was on a mission, which, of course, he was. "Chris, glad you could make it. Joel is eager to meet you. He's already got a table. Hope you don't mind eating inside; it's too steamy for Joel on the deck. He has to work in this heat and humidity every day at the nursery, so he likes to get inside whenever possible."

I said it was fine and followed him to BLU's nautically-themed indoor dining room. I was surprised to see Joel seated at a small table beside the window looking out on the outdoor bar and the Folly Pier.

"Aren't you joining us?" I asked Wayne as we approached the table set for two.

"Afraid not, got another appointment. I wanted to be sure the two of you got together and then head out."

Joel saw us and stood. He was roughly three inches taller than Wayne, slimmer, and his sun-bleached, blond hair contrasted with his campaign manager's. Other than those differences, Joel was dressed exactly like Wayne, with his blue blazer, light blue shirt, and gray slacks. He greeted me with a quick smile and a strong, confident handshake.

"Thanks for agreeing to meet with me, Mr. Landrum. I know you must be busy."

The handful of times I had talked with him previously, he'd called me Chris. He was now in political mode. I told him it was my pleasure.

Wayne put his arm around my shoulder and said, "I'll leave you two to talk. Again, thanks for agreeing to this meeting, Chris."

Wayne turned to the exit and Joel motioned for me to be seated opposite him. A waiter was at the table before I could place the black napkin in my lap and asked if I wanted anything to drink. There was a half-empty white wine glass in front of Joel and I said I would have the same.

"I'm terribly sorry that your gallery closed. I should have been in more often, but you know how work sometimes gets in the way of what you would like to do. Wayne told me wonderful things about your talent. I know he's purchased several photos."

Since Joel had never been in the gallery, I thought *should have been in more often* was over the top, but I appreciated his kind words.

"Yes, Wayne was a regular. I know his wife wanted to paint some of the photos and he enjoyed talking photography."

"Again, I am sorry you were forced to close. That's one of the key issues that precipitated my desire to run for mayor. Small businesses have a challenging time staying viable on Folly. The island is inundated much of the year with hordes of what I call non-spenders—college students, adults with little disposable income, others who can only afford enough beer to get them through the day, and even then buy the drinks before arriving here. A business like yours was a perfect example. Forced out because of that kind of people. It galls me."

My wine arrived, and my only thought was that the "successful," local resident sitting across from me had never stepped in my gallery, yet he was blaming outsiders for its demise.

"I apologize for hopping on a soapbox," Joel said and leaned back in the chair. "I'm passionate about the topic, and I sometimes get carried away."

I took a sip of wine, and lied when I said, "That's okay. Is that why you're running?"

He shook his head and frowned. "Over the last few months, I have been approached by numerous residents who have shared their dissatisfaction with the happenings in City Hall. I can't divulge their names at this point, but am certain you would know most of them, either personally or by reputation. They have offered their support, monetary and otherwise, if I would run." He paused and finished his wine and held the glass up for a refill. The waiter was quick to the table and said he would take care of it. Joel turned back to me. "I considered their requests with mixed feelings. I do agree with their position, but I believe Mayor Newman has been an exceptional leader. He brought a wealth of experience to the job. He has a good handle on the city departments. He's considered to be fair to his employees and presents a professional appearance to his constituents. Honestly, I like the man."

"But?" I said.

"Shall we order supper first? It's on me, of course."

The waiter returned with Joel's wine and waited for us to order. Joel either had studied the menu before I had arrived or was a regular. I had neither advantage and perused the menu while he ordered a tomato and crab salad and I decided on a Caesar salad. Joel told the waiter we would decide on our entrees after the salads arrived.

"But?" I repeated after the waiter headed to the kitchen.

Joel smiled. "Mayor Newman has given most of his life to public service. He was serving our country before I was born, and I admire and praise him for that. He's a true patriot. And, he has spent more than twenty years serving our community as either director of public safety or mayor." Joel's smile faded. "But sadly, his ideas for governing and his views about the future of Folly are stale and outdated, or so I believe as those who have asked me to run also believe."

I wanted to challenge him but knew this wasn't the time.

"Chris, I know I'll be a dark horse candidate. I know I'll be going up against lethargy on the part of many voters, the vast experience of Mayor Newman, and the current establishment, but I feel I must, as do those who support me. There are also council members we feel should be replaced."

Our salads arrived, and Joel quickly told the waiter he wanted the crispy snapper and I settled on the grilled Mahi Mahi. Joel nodded as if he had approved my selection. That was probably the only thing we would agree on tonight.

"What are you proposing? What's your platform? What will you do differently?" I asked.

"First, we must crack down on those who flaunt the law.

Drinking on the beach is illegal, yet you can go out there any day and find violators. Public drunkenness is illegal yet walk down Center Street any night of the week and see people under the influence of alcohol or other substances. It should go unsaid, but littering not only is unsightly, but a health hazard, yet, look how many yards of our fine citizens are dotted with trash daily. And we must do whatever we need to keep bums and college students away who have no reason for being on our beach other than to drink and cause trouble."

I could point out that everything he mentioned had been discussed, addressed, over-and-over since I had moved to Folly, and from what I had heard, that had been the case for many years prior to my arrival. I had several conversations with Brian Newman about each of these issues. Yes, they were concerns, but the city didn't have the budget to hire enough law enforcement officials to stop it, and so many of the times the violations were marginal and could go either way. Folly was a beachside community, open and welcoming to everyone, and some inconveniences associated with that were part of what makes the island special.

"What do you propose to do to stop the violations you've mentioned?"

Joel looked out the window at the Folly Pier. "I'm not naïve enough to believe there are simple solutions, but innovative approaches must be tried."

"For example?"

"We must dissuade outsiders from using our beach community as their debauchery location of choice."

His platitudes were beginning to irritate me. "How?"

Instead of becoming angry, he smiled. "It will take time and dialog among many constituent groups. And that leads to one of the reasons I wanted to have this candid talk. I would like your support and for you to become part of one of my small groups of advisors who can work toward solutions."

Our food arrived, and my first bite gave me time to craft my answer. "Joel, I appreciate the supper invitation and the chance to hear your concerns. I suspect you also know Brian Newman and I are friends and I supported him in the last election. I think you have the same concerns that have been addressed numerous times, many of them by Mayor Newman himself. To be honest, I haven't heard anything that would make my support for the mayor waiver."

"Chris, I didn't come into this meeting blind. I am aware of your connections with the mayor and doubted I could persuade you to change horses over one meal, but I also thought it was important you got to hear my ideas first hand. There's an old saying that it's funny how the people who know the least about you, always have the most to say." He took a bite of his fish and laughed. "Maybe if you know me a little better, you won't say too many bad things about me."

I smiled. "I believe you also said there were a couple of council members you felt needed to be replaced. Who are they?"

"Houston Bass and Marc Salmon?"

"Why?"

"Again, it's nothing personal against either man. They have been on the council for years; they've devoted countless hours to the city's business, and quite frankly, I like each of them. But, they appear to be puppets of the mayor rather than effective leaders. To make the kind of changes that I will be promoting, I need support and forward-thinking council members. That would not include Marc and Houston."

I thought of Charles's comment about me needing to spy on the opponent. "Who would run against them?"

"I'd love to say, but I'm sworn to secrecy. But again, you'd know them."

"What do you think your chances are of winning?"

"As I mentioned, I'm the dark horse candidate, as will be the new candidates for council, but I like to look at it like I would crabgrass in my business. It—like the mayor and council—are deeply rooted and difficult to eradicate but can ruin a yard. It will not be easy to overcome the past and the harmful decisions being made, but that's why I am starting my campaign earlier than has been the tradition. Several treatments of herbicides are often needed to kill crabgrass and it will take several months, and way more than several dollars, to unseat the current mayor and the two members of the council." He paused and smiled. "But I believe I can be successful."

Not if I have anything to do with it, I thought, but returned his smile.

He nodded and gave me a serious look. "I've talked a lot, but what I wanted to do was give you a chance to ask questions you may have."

"I have a good idea of what you want to do as mayor," I said, although I didn't. I wanted to get him off the crabgrass analogy. "Tell me a little about who you are. I've seen you around town and your landscape trucks seem to be everywhere, but I don't know much about you."

He chuckled. "Yes, my gasoline bill lets me know how much the trucks are driving around Folly and James Island." He gave me a capsule version of his businesses—nothing I didn't know.

"Are you married?" I asked, already knowing the answer.

He bit his lower lip and gave an almost imperceptible shake of his head. "I've reached my mid-forties without finding the right lady. Came close a time or two. Recently I had been dating a wonderful young lady until … umm, no, to answer your question, I'm single."

I felt Charles channeling through me. "Until what?"

He looked at me and I was afraid he wasn't going to answer, but then he said, "Have you heard about the woman who died of a drug overdose near the county park the other day?"

I said, "Sure."

"Her name was Lauren Craft. She and I had been dating."

I acted surprised. "Oh. I'm sorry."

"She was a wonderful person. I knew she had a history of drug abuse, in fact, she'd had a couple of stays at rehab, but I thought she'd kicked the horrible habit." He paused and shook his head. "I believe drug use and the horrible consequences of it is one of Folly's biggest problems—quite frankly, that's not only on Folly but everywhere in this country, and I want to make it a big part of my campaign. And then something like this happens. I knew Lauren had become distant lately, and had avoided me on several occasions, but it wasn't until a few weeks ago I learned she was using again." He hesitated. "Using heavily."

"Heroin?" I asked.

"Yes. The last time I saw her—I guess a couple of days before her … umm, her death, she confided she was back where she had been a year ago, struggling with staying away from the evil drug. She was avoiding me, and, well, allowing the drug to kill her."

"Sorry," I repeated.

"Two days before she left us, I talked to her into going back in rehab. She said she'd think about it. That was the last time I saw her."

I thought about what Cindy had said about there being only one needle mark on Lauren.

"Joel, you're certain she was using?"

He cocked his head and looked me in the eye. "She said she was. I had no reason not to believe her. Of course, I never actually saw her shooting up, but the last time I saw her she was grabbing her cell phone out of her purse and I saw a couple of needles in there. God, what a tragedy." He turned and stared at the beach.

"Yes, it was," I said, not knowing what else to say.

We finished our entrees and Joel turned back to me. "Chris, I didn't mean to get into any of this about Lauren. I apologize and hope I haven't dissuaded you for considering my candidacy over such a tragic event regarding Lauren."

I told him it hadn't, but I also didn't tell him I wouldn't have considered supporting him regardless what he'd told me. He said he wasn't in the mood for dessert or an after-dinner drink, but I was welcome to have some. I declined, and he asked for the check. I usually was the one who was stuck with paying, and it felt good to see him pulling out a credit card.

He thanked me for taking the time to meet with him and hoped I would consider supporting him. I lied and told him I would consider it.

After he had gone, I headed to BLU's outdoor dining area, leaned on the wooden bar, and stared at the waves rolling in as they were illuminated by the amber colored lights from the Folly Pier. I thought back on tonight's conversation and could see how Joel could be a viable candidate. He was likable, more likable than I had anticipated. He would be well financed. His platform, while short on answers, would resonate with a sizable portion of the voting public. And he was starting his campaign early enough to pull together a significant amount of support. He might be a dark horse candidate, but he had a shot.

CHAPTER FOURTEEN

Heavy thunderstorms cascaded through the area overnight and steam rose from every wet surface as the sun peeked over the horizon. The slight smell of sea air oozed in the house through cracks under the front door. The temperature was supposed to reach triple digits and combined with sky-high humidity, it would be a great day to stay in air-conditioned comfort. Besides, I had nowhere to go or to be. Retirement was a wonderful thing, and my only regret was I couldn't have begun it years earlier when I had energy and a stronger desire to travel and experience more new things and places. So, instead of booking a flight to Tahiti or rushing out and buying a jogging suit so I could start training to run a marathon, I sat at my kitchen table, gripped a mug of steaming-hot coffee, and replayed much of last night's conversation with Joel.

He had been clear and outspoken about wanting change both in the position of mayor and two of the council members. He was clear about what he saw as Folly's problems. Clarity ended when asked what he would do to solve them. And, when I had asked him about himself, he had shared little. In fact, he didn't tell me anything I didn't already know about his businesses. The one thing he had said that threw me was about Lauren. Joel said he knew she had begun using heroin again, that she had told him so. Yet there was only one needle mark on her body when she was found near the park. Why would she have lied to him? Or, why would he have lied to me. If he hadn't told me the truth, could there be other things he might not have been as forthcoming about?

Perhaps the most world-altering invention that had been created in my lifetime was the personal computer, more specifically, the Internet. The extraordinary tool provided everyone a window into worlds, information, and opinions previous generations could have only imagined. I moved to my spare bedroom that served as my office and turned on the computer and Googled Joel Hurt.

A downside of the Internet was it often provided too much information. In fewer than three-seconds, I learned there were more than 25,000 references that mentioned Joel Hurt. Many of them were about a Joel Hurt who was an influential businessman in Atlanta. I used my brilliant power of deduction to eliminate him since he died in the 1920s. After limiting my search to South Carolina, I started finding references to the Joel Hurt I had shared a meal with. He was a more successful businessman than I had been led to believe. There were lists of charities he had donated thousands of dollars to, everything from childhood diabetes to Alzheimer's research. There were a dozen photos of him at various charity events dressed in a tux and smiling at the camera. There were four different young ladies latched onto his arm in the various photos; none of whom were identified as Lauren Craft.

Other than learning he liked to party, dress well, give to charities, and share the special events with various women, I didn't learn anything significant. I was about to turn the computer off when I noticed the cutline on one of the earlier photos that read: *Joel Hurt, and his date Samantha Forest. Mr. Hurt recently moved to South Carolina from Lafayette, Louisiana.* I had assumed Joel was a native South Carolinian. Out of boredom and my continuing lack of desire to go outside, I added Lafayette, Louisiana, to my Google search criteria, and a half-dozen references to Joel Hurt popped up. Two were about a Joel Hurt who had died at age eighty-four after a long bout with cancer, the other four were about a young landscaper who had bought a well-established garden center from the owner who was retiring after fifty years in the business. A head and shoulder photo of the landscaper showed a younger version of the Joel Hurt running for mayor.

I quickly forgot the other articles when I found the last mention of Joel Hurt. It was in an extensive obituary for the daughter of a prominent Lafayette attorney. According to the article, the daughter was a junior at the University of Louisiana at Lafayette and had "succumbed to an accidental overdose." A sentence at the end of the obituary read: *At the time of her tragic death, she was engaged to Mr. Joel Hurt.*

I stared at Joel's name and reread the obituary. The only mention of cause of death was the benign *succumbed to* statement which didn't indicate an overdose of what, most likely the wording dictated by her father, the influential attorney. Joel was mentioned briefly, but that was enough. It didn't take much imagination to see the similarities between the death in Louisiana and that of Lauren. A coincidence, possibly, but to me, a highly suspicious one.

I grabbed the phone and punched in Cindy's number.

"You saved me a call," the chief said before I could say anything. "Just got the ruling on Ms. Craft's death."

"Murder?" I said and crossed my fingers.

"Was that a guess or are you psychic?" Cindy said.

"Guess. Why?"

"Then you're a sucky guesser. The coroner determined it was an accidental overdose of heroin."

"But—"

"Let me finish, sucky guesser. He said there were no signs of a struggle and her blood alcohol level was almost off the charts. She was drunk and misjudged the dose. Tragic, but accidental. Now you can add *but*."

I sighed. "But what about the lack of prints on the passenger door handle? And, wait until I tell you what I found this morning."

"Hang on. I'm from the hills so you know I can't multitask. Let me answer your question first."

Despite Cindy's self-deprecating comments about where she was from, she was one of the brightest people I knew. "Yes, Chief, answer away."

"Detective Adair speculates one of the EMTs grabbed the handle and since he wore gloves, it wiped off any prints that may have been there. And before you ask, yes, the detective did talk with the EMTs and one of them said he did open that door to get a better angle on Ms. Craft, and that he could have rubbed the door handle. It could have also happened if someone saw the car, grabbed the handle to bend down and look inside, saw the late Miss Burton, panicked, wiped the handle clean so no one would tie him or her to the scene, and ran like ... like someone running fast."

"Do you agree with him?"

"Seems unusual but does make sense."

That didn't answer my question, but thought it was time to tell her what I'd learned and that might help make up her mind.

"Ready to hear why I called?"

"Do I have a choice?"

"No."

"That's what I thought."

I told her about my Internet search and what I'd learned about Joel's *fiancé*.

"Chris, right up there with piss-poor insurance reimbursements, and damned medicine commercials on television, do you know what doctors complain about the most?"

"No, but I bet you're going to tell me."

"It's their competitor: Dr. Google. Seems most of their patients come to their office certain they know what's wrong with them. They've looked up some of their symptoms on the Internet and are ready, willing, and able to tell the docs who have wasted all those years in medical school when all they had to do was look it up and write a prescription for whatever Dr. Google said they needed."

"You made that up," I said.

"Gee, give me some credit, Mr. Citizen. I read it in that highly respected medical journal, *People Magazine*."

I smiled but didn't let Cindy know I found it amusing. "So, what's that have to do with Joel?"

"So, you're going to take an accidental death, stir in a little ancient history off the Internet about some chick from somewhere in Louisiana, and leap to the conclusion Ms. Craft's death —her *accidental* death—had something to do with Joel Hurt. Oh yeah, did I mention *accidental* death?"

"Cindy, all I'm saying is it seems like a large coincidence. Don't you?"

"Yeah," she said.

"So, what are you going to do about it?"

"I'm going to hang up, go to a meeting with our mayor that I'm five minutes late for, say 'Yes sir, yes sir, whatever you say sir,' leave the meeting, and call Detective Adair and share your harebrained coincidence. Then when he says it's absurd and asks what idiot came up with it, I'm going to tell him it was you, and hang up on him before he calls me names."

"Thank you," I said before she could hang up on me.

It may not have sounded like it to anyone who may have been listening to our conversation, but I knew Cindy had heard me, was taking it seriously, and would follow through with Detective Adair. What I didn't know was how seriously he would take it.

CHAPTER FIFTEEN

I barely had time to ponder if the Charleston detective would take my information seriously when the phone rang.

"Good," said Bob Howard. "Glad I caught you alive. Meet me at Al's at noon."

Sorry Bob, I'm busy. Why, Bob? Good morning, Bob. How are you today? All were responses I would have liked to share with the realtor, but I couldn't because he'd already hung up.

Al's Bar and Gourmet Grill was located a block off Calhoun Street, a main road that crisscrossed downtown Charleston, and three blocks from the hospital district. It was in a section of town Realtor Bob referred to as being in its pre-gentrification period. After three beers one night, he'd revised his terminology and classified the houses surrounding Al's as being slummy dumps still standing because termites were afraid to live there. It shared a dilapidated, concrete-block building with a Laundromat.

Bob was already in the bar, and probably had been for some time since his deteriorating dark-plum colored PT Cruiser was parked in front of the door. Bob had been driving the convertible ever since I had known him. It looked more like the vehicle an underpaid short-order cook would be driving than a successful realtor. Bob had once told me he drove it, so his clients would know he was only out for their best interests rather than making money off them. I didn't agree but trying to argue with Bob was like trying to convince a rhinoceros to play Scrabble.

I was greeted by near total darkness as I stepped from the sunlight into the bar. I was also greeted by Al who looked as worn as the exterior of the building and the yard-sale tables and chairs that filled the room. His skin, somewhere between deep brown and light black, appeared paler than usual and his hand-shake weaker than I had remembered. What hadn't changed was his high-wattage smile as he hugged me.

"It's great to see you, Chris. It's been too long."

Bob had told me about Al's declining health, and it'd only been a few weeks since I was in, but the change in his appearance was distressing. The Four Tops were belting out "Reach Out I'll Be There" from the jukebox, but not loud enough to mask Bob's voice coming from a booth near the back of the bar, "Dammit old man, stop huggin' on the boy. Let him get over here and buy me lunch!"

Three tables of diners stopped their conversations and glanced at Bob who was spread out on one side of the booth he had staked a claim to years ago and grumbled if anyone else had the nerve to sit in it. They turned to Al to see how he would react to the burly, bag of hot air.

Al pointed at Bob, smiled, and said, "Shut up and stick a fry in your face."

Bob and I were the only Caucasians in the room, so Al's generous smile had probably prevented a race riot. Two of the diners whose ages approached Al's clapped and some of the others in the room laughed and hoisted their beer bottles to Al.

Ray Charles was singing "Hit the Road Jack" and I wondered if I should follow his advice, but instead I told Al I was glad to see him and weaved my way through the tables and squeezed into the seat opposite Bob.

He waved his hand around and said, "See, they love me."

Not exactly my interpretation, but I let it go, and said, "Al is looking bad."

"Isn't that what I already told you?"

I said it was but didn't realize how bad until now. I glanced back and noticed Al was leaning heavily on a chair and appeared to be breathing heavily.

The music from the jukebox had switched from R&B to Connie Smith singing the country classic *Once a Day*. As a concession to his friendship with Bob, Al, to the consternation of many of his regular customers, had salted his jukebox with several country music tunes, which Bob had often and loudly proclaimed to be the only kind of real music.

"Thank God, my ears will stop bleeding now," Bob said, loud enough for all to hear.

I leaned closer to the table and said, in a voice I didn't want anyone other than Bob to hear, "Does everyone know about you buying the bar?"

"You talking about everyone, like all the monks in Tibet and whoever those short people are who live in Australia, or are you limiting it to Al's customers?"

I stared at Bob.

"No," he finally said, "Al wants to wait until the damned lawyers get all the I's dotted and Q's sliced before announcing it." He tilted his head toward the door. "And speaking about the damned old codger, look who's here?"

Al was three feet from the table and leaning on a rickety chair.

"Park your bony ass, old man," Bob said.

Al moved from leaning on the chair to the space beside me and said, "How could I pass on such a nice invitation. Chris, I went ahead and told my cook to fix you a cheeseburger and to bring you a glass of white wine. Hope that's okay."

I told him it was perfect but was surprised that he was having the cook bring the burger and wine to the table. Al had always taken pride in delivering the food.

Al took a deep breath. "Heard about the big corporate takeover?"

"Yes, if you mean your buddy here purchasing the best cheeseburger restaurant in South Carolina."

Al chuckled. "That's the one. Tubby here said he was going to keep the name of the place Al's. He said—"

Bob interrupted. "Thought about changing it to Bob's Burgers but figured that was too classy a name for this dump and that Al's had just the right dumpy ring to it."

I ignored Bob, a talent one must acquire to be able to spend time around him. "I hear you've agreed to help him."

Al shook his head. "I'll stick around, but don't know how much help I'll be."

Willie Nelson crooned "My Heroes Have Always Been Cowboys," my cheeseburger and wine arrived, and Bob said, "He'll always be welcome and is a tremendous help."

I was pleased by Bob's admission. I knew he felt that way about Al but figured it would take a mule train to pull it out of him with Al close enough to hear.

Al waited for me to bite into my cheeseburger, and said, "Blubber Bob here told me the other day that you're sticking your nose into another strange death on your island. He said you were suspicioning that it may be more than an accident, something about lack of prints or something."

"Not really," I said. "The police are saying it was an accidental heroin overdose. There wasn't any evidence it was forced. I took an interest because the woman's parents live next door to me."

Al slowly nodded. "Yes sir, I hear that. Her dad's that detective you called lazy and incompetent."

"A worthless sack of dog dung," Bob added.

Al's physical health may be fading, but there was nothing wrong with his memory. It had been a year or more since I'd said anything to him about Detective Burton.

Al rolled his eyes at Bob and said, "I was telling Tanesa about it. She said she's seen way too many ODs in the emergency room. I asked her if someone could force another person into sticking themselves and squirting enough H into the system to kill them. She said if the person had enough to drink, it'd be possible."

Cindy had said Lauren had been drunk. "That's true I suppose, but I think there's bigger news around here than what's happening on Folly. Al, I'm glad you'll be getting help with the bar. I know—"

Bob interrupted, "Bar *and Grill*. This ain't only a drinkin' dive. It serves the best cheeseburgers in the civilized world. I see great things happening when I sprinkle my dining-extraordinaire marketing talents to the business. This fine establishment will be reeling in five-star reviews. I can picture the Food Channel broadcasting live from here and that famous chef who goes around the country getting stomped by local chefs and chefettes when he tries to fix their specialties." Bob tapped his forefinger against his temple. "Before you know it, that TV channel will want to pay me, I mean us, a zillion dollars to host a series on their soon to be famous network."

Al laughed. "I can picture it too, Bob. You'll stand out front and when anyone sees your ample stomach they'll figure you must be an expert on cheeseburgers. Then you'll slop on the charm you're famous for and look at the potential customers— umm, excuse me, Food Channel audience—and woo them with something like, 'Get your damn ass in here and eat one of these famous burgers, or get out of my face.' Yes sir, I can see it now."

I leaned back in the booth, gazed at Bob as his face turned red, and ramped-up my admiration for Al another hundred percent.

Instead of exploding in a patented Bob rant, he grinned and leaned his *ample stomach* against the table to get close enough to reach Al's hand. Bob patted the thin, bony hand and said, "Great idea, former owner, and soon-to-be official greeter."

Bob and Al continued to exchange brilliant marketing ideas, I enjoyed the rest of my cheeseburger and especially my wine, and from the jukebox, Freddy Fender's accented voice reminded us what would happen "Before the Next Teardrop Falls."

CHAPTER SIXTEEN

Over the last few days, I'd noticed Brad Burton walking past the house on his way to or from Bert's. I suppose he had made the walk many times, but I had never paid attention to him until the tragic death of his daughter. I had been tempted to step outside and say something to him but knew there wasn't anything to say. He was devastated and there was nothing I could say that would lessen his misery.

Who I talked to several times in the last forty-eight hours leading to tonight's fundraiser was Dude. We had more telephone conversations than during the entire eight years I'd known him. A week ago, I shared with him the idea of him hosting a fundraiser for Brian. After listening to him vacillate between laughter and fear about hosting the event, he finally said, "Okee-dokee. Dude be kingmaker."

The closer we got to the event, panic had overcome any enthusiasm my surfer friend had for the fundraiser. One of his nonnegotiable conditions for holding the event was that it must be catered by Cal's. I hadn't argued, but having the singing cowboy cater anything was like having Bob as the keynote speaker at a Weight Watchers convention. Regardless, Dude asked me to negotiate the catering with Cal who had reluctantly agreed to have his staff of fine culinarians—one underpaid short-order cook—prepare hors d'oeuvres, which when he said it, sounded like *horse nerves*, under the condition he would be able to sing a few songs. He'd reminded me that, "Political types always have music at their shindigs."

I thought it was a small price to pay for having *fine culinarians* catering the event.

I picked Charles up and headed to his girlfriend's apartment building a short distance away. Charles told me to keep driving and that Heather wasn't going. I was surprised since they had been nearly inseparable over the last couple of years.

"Is she feeling bad?"

Charles stared out the windshield and I wondered if he'd heard my question.

"Charles?"

"I heard you," he mumbled. "She's been down, up, and down, since we got back from Nashville. More downs than ups. I've tried everything, but she seems immune to being cheered up."

I knew she had been depressed and while in Tennessee had attempted to take her own life after being arrested for a murder that she hadn't committed. I had been with the two of them three or four times since they had returned from chasing her dreams in Nashville but hadn't seen evidence of continued depression.

When they returned, I shared the name of a counselor who had helped William Hansel, another of my friends after he'd suffered depression. "Has she met with the counselor William recommended?"

Charles turned toward me. "Don't think so. She keeps saying

she's going to make an appointment, but I'm not sure she means it."

I asked if there was anything I could do to help. He said he wished there was but didn't know what it could be. He returned to staring out the windshield as we approached Dude's small, elevated house located a couple of blocks east of Center Street. It would've been hard to miss. His light-green, rusting, 1970 Chevrolet El Camino was parked in the front yard. A four-foot by four-foot sheet of plywood was propped up between two concrete blocks in the vehicle's bed. The plywood was painted white and hand lettering said *BRIAN'S CASH BASH* in fluorescent red paint with a red arrow pointed at the house.

"Dude be subtle," Charles said, mocking the surfer's command of the English language.

The party—cash bash—wasn't to start for another half hour but there were already a half-dozen cars parked in the front yard. I found a spot a block away and was sweating before we made it to Dude's front steps. It was in the low nineties, with high humidity. The only saving grace was thick, black clouds looming overhead. Rain was predicted.

There was a note on the front door that read *IF YOU BE DONATIN' BIG BUCKS, COME IN.*

"Yes, subtle," I said.

I had never been in Dude's house but after knowing the surf shop owner for several years, I was prepared to not be surprised by anything. His décor didn't disappoint. The door opened to the living room that looked like a museum devoted to the 1960s. Bright-green shag carpet covered the floor and the seating grouping consisted of an orange, a green, and a yellow beanbag chair. Three framed photos of a much-younger Dude standing beside other surfers were hung on the wall in an erratic pattern. After my eyes adjusted to the colors, I looked through the door leading to the kitchen and a large wooden deck. This was clearly where the action was.

Dude was waving his arms, his multi-colored tie dye shirt flapped in the breeze, and the subject of his gyrations, Dennis, Cal's short-order cook, pointed to an aluminum pan holding what looked like mini-hotdogs wrapped in dough, covered in freezer-frost.

"Fine chef and host be disputin' something," Charles said.

I elbowed him and headed to the patio. The Doors were screaming "Light My Fire" from an eight-track tape player on a table at the corner of the deck. And Dude was also screaming something about lighting a fire, but for the mini-hotdogs. Cal was standing stooped-shouldered behind his cook and nodding at everything Dude was saying. Five classic surfboards were hanging vertically on the wall by the door.

About that time, Mother Nature added her two-cents to the conversation in the form of a torrential downpour. Dude, the cook, Cal, and three other early arrivers grabbed their drinks, the eight-track boom box, and what was left of their dry clothing, and scampered inside.

Dude was in his early sixties, about five-foot seven, thin, and with his long, mostly white, stringy hair, looked like a shorter, thinner version of the folk singer Arlo Guthrie. He shook his head like a dog and noticed Charles and me.

"Whoa, cool T," he said and nodded toward Charles's long-sleeve T-shirt.

I made a conscious effort years ago to ignore the many long-sleeve, predominantly college logoed, T-shirts that Charles felt compelled to wear. Many others chose not to ignore them. Tonight, he had on a gold T-shirt with the word *Gauchos* written in script on it.

Charles smiled. "University of California at Santa Barbara."

Dude returned his smile, and said, "*Numero Uno* bestest surf college in US of A."

Okay, I couldn't resist asking, and turned to the host, "How do you know that?"

Dude looked at me like he'd seen me for the first time. "*Surfer Magazine*, duh!"

How had that fact slipped by me?

Dude and Charles's enlightening conversation was interrupted by the arrival of three more people who I assumed were here to be *donatin' big bucks*. Todd Livers, who I'd met last year, and was a surfer friend of Dude's, shook the rain off his ball cap and looked around the room. Behind him stood Stephon, one of Dude's employees and a perennial candidate for the East Coast rudest employee of the year. Both men were half my age. The third member of the trio of arrivers was much closer to my age. Mel Evans, better known for reasons that quickly become obvious as Mad Mel, shoved his way past Stephon, waved his camouflage hunting cap in the air throwing water in all directions, and glared at Dude, "Why in the hell didn't you have this shindig on a dry night, you damned, draft-dodging, hippy, druggy?"

Dude appeared nonplussed and nodded. "Welcome Melster. Crack a grin or skedaddle."

I saw Todd look around, probably to grab anything breakable before the earthquake hit. There was no need when Mel laughed. Mel and Dude had become friends more than two decades ago when Dude had saved Mel from being pulled out to sea in a rip current.

Dude looked behind Mel. "Where be Caldwell?"

Caldwell Ramsey was Mel's significant other and a music promoter in Charleston.

"Said he couldn't think of a single reason he wanted to see you tonight. Decided a colonoscopy would be more fun."

Dude shrugged. "He be sorry."

"Doubt it," Mel said. "He sent a check."

"Be better if Caldwell be here, better than have camera stuck up in butt. You send a check, if it no bounce."

The Doors sang "People Are Strange" from the boom box Cal retrieved from the rain. I agreed, and Brian Newman, the reason for the gathering, stuck his head in the door.

"Yo, Mr. Mayorster," Dude said. "Welcome."

As if on cue, Dude's Australian Terrier, Pluto, stuck his head out of a red, tiny, domed, camping tent, with a glow-in-the-dark peace symbol on the side, and barked.

"Be saying howdy," Dude translated for the pup that looked like a shorter version of the surfer.

Brian looked to see who was in the room and, like all good politicians, leaned down and let Pluto lick the side of his face. There were no babies to kiss.

If anyone else arrived, we would be standing on each other's toes, so I was happy to see that the rain had stopped, and rays of the setting sun filtered through the window. Dennis was putting the thawing hot dogs in the oven, and Mel was rooting through the tub holding the beer. I suggested we should migrate back to the deck. Cal took the hint and said he'd begin singing as soon as a crowd gathered outside. Mel rolled his eyes and grabbed the beer tub and hauled it outside. Others followed, most likely following the beer rather than the country crooner. Dude told Stephon to wipe the rain off the chairs. Mr. Rude snarled at his boss but grabbed a dry rag and started slapping the ponded water to the deck.

Barb arrived next. She looked lovely in one of her red blouses and linen slacks. She had a bottle of white wine in her hand, winked at me, and said it was for emergencies in case Dude didn't have any of my drink of choice. I kissed her on the cheek and thanked her for the care package. She asked if I knew everyone at the fundraiser and I said yes, some better than others. I took it as a hint and introduced her to Mel who acted civil and said he'd heard a lot about her and her bookstore. He backslid a bit when he asked her what she was doing with such a stuffy, prude like me. She said all the charming guys were taken and I was all that was left. He said all the charming straight guys may be taken, but there was one charming gay guy in the room. I looked around to see who he was referring to, he said, "ha ha," and moved away to pester Dude. Barb already knew Stephon and Todd from the surf shop.

A younger version of Barb came around the corner. She was thin with stylishly-cut, short blond hair, wearing a white and light-blue sundress and looked more like she was going to a cocktail party than anything at Dude's. She spotted the host and headed his way without stopping to talk to anyone. Barb asked me who she was, and I told her I didn't know.

"Then let's find out, shall we?"

Barb was normally reticent to meet strangers and had a reputation among those who didn't know her well of being standoffish. I followed her to Dude and the stranger who had knelt and was petting Pluto.

"Howdy, Barbstress," Dude said and shook her hand. Barb gave it a brief shake and hugged the host.

Dude smiled and said, "Woe, make me woozy."

Barb returned his smile, didn't comment on her level of wooziness and thanked him for inviting her.

"Me be invitin' all big-buck peeps. Need to keep el mayor mayor."

Pluto drifted toward his food bowl and the newcomer stood

and looked at Barb. "Book store lady, right?"

Barb said she was right and said, "And you are? I don't recall seeing you around."

"I'm Katelin Hatchett." She stuck out her hand. "Dude invited me. We met in the surf shop. He's a nice old hippie."

"Whoa," Dude said for the second time. "Me be hippie, but young compared to age of rock—stone one, not rock and roll one."

He said something else, but I didn't catch it—not that rare an occurrence. I was trying to remember where I'd heard her name. It struck me about the time Cal struck the first notes of "Hey Good Lookin'" as he channeled Hank Williams Sr., one of his idols. Katelin was one of Lauren Craft's housemates.

Cal tried to get everyone in the spirit of Dude's house and sang "Surfin' U.S.A." His rendition fell under the category *it's the thought that counts*. Country music was in his blood and in his voice. His vocal range began and ended there. He finished, and Dude applauded and said, "Boss!" The only reaction from everyone else was to look at Dude and, I suspect, wonder what music he was listening to. Cal slid back into his genre and began Ricky Van Shelton's "I'll Leave This World Loving You," and the rest of us continued our conversations. I tried to think of something to say to Katelin, but she moved away to talk to Stephon before I had a chance.

I was surprised to see Brad Burton at the back of the patio. He must have arrived while I was talking to Katelin. He was looking around like he didn't know anyone, so I sighed, and as much as I hated to admit it, felt sorry for him and wandered his way and said it was nice seeing him.

He continued looking around the deck, and said, "I've always liked the mayor and Hazel said I should make an appearance to show our support." He hesitated and smiled. "And give him a check."

The only positive encounter I had with the former detective before he'd moved here was a couple of years back when he had shared with me some damning information about the unpopular previous mayor, and I used it to get him to resign, thus opening the door for Brian to be elected.

"It was nice of you to come. I know how difficult this must be."

Brad saw Brian Newman talking to one of the surfers. "That's why I'm going to say hi to the mayor, leave my check, and get out of here. Excuse me."

I again thanked him for coming and watched him move to Brian.

I looked for Charles but instead saw William Hansel peeking in the door. He looked around and smiled when he saw me. The sixty-four-year-old professor at the College of Charleston had been one of the first people I'd met when I got to Folly. We were about the same age, and even though he'd lived on Folly for more than ten years at that time, we in many ways had been outsiders. I was new to the community and William was African American, one of only a couple of hand-fuls residing here at the time. He had made a few good friends since his wife died seventeen years ago. I was honored to count myself as one of them.

"Chris, I am heartened to see you among the guests at this event."

William's navy-blue dress slacks and tan, button-down, dress shirt were as formal as his speech. He could be as difficult to understand as was Dude, but for the opposite reason.

"Glad you could make it," I said. "Brian will be pleased to see you."

William looked around the room. "It appears I am amid several people to whom I am unfamiliar."

I pointed out he knew the mayor, Charles, Barb, and Dude, and offered to walk with him to the bar.

"That would be appreciated."

Charles had seen William and ended his conversation with Mel and met the two of us at the drinks.

"Evening, Professor," Charles said and nodded in my direction. "Couldn't find anyone better to hang with?"

William chuckled. "Mr. Fowler, you were in deep conversation with Mr. Evans and I didn't want to interfere with your social intercourse."

"If you mean that Mad Mel was blabbing on about how great he was, you're right."

Cal finished "On the Other Hand," and waved Dude to stand beside him and said, "Guys and Gals, Dude here invited us to share in this gala, so we could support the reelection of our mayor. So, let's give Dude a big hand and let him say a few words." Cal smiled. "And if I know Dude, it'll be very few words."

Applause for Dude wasn't quite as strong as was the laughter at Cal's remark. Either way, Dude moved to where Cal had been standing.

"Thanks for coming. Lay oodles of dough on getting the mayor reelected." Dude gave a bow like he'd recited the Gettysburg Address and stepped aside.

Brian put his arm on Dude's shoulder. "Thank you, Dude, for hosting this event, for giving me a chance to share why I am running for reelection, and for your, umm, words of encouragement."

Barb had moved to my side and was surprised to see Katelin and Stephon on my other side. Brian began by sharing what he considered his main accomplishments since being in office and a little about his background as police chief. He told us since there was an opponent—a well-financed opponent—who had already started his campaign, that Brian needed to start early. He confided he hated asking for donations, but he would have to get over it since it appeared that record amounts would be spent on the election.

"Now don't get me wrong," he said. "My opponent appears to be sincere, with the best of intentions." Brian was following the current political strategy of not mentioning his opponent's name. "Many of us already know him through his businesses. He's telling everyone he's a long shot or a dark horse in the race, but don't believe it for a second. He's got money and a message that sounds better than it is. I believe he is a fine man, but we simply have different visions of what Folly should become."

"Fine man, shit," mumbled Katelin, louder than she had intended.

I glanced around and no one else appeared to have heard her.

Brian continued with how he differed with his opponent, and ended by asking for our support and turned it back over to Cal.

"Now friends and neighbors," Cal said, and pointed to a small table by the door "I hear there are empty envelopes back there on that table. Before y'all leave, grab one, stuff it full of cash, checks, gold nuggets, whatever, and fill out the pesky paperwork. Our mayor, Brian Newman, needs our support." He picked up his guitar and back in the spirit of Dude, he started strumming and poorly singing "Fun, Fun, Fun."

CHAPTER SEVENTEEN

T he day after the fundraiser, I was having breakfast at the Dog, joking with Amber, and watching Marc Salmon and Houston Bass arguing about a parking ordinance the council had been debating. Were they as worried about the upcoming election as Brian was? I also replayed parts of last night's fundraiser and what I had told Charles about how Katelin had reacted to Brian's complimentary comment about Joel. Charles had been so distracted about Heather that he failed to do what he does best: ask thousands of questions about what I was telling him, most of them irrelevant. I hate to admit it, but I missed his interruptions.

I had noticed a change in Charles since he and Heather had returned from Nashville. He had been one of the most upbeat people I'd ever come into contact with from the day I'd met him until the day they loaded up his car and moved to Music City. Folly had been his home for years and he had embraced it and had become one of its biggest supporters. To be honest, Charles was the walking, talking personification of the kind of person the island I had fallen in love with represented. He liked almost everyone, could find good in the most obnoxious resident, and was a chameleon when interacting with the wide range of personalities with which he came in contact. And I knew from personal encounters with evil that he would put his life on the line for his friends. Charles had said he was glad to be back after their move to Tennessee, and at times I recognized the Charles of old, but while others had said he was the same, I knew differently. I hoped time would bring out the old Charles, for both his and my sake.

Amber had refreshed my coffee when Katelin stepped into the crowded restaurant, glanced around, and headed in my direction. She looked exhausted. Her stylish attire from the fundraiser was replaced by ratty shorts and a wrinkled, black T-shirt with Nike written below the company's iconic swish.

"Mr. Landrum, umm, Chris, could I join you?"

I nodded toward the seat on the other side of the table. "Of course. Want coffee or something to eat?"

Amber had seen Katelin arrive and was quick to the table.

Katelin started to answer me but looked up at Amber. "Maybe some coffee, yes, coffee please."

Amber headed to the kitchen, and Katelin tapped her fingers on the table. "Pretty day, isn't it?"

"Beats last night's weather," I said. I wanted to jump into the reason she was here, but it'd be better for her to get there at her own pace.

She looked at the framed photos of dogs on the wall beside me. "Lots of dogs in here."

I agreed as Amber returned with Katelin's coffee and a second refill for me. Amber asked if Katelin wanted something to eat. She said no, and Amber moved to the next table to share her endearing smile and helpful attitude.

"Umm," Katelin said, "saw you talking with Lauren's dad, umm, Mr. Burton, last night and figured you were friends."

I acknowledged that we were *acquaintances* and had been talking at the fundraiser.

Katelin took a sip of coffee. "Well anyway, I wanted to tell him something, but he disappeared before I could get to him."

I told her Brad wanted to support the mayor and wasn't there long.

She looked in her coffee mug and in a lower voice said, "I was afraid he'd be mad at me, or try to blame his daughter's death on me."

"Why would you think that?"

"I'd only talked to him a couple of times when he came to the house Lauren and I shared. He didn't say anything bad, but I could tell from his expression that he didn't approve of where we lived. I figured he thought I was a bad influence on Lauren."

I wanted to repeat "why would you think that" but didn't and nodded for her to continue.

"I don't know if he knew it or not, but I had gone through rehab with Lauren a couple of times." She shook her head and frowned. "We shared some rough patches. If she told her dad about our history, he probably would've thought I was bad for her." She looked up from the mug. "Chris, I wasn't bad. Lauren was good and most of the time real clean. I was sort of between waitressing jobs a while back and we had more time to spend together. She had a good heart and was funny, not jokes funny, but said funny things about what was going on around her, if you know what I mean."

"I think I do. You said she was clean most of the time."

Her head dipped, and she returned to staring at the coffee mug. "Umm, I hate to admit it, but over the last two months, she relapsed. She was back on H big time. It was so sad. I tried to talk to her, remind her of all the, excuse me, shit we'd gone through getting off the stuff. She wouldn't listen."

I thought about what Cindy had said about only one needle mark. "Are you sure she was using again?"

Katelin sighed. "Yeah, I'm certain. She was shooting up worse than ever before; shooting up right in the living room, not even trying to hide it. Drinking heavy too."

"Do you know why?"

"She never said it, but I'd put money on her a-hole boyfriend, Joel."

"Why?" I asked, and decided I was becoming nosy Charles.

"He's not good for, umm, not good for Lauren. He had a way of putting her down. Condescending, I think that's what you call it. One minute he was all lovey-dovey and the next he was saying he was ashamed of her, hinting that her drugging was going to give him a bad name."

I also remembered how Katelin had reacted to Brian Newman's remark about him last night and wondered if his treatment of Lauren was what precipitated her strong reaction.

"Last night I saw how you reacted when the mayor was complimenting Joel and saying he was a good guy."

"I was afraid you might have heard me. I couldn't help it, just blurted it out."

"Was it because of how he acted with Lauren?"

She glanced around the room and at me. "Sort of."

"Sort of?" I said.

Her face looked like she'd been sucking on a lemon.

"I dated him before she did." She shook her head. "No, that's not accurate. He dated both of us at the same time and I didn't know about it. Joel and I were getting serious, or so I thought. I was working a lot of double shifts and wasn't ever home." She sighed. "Crap, I don't know why I'm telling you any of this." She paused and looked at me like she was expecting an answer.

"It's okay," I said.

That seemed to satisfy her. "Anyway, Joel's a lying two-timer. He was trying to juggle both of us. Can you believe that? We were housemates. The only reason he dumped me was I found out about him and Lauren. He blew a gasket. I was afraid he was going to hit me." She gripped her fist so tightly I thought her fingernails were going to draw blood. "Thank God, he didn't. He seems so sincere, even sweet, but the more I got to know him, I realized he would lie about anything. It was my good luck that he dumped me. Enough about that. I wanted to tell Mr. Burton I was sorry about Lauren, that's all."

"Katelin, do you think her death was accidental?"

"Sure, why? Do you think she killed herself on purpose?"

"I'm not saying anything. You knew her better than most anyone, maybe better than everyone, so I thought you might have an opinion. Just asking."

"If she killed herself, it was over Joel. She thought they were close but was wondering more and more where he was when she thought he should be with her. That shouldn't be reason enough to harm yourself. Should it?"

Good question. I wish I had an answer. I told her I didn't think so and it seemed to satisfy her.

"Chris, do you think Mr. and Mrs. Burton would mind if I stopped by their house to tell them how sorry I am?"

"They would appreciate it."

She took another sip of coffee and clunked her mug down on the table. "Think I'll try to do that now while I've got my courage up."

I told her I thought it was a good idea and said I'd pick up the tab on her coffee.

"Thank you for letting me mouth off. I hope the mayor got enough money last night to stomp Joel. If you excuse my French, he's an asshole."

She pushed away from the table and was gone before I had time to excuse her French.

CHAPTER EIGHTEEN

I called Charles twice over the next two days. Each time, he was abrupt and said he was busy making deliveries for the surf shop and would call me when he had time. He didn't ask if I knew anything new about Lauren's death or Brian's candidacy. His behavior was so un-Charles-like that I wondered if I'd gotten the wrong number. It sounded like I was talking to a stranger, and he never called back.

I hadn't heard from Charles and the fundraiser at Bob's house was this evening, so I called to see if he was going. When the topic of fundraisers was originally discussed, he had said nothing could keep him away, but he knew the event was tonight and hadn't said anything about it recently.

"What?"

"Good afternoon," I said. "Are you going—"

"No," he interrupted.

"You don't know the question; how can you say no?"

"You're going to ask if I'm going to Bob's thing."

I hated him knowing what I was going to say before I said it. "So, you're not going?"

"That's what *no* meant," he said, without a hint of warmth.

"Charles, what's wrong?"

"Nothing, I'm busy, that's all."

"Busy?"

"Okay, not that busy. It's just Heather says she doesn't like to be around all those hoity-toity rich people, and she's been in such a sour mood I don't want to leave her tonight." He hesitated, and said, "Sorry I've been short with you."

I was surprised. "She thinks rude, obscene, politically incorrect Bob Howard is hoity-toity?"

"Okay, you got me there. Not him, but she means the kind of people Bob will invite. For reasons I can't figure out, he does have some snooty friends. Even if he doesn't or if none of them show up tonight, Heather thinks they are and flat out won't go. I need to stay with her."

There was no sense in trying to convince him otherwise, so I wished him luck with Heather and he told me to let Bob know he wasn't there because he hated Bob's guts. I knew that was one-hundred percent incorrect but said I would share his sentiments. On a more pleasant note, Barb had said she had to work late, but would join me at Bob's.

On the short drive from Folly to Charleston, I realized I had never been to Bob and Betty's new house. They'd moved about three years ago from James Island to a ritzier section of Charleston a few blocks west of King Street and three blocks north of Broad Street. My navigation system still managed to lead me to their house even though it'd also never been there.

The predicted late-afternoon showers failed to appear, and the humidity was lower than usual as I pulled up to the address. I knew Bob was a successful realtor, but was still impressed by the large, two-story, Georgian style home that had Bob's street address beside the front door. I was more impressed when a college-aged gentleman, dressed in a red blazer, and black slacks waved for me to pull to the curb between two orange cones— illegally placed there by Bob, I suspected—and said he would valet park my car.

"This is Bob Howard's house?" I said, feeling more like I'd parked in front of the White House.

"It is the residence of Mr. Howard," said the polite valet. "I'm not certain of his first name."

I said I supposed it would have to do and left him with my car, and hoped he wasn't an industrious car thief.

I took a moment gawking at the house and passed through a decorative, traditional Charleston wrought iron gate and walked up a pea gravel path to the front steps where I was greeted by a grey-haired, older gentleman wearing a white server's jacket, black slacks, and black shoes so highly polished that they could've been made of glass.

"Welcome, Sir," he said, and honest-to-goodness, he bowed.

I was now certain I was at the wrong house, but he reassured me it was indeed the residence of Mr. and Mrs. Robert Howard, the "fine couple who are hosting tonight's political gathering." I was starting to agree with Heather.

"Other ladies and gentlemen are gathered on the back patio," said the doorman. "Please allow me to aid you in finding your way."

I did. On the walk through the hallway I peeked in the formal living room on the right and formal dining room to my left, before we arrived in the larger, and more casual, family room.

All the rooms were filled with antiques and fine furnishings that made the house look more like a museum than where real people lived. The one hint of reality was a flat screen television on the wall of the family room. The set was the size of an Interstate billboard. I suspected that was Bob's decorative touch.

Two sets of French doors led from the family room to an expansive brick patio that sat on a more expansive manicured lawn. Twenty people were milling around a six-foot-tall version of the distinct Pineapple Fountain located in downtown Charleston's French Quarter. Most of the attendees were all smiles with a drink in one hand while trying to balance a china plate of finger foods in the other.

Of the group, I only recognized a half dozen and was tempted to turn and leave when I heard Bob yell, "Well it's about damned time you got here."

He scurried—more like a slow walk for most everyone else —around a couple of the guests and headed my way. He had made major concessions to his normal attire since he had on long pants instead of shorts, and his extensive Hawaiian flowery shirt collection had given way to a yellow dress shirt. I nearly reached for my phone/camera to record Bob in sartorial splendor, truly a historic event, but he had already put his arm around my shoulder. "Where's piss ant Charles?"

You could lead Bob to a classy event, but you couldn't make him classy, or something like that. I explained Charles was staying with Heather and she'd been a little under the weather. I doubted he'd believed me, but he didn't press it. A waiter arrived about the same time Bob had and offered me a glass of Champagne. I took it, thanked him, and gave Bob a sideways glance.

"All Betty's idea. You'd better enjoy that damned drink. You know they don't even sell that stuff in boxes?"

I told him I didn't know that, but I thought it was classy. He told me she made him hide the beer cooler behind the shrubs that were aesthetically placed around three sides of the patio.

A second waiter magically appeared carrying a silver tray with a selection of finger foods that looked more colorful than appetizing. I took one that looked familiar and thanked the smiling waiter.

Bob waved his hand in front of me. "Don't even think about asking me what that crap is. I can tell you it costs more than a new Dodge Dart."

I told him that I appreciated his fiscal analysis, and turned more serious, and thanked him for the generous offer to host the event.

"Don't thank me," he said as he turned to look at the group gathered near the outdoor bar. "Betty said if I didn't make this a memorable shindig I'd better have one of my builder friends start on an oversized doghouse."

I didn't catch everything he'd said about the doghouse; I was stuck on him having friends, builders or otherwise. I also knew he was doing little more than blowing smoke, because he would have done anything for Brian.

"It's still kind of you. So, who are these people?"

"Most are realtors who spend all their time slinking around looking for potential clients. Free booze and little clumps of food that no normal person can recognize drew them in." He chuckled. "They also have money and with the right twist of the arm can be convinced to give a chunk of it to the right political candidates."

"And that would be Brian Newman?"

"Hell, Chris, they don't have a rat's turd idea who Brian is. They do know me, and if I suggest they donate to him, they'll smile and take the duct tape off their checkbooks and scribble out a check for the legal maximum amount."

I smiled. "I didn't know you had that many good friends."

"I don't. Half of them work for me, and most of the others work for people who owe me favors. You're beginning to bore me, so let's go, I'll introduce you to some of them."

I was once again reminded why he didn't have many good friends. Bob told me I wouldn't have to remember any of the names since most of the realtors had money and since I was old and broke I wouldn't see them again. He was wasting his words since names and I had never been on remembering terms.

He dragged me over to a couple of gray-haired men in deep conversation. Bob, being Bob, was oblivious to what they were talking about and shoved his way between them, told me the taller one was Gordon something, and the "skinny, malnourished little twerp" was Lawrence Brockman. He said they were two of his employees which apparently gave him authority to interrupt and insult to his heart's content. Bob told them I was a good friend of tonight's guest of honor, Brian Newman. They smiled and pretended to care who I was and probably who Brian Newman was.

I held their smile and looked around to see if the *guest of honor* had arrived, but he either wasn't here yet or was hidden behind some of the other guests of lesser honor. Bob told the two realtors that he'd love to stay and talk longer but had to mingle. They didn't appear to be sad to see us go.

A violinist, not more than a teenager, was plying her trade on the other side of the patio. Her eyes were closed and she was lost in the music. That was good because I doubted anyone could hear her because of the water splashing in the fountain and the din of several people talking over each other. The succulent smell of late-blooming flowers flowed through the air.

Bob pointed at the musician. "I wanted a fiddle and guitar, so we could have real music—country music—but Betty vetoed my brilliant idea. There's no king at this castle. Betty rules with a firm skillet."

Our next stop was one I did look forward to. Al and his daughter Tanesa were standing by themselves near the violinist. I realized it was only the second time I'd seen Al outside his bar/restaurant and the first time I'd seen Tanesa in something other than her medical scrubs. She wore a knee-length yellow and white sundress that contrasted nicely with her coco-brown skin and black, curly hair. She looked more like a doctor's daughter rather than the highly skilled ER doc I knew her to be. Al had on a black dress shirt, gray slacks, and an expression that screamed *I'm uncomfortable as hell.*

"Well if it ain't beauty and the damned ugly old beast. Hope none of my fine Caucasian neighbors saw you two sneaking in," said Bob, warmly welcoming the Washingtons to his house.

Tanesa ignored Bob's comment, smiled, and gave the burly politically incorrect realtor a kiss on the cheek. Al also smiled, his coffee-stained teeth contrasting with Tanesa's gleaming white ones.

Bob looked at Al and took a step back. "Don't you even think about kissing me, old man." He looked around and waved one of the waiters over. "Get this old man some of those food clumps before he dies of starvation right on Betty's manicured lawn."

Bob made a few ruder remarks, hugged Al, showing a glimmer of his true feelings about his friend, and said, "Gotta spread more joy among the others, so I'll leave so you can talk about me."

Al and Tanesa thanked him for inviting them, Bob mumbled it wasn't his idea, and left the three of us. Tanesa suggested her dad may want to sit on one of the stone benches along the perimeter of the yard. Al didn't pretend to argue with her and moved toward the closest resting spot, leaning on Tanesa's shoulder the entire way. And yes, we did spend some time talking about out host, but regardless what Bob might think, it was all positive.

After talking about Bob and how lovely his house was, Tanesa said she wanted to get another drink and asked if I would walk with her to the bar. I didn't want to leave her dad, but figured she wasn't asking just to have an escort so I said "sure."

"He's not doing well," she said once we were out of earshot of her dad. "You don't know how thrilled I am that Bob bought the bar. Dad wouldn't say it, but we all knew he was on the verge of bankruptcy. The bar means everything to him and if he lost it that way it'd kill him. I just hope—never mind, I hope he'll be okay."

"But you're worried?" I said, to keep her talking.

"He needs a good checkup, he's getting weaker. I can tell that from how much he's having to lean on me, and how much trouble he's having catching his breath after taking a few steps."

"What does he say?"

"He laughs and blames it all on his arthritis and age *sneaking up* on him. He seems to forget he helped pay my way through medical school. His problem is much worse than age and arthritis, but it'd be easier to get Bob to lose 100 pounds than to get dad to the hospital."

We'd reached the bar and grabbed three more drinks and headed back to Al. His eyes were closed and for a second, I thought maybe he was sick, or worse. He opened his eyes, smiled, and thanked Tanesa as she handed him his drink.

I saw Brian come through the French doors onto the patio. He was dressed in a sports coat and tie and I started to head his way, but Bob, who had been talking to and probably insulting a man and a woman I didn't recognize, cut off their conversation and headed toward the guest of honor. I would let him handle the introductions since I still didn't know many of the guests. Barb was next through the French doors. I wasn't going to let anyone, especially Bob, greet her and excused myself from Al and Tanesa and walked around the fountain to meet Barb. She had on another of her red blouses but wore a white, linen jacket over it. She smiled when she saw me and gave me a hug as she looked around the patio.

"Just like Dude's party," she said with a large dose of sarcasm.

"Hard to tell the two apart," I said.

She stared at the fountain. "I knew Bob was successful, but you never mentioned he lived in a palace with a fountain he must have stolen from a square in Rome."

"If it wasn't for someone who is the most patient woman in the world, Bob's wife, Betty, he'd be just as content living in a three-room shack at the beach, that is if the shack had air conditioning, cable TV, and a refrigerator stocked with thirteen cases of beer."

Barb looked around. "Where is Saint Betty?"

"Bob said something about it taking her longer to put on her face than it took him, and she'd be making a grand entrance at any moment."

"In honor of our host, I'll refrain from commenting on Bob's face."

I nodded, and Bob yelled for everyone to pay attention to what he was about to say. The violinist stopped, the smattering of conversations stopped, and all that could be heard was the fountain. Bob glared at the flowing water like it should have obeyed his command. It refused his order, he faked a smile and introduced the person the fundraiser was created to assist.

Brian thanked Bob and stepped on a nearby stone bench. "First, let me thank Mr. and Mrs. Bob Howard for hosting such a magnificent event." Betty had stepped out on the patio and waved acknowledgment to Brian. The rest of the guests applauded, but not as loud since most of their hands were holding food and drink. Brian gave nearly the identical speech he had shared at Dude's house.

He finished his remarks and Bob tried to step up on the bench and failed. He mumbled something about the bench being too high and "reminded" those gathered that there was a table near the door to the house, and there were several empty envelopes on it, and said, "As you know, our insightful, helpful lawmakers have dictated the maximum amount individuals can donate to Brian Newman's reelection campaign is a mere thousand dollars. I know all of you carry more than that in your wallet and consider it petty cash. So, I expect—I repeat, expect —you to slip your measly thousand bucks in an envelope before you leave."

I wondered how many of us had that much in our pockets. I know I didn't, but I also didn't know the rest of Bob's friends that well, so they could have. There was a smattering of applause, most likely because Bob was finished speaking, and the host drifted back to the couple he was talking with earlier.

Barb and I walked around the edge of the lawn as she admired the weed-free flower beds. She asked if I knew what kind of flowers had such a pleasant aroma. I told her I knew as much about flowers—and trees for that matter—as I did about the founding of Finland. She smiled at my ignorance, something she was learning I had no shortage of, and started to say something. Bob, often oblivious to conversations not involving him, interrupted as he dragged the couple he had been talking with over to us.

"Lovely Barb and, well, not so lovely, Chris, meet Lisa and Jeff Holthouse. They're a husband and wife realtor team who're always trying to steal my listings. Despite their larcenous ways, they're not bad blokes."

In Bob-speak, that meant the middle-aged couple, whose last name seemed quite appropriate for realtors, who I had seen him speaking to earlier, were friends. Lisa nodded to Barb and me, and Jeff held out his hand for each of us to shake.

"Enough bonding," said Bob after I shook Jeff's hand. "Jeff's got something to tell you about the ball of crap who's trying to knock Brian out of office. Well, don't stand there, Jeff, tell him."

Who wouldn't want to be friends with such a charming guy?

Jeff was around six-foot three and leaned toward me and glanced around before speaking. "Lisa and I specialize in high-end properties."

"Try to steal them from me," Bob interjected.

My thought that Bob and Jeff were friends was confirmed when Jeff ignored Bob and continued, "High-end residences, of course, are slower to sell than smaller homes with a much-more palatable price point."

Bob interrupted again, "Cheaper."

"Anyway," Jeff continued, "because they are often on the market so long and are occasionally vacant, we contract with a lawn-care company to do the routine yard work, and if the exterior needs sprucing up, the company adds additional landscaping or cheers up the tired existing landscape."

"We call it exterior staging," Lisa added.

Bob threw up both hands. "Get to the damned point before Chris and Barb fall asleep."

Jeff glared at Bob and turned to me. "For the last three years, we've contracted with Joel Hurt's lawn service company and garden centers. He and I are graduates of the Citadel and met at a cocktail party hosted by the alumni association. Nice fellow, or so I thought."

"Now to the point," Bob said, as he pointed at his watch.

"The point is I met with him last week at a residence on Tradd Street that needed extensive exterior staging. The owners had moved to Arizona and thought their house was worth more than I had estimated it to be worth. They told me to do whatever I needed to do to bring it close to their expectations."

I was ready to join Bob in asking what the point was but waited for Jeff.

Jeff put his arm around Lisa's bare shoulder. "Lisa was with me and after we walked through the property we were cooling down on the lanai when—"

"Cripes, Jeff, it's a damned porch. You gotta dumb-it-down for Chris."

"I know what a lanai is, Bob. Jeff, you were saying."

"I was *trying* to say that Joel started talking to us about running for mayor of Folly Beach. He wanted us to donate to his campaign. But the funny thing was how he started badmouthing the current mayor." Jeff paused and nodded his head toward Brian Newman who was standing near the fountain and talking to Betty. "You have to understand, we barely know Joel, only talked with him at the cocktail party and at six or seven work sites, and he starts mouthing off about the mayor we had never heard of. Thought it was strange and inappropriate."

I waited for Bob to interrupt, but he remained silent, so I said, "What kind of things was he saying?"

Lisa moved a step closer. "Joel said everyone knew Mayor Newman was taking bribes from bar owners, so his police would look the other way about under-age drinking. He said Mayor Newman often played favorites for his friends. Even said Mayor Newman had been a suspect in some horrible murder when he was in the military police and stationed in Europe."

I was shocked. "Are you sure Joel was talking about Brian Newman?"

Jeff answered for Lisa. "No doubt. He kept saying Newman."

I thought back to my meeting with Joel when he praised Brian for the job he had done as mayor and for his stint in the military.

"It didn't bother us too much," Lisa said. "Politicians are always saying terrible things about their opponents, but what surprised me was we didn't live on Folly, couldn't vote in the election, had never heard of your mayor, and barely knew Joel. He wanted our money, but he didn't have to be so, how shall I say it, umm, vile about his opponent." She turned to Jeff.

He took the handoff. "When our friend Bob invited us to this gathering, we wanted to come to learn more about the devil incarnate you have as mayor. Then, as Bob can often do, he screwed up everything when he told us a little about Brian and how good a guy he was. Bob said you were a friend of the mayor and an inquisitive gentleman—"

Bob interrupted, "I said damned nosy, not inquisitive."

Barb didn't say anything but put her arm around my waist.

"Since you were the mayor's friend and *inquisitive*, Bob suggested we tell you what Joel had said."

Lisa looked at her husband. "Jeff, tell him what Joel said about the police chief and those other council members."

"Joel went on to say the police chief wasn't even from the area and the only reason the mayor had hired her as chief was because she would do anything he told her to do—legal or not. Joel said she had to go, before she made even a bigger mockery of law enforcement over there."

"The other elected people," Lisa prompted.

"Two council people, names I don't remember, had to go. Joel said they were nothing but puppets of the mayor."

"Houston and Marc?" I said.

"Think that's them," Jeff said.

Lisa nodded.

Bob held up his empty glass. "Enough boring political talk. We need to get back to the bar. Anything else?"

Jeff and Lisa said that that was it and repeated how unprofessional they thought it was that Joel was telling them what he thought about Brian. Bob had heard enough and herded the couple toward the bar.

Interesting, I thought, and wondered if it had meant anything other than a politician doing what many of them do so well—lying.

CHAPTER NINETEEN

The rest of the evening was a haze. The roar of water from the fountain mixed with the soothing violin music; conversations from those I didn't know melded into the words from Betty, Bob, and Brian. I told Barb I had spent as much time socializing as I could without pulling out my remaining hair. Al and Tanesa had already departed, so I said my goodbyes to Bob and Betty, and Barb and I headed to the front of the house to ask the smiling valet to collect our vehicles.

Barb asked if I wanted to have a drink on her balcony, I agreed and followed her back to Folly to her condo overlooking the Atlantic and the iconic Folly Pier. On the drive, I mulled over the thought that if Joel had been telling such blatant lies to people who had no interest in the election, what could he be telling people who could make a difference? I tried to push it out of my mind and focus on the lovely evening with a lovely lady.

It was warm on the deck but the breeze off the ocean made it tolerable. Barb said for me to fix each of us a glass of wine while she changed into something more comfortable. My culinary skills were limited, but pouring wine was one of my specialties, perhaps my only one. Moments later, she returned and had changed into tan shorts and a red T-shirt with the cover of *The Great Gatsby* printed on the front.

"You're not going to start competing with Folly's 759 stores that sell T-shirts, are you?" I asked and handed her the wine.

She glanced down at the shirt and said, "No, but because I have a bookstore, a wholesaler from Virginia wants me to. This was a gift, bribe, to get me to carry their famous books and authors' collection. I think *Le Petit Prince* would have a tough time competing with *I'm not awesome; I'm awe every day!*"

I agreed and told her that when it came to selling books, she had little competition. She joked she had nearly as many books in her store as Charles had in his apartment. My friend had more books than a small-town library, so Barb wasn't far off although she was teasing—or so I thought.

We watched the lights from a shrimp boat gently bob in the waves a few hundred yards off shore, and three people carrying flashlights walking on the beach.

"Changing the subject," I said, "what do you make of what those two realtors said about Joel?"

She turned from watching the trio on the beach and stared at me. "I think the guy running against your friend was doing what politicians have done since the beginning of democracy in Athens during the sixth century B.C.: lying about their opposition. Nothing more, nothing less."

"Sixth-century B.C. You learn that in law school?"

"Sixth grade studying Greece. I was interested in history then slept through most things related to it in law school. What's your take?"

"You make a good point, but it galls me. I sat across from Joel the other day and listened to him go on and on about how nice a guy Brian Newman was. He praised his military service, his service as chief of police, and even his work as mayor. He was convincing. Now I hear what he told those realtors, the opposite of what he told me."

Barb nodded. "You're taking it personally. You can't do that with politics. Could your feelings have something to do with learning Joel had been dating Lauren? Could it be clouded because of what her roommate Katelin had said about Joel dating both of them at the same time and her anger toward him?"

I turned my attention to the Folly Pier. "And now Lauren's dead."

"And the only reason to think Joel had anything to do with her death could be because she may, and I emphasize may, have been distraught over their breakup when she killed herself."

"But what if her death wasn't accidental or suicide? What if—"

Barb jerked her head my direction and interrupted, "It wasn't long ago that I heard your friend Bob accuse you of sticking your nose in every death over here regardless if it was caused by someone else's hand or natural causes." Her voice rose with each word. "I thought he was kidding, but I'm beginning to wonder."

"Barb, I'm only trying to see how the pieces fit together. I don't know that they do."

She sighed. "You said Detective Adair was looking into Lauren's alleged OD. You said he was good at his job. You said your friend Cindy was a good police chief and wouldn't let go until she got to the truth. Right?"

I knew I was being backed in a corner. "Yes, it's in good hands. I know Lauren's death looks like an accidental overdose or suicide. Her friend Katelin said she was using again and drinking. I know all that and so do the police."

"Then let them do their job." Her voice was calmer, and she

put her hand on my arm. "Chris, I don't know where our relationship is going. I doubt you do either, and that's okay. I'm still not over what my ex did, and it gave me a sour taste in my mouth for men, a taste that I thought would last for a long time." She stopped talking and returned her gaze to the pier.

I understood what she had meant and decided to wait her out and sipped my wine and stared at the pitch-black horizon.

She lowered her voice and said, "You screwed up my plan to avoid the opposite sex. My ex was great at the law; he sucked when it came to listening to me. It took him being hauled off in cuffs for me to realize that he was as devious as hell. So I got here, avoided any interactions that would make it appear that I had any interest in a man, and then that damned body was found behind my store and you stumbled across it and shot my plans to hell."

I nodded.

She continued, "I know I'm not making much sense, but what I'm trying to say is you came along and seemed about as opposite from my ex as one could be. You listened to me. God, I appreciated that." She broke a smile. "And unless you're a much better liar than I think, you're as open and honest as anyone." Her smile faded, and she squeezed my forearm. "Chris, I like you and I'm scared. Bob may have exaggerated, but you have an innate sense of right and wrong and for some reason you feel the need to right as many wrongs as you can. I don't think it was, but if Lauren's death was murder rather than accidental or suicidal, have you thought about what that means?"

I nodded. "It means there's a murderer out there."

"Yes, and the person sitting next to me is wondering if it could be Joel."

"Not really," I said. "It's that he might have a reason to want her out of the way."

"I'm no expert," Barb said, "but murder is a huge leap from breaking up with someone."

"I know. What do you think I should do?"

"At the fundraiser, you learned Joel was a liar, but that's all you learned. If you told that to the police, and to a cop who doesn't know you well, he would probably say, and rightly so, 'So what? What's that have to do with Lauren's death?' You and Cindy are close, so tell her. It may mean nothing, but you'd have told someone, someone in a position to do something about it."

"And then?"

"And then drop it. It's none of your business. You didn't know Lauren."

She was right. In the past when I'd become involved in things that should have been left to the police, the only reason was because I had witnessed the murder or it had touched a friend of mine. Lauren's parents were my neighbors, but I had no allegiance to Brad Burton. But I couldn't shake the feeling something wasn't right.

I put my hand on Barb's shoulder. "I'll tell Cindy what the couple at Bob's said about Joel."

"Good."

What I didn't say was I would drop it.

CHAPTER TWENTY

I called Chief LaMond the next morning to share what I had heard at Bob's house. From the voices in the background I knew she wasn't alone.

"Hello, Mr. Landrum, how may I be of assistance?"

She didn't begin with an insult, so I knew she was with someone who didn't know about our friendship and she couldn't speak. So, instead of getting into what I had called about, I asked if she could call me when she had a free minute.

"Sir, I will pass that message along. Thank you for calling."

The mayor had been trying to get his chief to act more *chiefly*, as Cindy had called it. For that brief conversation, I would say Brian was succeeding. *Too bad*, I thought.

Five minutes later the phone rang, and I was glad Cindy had gotten rid of whomever she had been talking with. My happiness was short lived when instead of the chief, Charles was on the other end.

"I need to hear about the party, every detail. I'm on my way to the Dog. Will probably beat you there." He had hung up.

I wondered how difficult it would have been for him to ask if I could meet him; and I wondered why I had wasted my time wondering about it. Coming from my life in a boring, bureaucratic work, and truth be told, life environment, I must admit Charles's quirks were some of his most endearing qualities. If I'd given it more than a cursory thought, the same applied to most of my friends on this enchanting island. Regardless, this was not the time to think about it, and wouldn't dare tell any of them. Instead of going down that path, I started down the path—more accurately, road—to the Lost Dog Cafe, knowing when I arrived, my friend would scold me for being late. Maybe his quirks weren't that endearing after all.

Charles had secured my favorite booth along the back wall and was in conversation with a distinguished looking, white-haired gentleman at the nearby table. I slid in the booth opposite Charles and he introduced me to Alex, a "young man" from Gravenhurst, Ontario. He quickly went on to say Alex had recently retired and he and his wife Hilary were travelling along the east coast and had been on Folly for the last week. Alex only nodded as Charles rattled on about his *friend* like he'd known him for years. It may have been my imagination, but I thought I could detect a Canadian accent as Charles, the chameleon, went on to say that Hilary had slept in this morning and they were going to visit a couple of Charleston's plantations this afternoon.

Amber stood to the side as Alex said he had to be going and how nice it was to meet Charles, and me, and headed to the exit. She set a mug of coffee in front of me and asked if I was ready to order. I asked her to give me a few minutes.

Charles lifted his Tilley hat that was sitting on the seat next to his cane. "Alex liked my hat."

I smiled, and nodded toward his gold colored, University of

Minnesota T-shirt. "What'd he say about that goofy-looking gopher on your shirt?"

"Didn't mention it. He probably sees a lot of these shirts in his neck-of-the-Canadian-woods. Enough about my fine taste in attire, let's hear about last night. Everything about it."

I knew he meant it when he said everything, so I started from arriving and the valet parking. After that I had to tell him the color of the cones that had been reserving space along the street, what the valet had been wearing, and if the house had a single or a double door entry. Finally, he let me tell about entering the house. My coffee was cold before he let me catch my breath, take a sip, and regret not insisting he accompany me to the fundraiser. Amber returned to see if we were ready to order and Charles told her not yet because he didn't want me to slow up my story by sticking food in my mouth. I did manage to nod toward my mug and Amber said she'd get me coffee. I continued my narrative of everything—everything—that had happened at Bob's.

I was telling him in chronological order, so I had shared almost everything when I got to the part about meeting the Holt-houses and what they had said about Joel.

Charles raised his hand. "Whoa, let me interrupt a sec. When you're done, I've got something to tell you about Joel."

Interrupt a sec, I thought. He'd already interrupted my story 7,000 times. I said okay and continued sharing up until Barb and I left the party, and changed directions, something my friend had mastered decades ago and that he'd tutored me in.

"What about Joel?"

"I decided to get a laptop computer instead of one of those with that big black box attached. The guy at the store said the black box ones are obsolete and I can take mine everywhere and even can get Internet access with its Y-fly."

"Wi-Fi," I corrected.

"Whatever."

"About Joel?"

"I'm getting there. Be patient."

I didn't think he knew the word *patient*, and I knew he'd never followed it. "Go ahead."

"So, while you were hobnobbing with all the snobs at Bob's and before I spent the, umm, evening, yeah, the evening, with Heather, I was at the Surf Bar doing what you're supposed to do in a place with surf in its name. I was surfing the web from their free Y-fly—Wi-Fi."

"And?" I tried again.

Charles sighed. "John Quincy Adams said, 'Patience and perseverance have a magical effect before which difficulties disappear and obstacles vanish.'"

I stared at him. "Chris Landrum said *what did you learn about Joel?*"

"Chris, you're beginning to sound like me. There's hope for you."

I chose to follow the axiom, regardless who'd said it: Silence is golden.

"Anyway," he said, "Teri came in and asked where Heather was."

"Teri?"

"You know, Teri, the hairdresser at Milli's."

I didn't, but said, "Okay."

"I told her I'd see Heather later and she asked if I could give her a message. Guess what she told me?"

"Do you want me to guess?"

"No. We'd be here all day. She told me she was talking to Katelin yesterday in the shop and she—Katelin, not Teri—said Lauren told her she was afraid of Joel."

"Did she say why, and why did Teri want to tell Heather?"

"She said Heather had been asking everyone who worked at the salon about Lauren. Teri said she figured I had put Heather up to it, because everyone who knows Heather knows I'm a pretty good detective and have helped the police crack some of their most difficult cases." Charles chuckled. "Heather had told them I was so good I'd cracked cases that weren't even cases."

That was the same Heather who thought she was a good country music singer!

"Why was Lauren afraid of Joel?"

"That's where it gets convoluted, if that's the right word. It seems Lauren told it to the other housemate, Candice Richardson. Candice didn't think anything of it but after Lauren turned up dead, she told Katelin, who told Teri, or maybe she told it to one of the other hairdressers who told Teri. Anyway, the story is Joel was angry about Lauren getting back on drugs. And get this about the heartless, selfish Joel, he wasn't upset for Lauren, but was worried her drugging would be bad for his campaign. I guess he's going to hang one of his campaign promises on being anti-drugs."

Amber returned and each of us ordered French toast, my breakfast of choice.

"I'm shocked," she mumbled as she headed to the kitchen.

"Did she say anything else about Lauren or Joel?"

"Nope."

"Was Teri, or Candice, or Katelin implying Joel might have something to do with Lauren's death?"

"After she decided she wanted an order of fries to go with her beer, Teri said she wanted to tell Heather because she knew Heather and I were close. Then she decided I didn't have to tell Heather because the only reason to tell her was, so she could tell me, and since Teri already told me, I didn't have to tell Heather."

It took me a moment to follow the trail of who told who

what, and I said, "Do you think Joel could have been responsible for Lauren's death?"

"Good question. Could have been. He could have split with her over the drugs and she decided she didn't have anything to live for and took the overdose. That would make him responsible, I suppose."

"Do you think he could have killed her?"

"Like on purpose?"

I nodded. "Yes, Mr. Detective."

"Since they'd been dating, she would have let him go with her that night." He paused and rubbed his chin. "She was drunk and could have been out of it enough for him to inject her. That could explain why there weren't prints on the door. It's something to think about."

"You're sure Teri didn't say anything else?"

"Other than *another beer barkeep* and a few burps, nope."

"I was going to tell Cindy what I learned from the realtors last night. Think Teri would mind if I give the chief her name? It sounds like what she said was consistent with Joel's character."

"Tell away."

"How is Heather?"

I had wanted to ask earlier, but he was too intent on hearing about the fundraiser.

"To be honest, I don't know."

Breakfast arrived, and Charles took two quick bites before he pointed his fork at me and started to say something, but instead shook his head and looked down at his plate.

"You don't know?" I said, prompting him.

He took a bite, rubbed his forehead, and said, "We had a good time last night. She brought up a couple of funny things that happened after we moved to Nashville. We laughed at some stuff she couldn't kid about when it happened. She talked about the singing buddies she met at her gigs at the Bluebird Cafe and that she missed them but was still able to laugh about not being there." He hesitated. "Yeah, we had a good time."

The look on his face told me there was more. "But?"

He moved his head from side to side. "Can't put my pinkie on it. There's something she's not telling me. She says she's glad we moved back. She says she's enjoying working at Milli's. She says she's happy that she can get back to singin' at open-mic night at Cal's. Umm, don't know what it is. I don't. Just a feeling."

Charles, along with being one of the quirkiest people I know, was also one of the most perceptive. He managed to see through the smokescreen that many people throw up when they're trying to mask their feelings. He recognized insecurities in others that most of us can't see and bolstered their positives. He could bring out good traits in others even if they couldn't see them in themselves. So, when he said it was just a feeling he had about Heather, I knew he was right. What did surprise me was he couldn't define it.

"Help me understand, what gives you the impression there's something she's not telling you?"

Charles looked around the crowded room and toward the outside door. I followed his gaze and didn't notice anything unusual. There were several people waiting for tables, but that was not unusual this time of day. My friend dropped his fork on the plate, waved for Amber to bring the check, and said, "Let's get out of here."

I paid and followed him out the door. He ignored the group milling around and walked past two large dogs drinking out of a water bowl provided by the restaurant. I knew something was wrong when Charles didn't bend down to let the dogs welcome him with slobbery licks—kisses.

CHAPTER TWENTY-ONE

I followed Charles across Center Street to the Folly River Park where he flopped down on a picnic table under the small covered pavilion. Unlike the area around the restaurant, the park was deserted, and Charles stared at the steady stream of traffic on the bridge. Two good-sized fishing boats motored past on their way upstream. The temperature had to be approaching ninety and the shade felt good on my aging bones.

Charles finally turned towards me. "You know how off-the-wall Heather is. She blurts out whatever's on her mind regardless how it may be taken." He chuckled. "She's stuck her foot in her mouth so often that if she was a cow she'd have hoof-in-mouth disease."

I nodded and smiled. "I'll be sure to tell her you don't think she's a cow."

"Ha, ha," he said and turned serious. "There've been more and more spells when she won't say anything; stretches of time that before she'd fill with who knows what. Silence is something she'd never taken kindly to. Chris, she gets this look in her eyes like she's staring into another world. She says she's a psychic, but before when she'd go into psychic mode she didn't stare that weird. I don't know what's going on."

"The other day you said she hadn't met with the counselor. Has she seen him yet?"

"Funny you asked. Last night when I was trying to figure out what was wrong, I asked the same thing. She would've reacted better if I'd asked her to go in the kitchen and slice her thumb off with a steak knife."

"Sorry. Does that mean she hasn't talked to the counselor?"

Charles looked at the ceiling of the gazebo. "Don't recall her saying no, but she left the room and slammed the door so hard I thought it'd knock the paint off the wall. I may've missed her answer."

"Sounds like no," I said and patted him on the shoulder.

Charles turned and looked toward Center Street. "Speaking of the devil."

We weren't, but with Charles it didn't matter. I looked in the direction he was facing and saw Chief LaMond's unmarked car parked in a parking spot parallel to the road. Cindy walked our way.

Charles said, "Howdy, Chief. What brings you out on such a lovely day?"

"Got a complaint about a couple of old, really old, farts hanging out and doing no-telling-what in the park. Figured I needed to earn my astronomical salary paid by the good citizens like the one who complained and came to check it out."

She stifled a smile, so I said, "You made that up."

"Yep, especially the astronomical salary part. I was riding by and saw you and thought there was no time like the present to share a nugget of news."

I patted to the empty space on the bench. "Join us."

"Thought you'd never ask." She pointed toward town. "You get kicked out of a restaurant or a store?"

"Us, kicked out," Charles said in mock exasperation. "We were at the Dog and they begged me to stay to add some class to the joint, but Chris insisted we come over here, so we could enjoy the sweltering, miserable heat."

Cindy rolled her eyes. "Then let me suck some of that enjoyment out of your day. Got off the phone about an hour ago with Detective Adair. Chris, I told him what you'd said about Joel and Kristin."

Charles interrupted, "What'd he say?"

"He said he didn't see how that changed anything. Said as far as he was concerned, the case was closed. He was confident Lauren had accidentally or intentionally overdosed. Said there's no way to tell which it was."

I was surprised. "It didn't matter that Joel had a reason for her death?"

Cindy watched a beer truck cross the bridge and turned to me. "Guys, I'm as frustrated as you are, but the case is with the Sheriff's office and I'm stuck with their conclusion. But tell you what, if you hear anything else, let me know. No guarantees that it'll do any good, but I'll try."

I said we would. She stood and said, "Gotta go stir up some crap in my office. The guys will think I'm goofing off if I'm not on their case about something. The mayor says it's superior administrative oversight."

We watched her pull back in traffic and Charles turned to me. "Why didn't you tell her what Katelin said to Candice, who told Teri, who told me?"

"And then you told me, and now wanted me to tell Cindy."

He nodded.

"I might later, but for now that's too many *who tolds* to hit Cindy with."

Charles shrugged. "If you say so. I've got to make a delivery for the surf shop, so I'll leave you here to ponder ... well, to ponder whatever you want to ponder."

He grabbed his cane and left me to ponder.

It was hot, humid, and the sun was out at full force, so I decided the shade of the pavilion was as good a place to ponder as any. At least, it beat walking anywhere.

I was amazed Charles didn't know what was going on with Heather. They were a perfect couple, or as close to perfect as a couple could be in this imperfect world. They were quirky beyond definition. They both marched to the beat of a different drummer, or guitar in Heather's case. They were kinder than ninety-nine percent of the people I'd ever met, and on the surface, it appeared their main interest was making the other one happy. I vacillated between telling myself that whatever was bothering her was none of my business and trying to think of what I could do to help them through whatever was going on.

All I accomplished by trying to figure it out was giving myself a headache, so I tried thinking about something else. What jumped to the forefront was Lauren and what had happened. Why was her death bugging me? The police were convinced it was either accidental or a suicide. Why couldn't I let it go at that? Since I had been on Folly, I had been involved in several murders. Was I beginning to see all deaths as being nefarious? There was no evidence of foul play, so why was it still on my mind. Sure, the lack of fingerprints on the passenger's door could seem suspicious, but there were logical explanations. Was Joel angry enough to want her dead? Possible, but it was also possible—maybe even probable—that I was looking at him through bias-tinted glasses. He was running against a friend and that could be clouding my opinion.

I took a deep breath, shook a couple of random thoughts out of my head, leaned back against the picnic table, and watched three trucks and a scooter cross the bridge. When I had gotten dragged into previous murder cases it was because of one of two reasons: I was nearby when the death occurred, or the murder involved one or more of my friends. So why now? I never knew or met Lauren Craft, and the only connection between her and someone I did know, was her father. Technically Brad and Hazel Burton were next door neighbors, so there could have been a friendship connection, but Brad and I were as far from being friends as were a worm and a catfish. There was no reason for me to get involved. No, not a single reason.

So why was I having to convince myself?

I headed home. After two blocks, I realized how wise I had been to stay under the shade provided by the park's shelter. Two more blocks and sweat was running down my face. I approached my house and saw Brad Burton sitting on his front step; a sight I hadn't seen since he had lived there. It was even stranger when he saw me approaching, smiled, and waved. For a moment I thought I was hallucinating from the heat. I returned his gesture and walked past my house to his yard.

Brad stood and shook my hand. I apologized for it being sweaty. He said his was too and asked if I wanted to join him. The front of his house shaded us from direct sunlight and I sat next to him. I didn't know what to say so I asked him how he was doing and realized how stupid a question it was. He had lost his only child, and by being nice to me indicated something was wrong with him. He glanced over at me and I imagined him saying something like, "How do you think I feel, you idiot?"

He started to speak, thought better of it, and lowered his head. I watched a squirrel foraging around in the side yard, before Brad finally said, "Chris, I've spent my entire professional life staring at dead bodies. After so long, I became calloused to the sight, smell, and revulsion. I had to do that, or I couldn't do what I was paid to do; find the person responsible and bring justice and some small degree of closure to the families of the deceased. At first, I took the images of the horrible transgressions home with me. I'm afraid I burdened Hazel with my gut-wrenching feelings. She was an angel to put up with it; nearly didn't … umm, well, I finally was able to block it out." He hesitated, watched a plumbing truck roll by, and again lowered his head.

I waited in awkward silence.

"I thought I could handle anything, but Chris, I was wrong, damned wrong." He hesitated again. "Lauren was such a sweet little kid. When I came home from work before she knew or could understand what I did for a living, she'd ask me how my day was. I'd smile, hoped she didn't smell death on my clothes, and told her I was great now. Those days became fewer and fewer. I was working all hours, but even then, and after she knew what my job entailed, she would still break out in a big smile, and ask about my day." He shook his head. "Most of the time I lied and said, 'great.' She was so sweet."

"It's got to be terrible for you and Hazel."

"My heart pained for her when she married Sebastian Craft. She was looking for someone who could be there when she needed him; something I couldn't do for her. I knew it was a mistake. I never felt good about him, but Lauren couldn't see it. I hold him responsible for her spiral into drink and drugs." He shook his head. "I'm just as responsible. Anyway, she ended the abysmal marriage, but couldn't end the debilitating habits that came with it. Chris, I thought we could help her by moving here. I thought we had. God, I was wrong, horribly wrong."

"You did what you could."

"I tried, and so did her roommates."

"How well do you know Katelin and Candice?"

"I only met them a couple of times when Lauren was … before her death. She spoke highly of them and they seemed like nice gals. Yesterday I went to the house they rented to pick up Lauren's possessions." He put his head down and put a hand on each side of his head. I waited silently. "Umm, Katelin was there and talked a lot about Lauren. She didn't say it, she talked around it, but I had the impression Katelin knew Lauren was back on drugs. I didn't want to press her."

"Did you find anything in Lauren's things to give you that impression?"

He raised his head and turned to me. "Chris, I've spent countless hours rooting through people's stuff, both at murder scenes and when searching houses of suspects. I know where to look and what to look for. There wasn't anything there, not a thing. But, that doesn't mean much." He shook his head. "I'll tell you what I did find. There were copies of online job applications from several stores in Charleston, and a couple of handwritten ones for places over here. They were recent, two were filled out the day before she … left us. She was hot and heavy on a job search." He looked at me, but with the such intensity that he was staring through me. "I can't fathom how she turned from hope to hopelessness that quick."

"How well did you know her boyfriend, Joel Hurt?"

"Hardly at all. He seemed a lot nicer than that shithead she was married to." Brad bit his lower lip and wiped perspiration off his brow. "I only met him once. I ran into him and Lauren in Bert's. He seemed okay and told me that meeting Lauren was the best thing that'd happened to him since he moved here."

I knew what I'd learned on the Internet, and wondered what Brad knew about his past. "Did he say where he'd moved here from?"

"No. I asked him, and he laughed and said something like, 'Somewhere that's not as nice as Folly.' I started to push him, but Lauren said they had to get going, they were late to something, and rushed out."

A motorcycle roared past and we watched it speed toward the Washout. Now would be as good a time as any to broach a delicate topic. "Brad, is it possible Lauren didn't take her own life?"

"Why would you say that?"

"Simply curious."

"Chris, there's nothing that makes me think that. And remember, I'm a retired homicide cop." He hesitated and stared at the road where the motorcycle had been seconds earlier. "Sorry, I can't go down that path. It's over. My little girl died ... died of an accidental overdose."

Brad looked around, patted his knee, and said he'd better be getting inside. Our relationship was so precarious that I wasn't comfortable pushing him somewhere he didn't want to go. I told him it was nice talking to him, that again I was sorry about Lauren. I told him to let me know if he needed anything. I knew he wouldn't.

CHAPTER TWENTY-TWO

The next morning began as a cool wave passed through the Lowcountry. The temperatures were still going to be in the eighties, but the humidity levels dropped. Over the years, I made halfhearted attempts to get in better shape, and while most failed, I convinced myself that walking was my best route to success. Anything more strenuous seemed like work, misery, and for me, unsustainable. Walking without direction also struck me as nonproductive, so most of my walks occurred on my way to or from restaurants where I usually defeated the benefits of walking by eating unhealthy foods. I'd convinced myself that the walks counteracted the evils of my diet. Exercise was one of my greatest weaknesses; the art of rationalizing was near the top of my strengths.

I was thinking about what to order and nearly ran into Dude who was dressed, well, dressed like Dude, carrying the latest issue of *Astronomy* magazine, and standing in front of the surf shop.

"Whoa, Chrisster. Where be daydreamin' off to?"

"The Dog."

"Boss! Birds of a feather, think like together. Me boogie with you."

Correcting Dude's expression would be as productive as trying to teach his dog Pluto to learn Konkahi, so I said, "I'd be honored."

He pointed the magazine toward the restaurant and skipped along beside me. On the three block walk he shared the latest updates about Dude's other favorite Pluto, the dwarf planet, from an article he'd read in the magazine, and about the latest tricks that his much smaller, and a zillion miles closer Pluto had learned. We reached the restaurant, and I thought how Dude was the perfect companion for me to get my mind off Brad and Lauren.

Amber was standing on the patio and asked if we wanted to sit outside or inside. Dude said, "Wherever the Amberster say."

The Amberst...., umm, Amber, pointed to a table she had finished cleaning and Dude and I moved to the vacant table.

Amber pet Dude on his long, stringy hair, and said, "How come you brought this old dog with you. Where's Pluto, the cute one?"

Dude shook his head, sat down, and glanced at me on the other side of the table. "Stray. Felt sorry. So, here he be."

Maybe I would have been better off thinking about Brad and Lauren. I smiled and told Amber it was good to see her too. She kissed the top of my balding head and said she would return with menus.

Dude watched Amber head inside and turned to me. "You be jabberin' with Kategal?"

"Katelin, Lauren's housemate?"

"That's what me said."

Close, and said, "Not recently. Why?"

"Thought you be detectin'. Fishin' for clues."

"Charles is the detective, remember?"

"Okeedokee, me not report what the Kategal said."

"You win. What did Katelin say?"

Dude grinned. "See, you be detectin'." He nodded like he'd discovered the secret of removing wrinkles. "The Kategal likes to gander in surf shop—not buy, just gander. She be in last daytime."

"Yesterday?"

"What me said. She be rantin' about her dead roomie. She be pissed."

"What'd she say?"

"Details not clear. Something about always discord in house. Temper tantrums. Two chicks pullin' at dirt guy's arms."

Where was Charles my Dude Translator when I needed him? So, I had to resort to guesses. "Lauren and Katelin were fighting about Joel Hurt?"

He nodded and probably wanted to say, *What me said,* but instead said, "The dirt guy dumped Kategal like load of monkey manure. He be Superglued to dead gal before Kategal knew she be dumpee."

Amber returned with menus and we quickly glanced at them and ordered Chicken salad croissants. Amber mumbled something about my order almost being healthy. I told her I'd get over it, and she left smiling.

"Dude, did Katelin say anything else about Lauren or Joel?"

Dude rubbed the stubble on his chin. "Squawked some about drugs, but drug words go in one auditory organ and wiggle out other." He patted his left ear, so I would know which auditory organ he was referring to.

As far as I could tell, much of Dude's past was filled with voids. If I were a wagering person, I'd lay a few bucks on him having more than a passing encounter with the drug culture of the 1960s. During the time I'd known him, he had the reputation as someone who could bridge the gap between the bohemian residents, surfers, and the more well-heeled citizens and law enforcement.

"Do you know the third housemate, Candice Richardson?"

"She be petite Barbie." Dude pointed at his eyes and out the door. "She be with other two once, she and me never shared words." He hesitated and rubbed his chin. "Heard something from Kategal. She—Kategal, not Candygirl—say third roomer never at house. Kategal say that's why Candygirl be good house-mate. Three pay rent, two share air."

"Did Katelin ever say anything about Lauren being depressed or being back on drugs?"

"Not recallin' anything."

"Know anything about Joel Hurt?"

"Other than two-timing two chicks?"

"Yes."

"Got more faces than Lernaean Hydra."

"The Greek water monster with many heads?" At some point, I must have paid attention in school.

Dude rolled his eyes. "How many other Hydras you know?"

"Good point. Do you say that because of some of his comments about our mayor or about Lauren and Katelin?"

"All."

"Is that everything you know about Joel?"

"He and his waterfowl friend moved here mucho full-moons ago."

Wayne Swan was the first waterfowl that came to mind, mainly because I had remembered that Joel had said he and Wayne went way back. "Wayne Swan, his campaign manager?"

"You know more waterfowl than you know Hydras?"

Some comments deserve nothing more than being ignored. Our food arrived, and Dude took two bites and started telling me something about the next solar eclipse. He was finished talking about dead citizens, politicians, waterfowl, and multi-faced mythical creatures. I also had stopped listening until he said that the third roommate, Candice Richardson, Candygirl in Dudes-peak, had worked for Joel and had been fired from one of Joel's garden centers. At least that was my understanding of what Dude had said. He used fewer than half that many words, so something could have been lost in translation.

"Anyone say she was fired?"

"Official reason, stealin'."

My understanding was she now worked for a real estate office in Charleston. If that was the reason for her termination, I was surprised she got the new job.

"Dude, you said official reason. Do you know that it was for something else?"

He nodded. "Rumor."

I nodded. "What?"

"Story spread like PB & Jelly on bread that she caught dirt man plantin' bod part where not belong, if you get my drift."

I did, and if true, could be how she got a positive reference for her next job. I doubted Joel, the dirt man, would have shared the real reason with someone asking for a reference. It also struck me that if mayoral candidate Joel Hurt was sincere about getting elected, he would have a reason for all three of the women to be silenced—one way or the other.

Instead of elaborating, Dude started talking about the dwarf planet Pluto, a topic he spent more time on than the rest of the Folly's citizens combined. I doubted he could shed more light on Lauren's death, but before I could ask him, the phone rang.

Bob Howard's voice bellowed out of the speaker. "Here's

your deal of a lifetime. Be at Al's at one thirty tomorrow afternoon and I—yes I—will buy you lunch. And, don't call the television stations to tell them about this historic event. If they show
up, I'll say *me buy, shit no*! *Where'd you hear that damned
rumor?*"

Bob's offer to buy was historic. I didn't need Heather's
psychic powers, or Charles's detective skills to know that there
was no such thing as a free lunch waiting for me at Al's.

CHAPTER TWENTY-THREE

I found a vacant parking spot much closer than on my last visit and stepped from blinding sunlight into blinding dark with minimal illumination coming from rays of sun sneaking over the top half of the front window. The lower half was painted black to keep nosy eyes from staring in the building. Budweiser neon signs provided a bit more light and a jukebox that appeared as old as the eighty-year-old proprietor, added a glimmer of colorful light to the corner. The lunch crowd had either come and gone or hadn't come at all. The bar was two diners shy of empty, and I was one of the two.

My first surprise was when I saw Al beside the front door sitting in a chair that belonged to the nearest dining table. He saw me enter, grinned, and leaned forward and used his hands to push himself out of the chair. Other than his visits to our table when the bar had few or no other patrons, I had never seen Al seated. And, even in the poor lighting, he looked worse than he had at the fundraiser. From the jukebox Jerry Lee Lewis was wailing about someone shaking his nerves and rattling his brain, so it was difficult to hear what Al had said, but words weren't needed as he wrapped his emaciated arms around me and squeezed.

I told him it was good to see him and started to say *you're looking good*, but he would have known I was lying. He looked horrible.

He leaned closer, so I could hear and said, "Thank the good lord you're here. Fatso's been asking every five minutes why you weren't here yet."

I glanced at Bob—Fatso—and leaned closer to Al. "He told me to come at one-thirty. Has he been talking to my buddy Charles?"

Al smiled. His coffee-stained teeth were illuminated by the neon signs. "Charles, the thirty minutes early to be on time, buddy?"

I said, "Good memory," and patted him on the back.

"Get on over there to shut him up," Al said. "If I had any customers he'd be running them off."

Jerry Lee Lewis finished his piano riff, but Bob's voice would have been heard over it if was still playing, "Welcome fine customer! Come join me."

"Extreme Mouth Makeover," Al said as he shook his head and lowered himself back in the chair. "Bob says his charm will bring in the customers by the boatload."

Lawrence, Al's part-time cook, laughed and asked if I wanted a cheeseburger. I told him of course and headed to the table. Bob was stuffed into his side of the booth, a normal sight, but what was not normal was a two-by-four-inch brass plate screwed into the top of the table facing the room and Bob holding a screwdriver—the tool, not the drink.

"What are you screwing up now?" I said before I was close enough to read what had been inscribed on the brass addition.

Bob said, "My first action to add a touch of class to this dump."

I slid into the other side of the table, no simple task because Bob's ample stomach had pushed the table to my side of the booth. I looked down at the shiny plate and read: *BOB'S BOOTH. WARNING: Sit at your own risk.*

I smiled. "Class?"

Bob followed my eyes. "You're not be making fun of the person who's buying your lunch, are you?"

I continued to smile. "Of course, I am, Bob. I didn't think you were going to be here until later."

"Don't remind me," he said. "Was supposed to show a frou-frou couple a three-million-dollar shanty south of Broad." Some of Charleston's most majestic homes were in the area between Broad Street and the Battery. "They called a little while ago and said they were going to 'reassign their resources to other opportunities,' whatever the hell that meant. If you ask me, which I'm sure you were about to do, they couldn't afford the house and probably had to reassign their resources to buying food to feed their two gigantic Mastiffs."

I stifled a smile and said, "Sorry."

"They damned sure are." Bob turned toward the grill. "Where in the hell's this damned ingrate's food? Snap, snap!"

Tanya Tucker's "Delta Dawn" drowned out normal conversation, but the cook uttered what appeared to be a string of profanities.

To try to prevent an employee revolt, I said, "So what's up?"

Bob harrumphed in the direction of the cook and turned to me. "Why can't I invite a friend to lunch? Why does it always have to be something?"

"Could be because in the eight years I've known you, you've never offered to buy me lunch, or anything else, for that matter."

Bob shrugged. "To quote that song written in 1964—which happened to be the last year any good music was written—by Bobby Dylan, "The Times They Are a-Changin'.""

Bobby Dylan, I thought, and showing more maturity than I possessed, I repeated, "So what's up?"

Bob pointed his thumb at Al who was slumped down in the chair by the door. "Anything look normal about that?"

"I was surprised to see him there when I came in. Is he okay?"

Lawrence, who was a couple of decades younger than Al, delivered my cheeseburger and glass of chardonnay and asked "Mr. Howard" if he needed anything. Bob told him he was Bob and not Mr. Howard and not to forget it. He also requested— demanded—another beer. Lawrence faked a smile at his new boss and scooted away.

Bob watched me take a bite and said, "Al called last night to talk about bar business, something about ordering from another vendor and an electrical issue with that doohickey that cooks the fries."

And I thought Bob wasn't an expert on owning a bar. "And?"

"Then he started repeating himself, but before that, he asked me something I had answered a few seconds earlier. The old man tried to laugh it off and said that he was testing to see if I remembered what I had told him. Chris, he laughed, but there wasn't a damned thing funny about it." Bob glanced back toward Al. "He lost his train of thought; not once, but several times. He started talking about something that happened in here in 1957 like it was last week, and he—"

"You talking about me?" Al said as he leaned against the back of a chair at the next table.

I moved over and waved for him to join us.

"Hell yes," Bob said. "Chris was saying you looked like you

just stepped out of a coffin. I told him to stop making fun of you." He shook his head. "You know how cruel some white customers can be—especially those young whippersnappers like Chris."

Al flopped down on the seat, wiped sweat off his forehead with a bar towel, and stared at Bob. "Don't know about customers, but cruel's talking too kindly about a white bar owner."

I smiled and kept my mouth shut, something Bob couldn't find it in his DNA to do. "That's no way to talk to your good buddy and person who singlehandedly will save this decrepit old bar and its more than decrepit former owner."

Al looked at the brass plate and at me. "Chris," he said and pointed an arthritis ravaged finger at Bob and at himself, "if there's only one thing this old, shriveled up, bar man can teach you, it's that friends, not the fair-weather kind who are with you when things are going well, and dump you like chewed gum when things go sour, but true friends will stick with you no matter what. They'll stand behind you and keep you from falling; they'll go to the ends of the earth to help you in your time of need. They'll do anything for you, yes they will."

Bob interrupted, "Get to the point, old man. The boy's burger is getting cold while he's waiting with bated breath for whatever you're trying to say."

Al continued to look at me and waved his hand at Bob like he would shew a fly. "I'm nearly there, Chris. The point is that cranky curmudgeon over there is the best friend this old man's ever had. Lord knows why; I sure don't. But anyway, he is."

In a move uncharacteristic for Bob, he reached across the table and touched Al's hand. Tom T. Hall's "Old Dogs, Children, and Watermelon Wine" flowed from the jukebox. And I felt like I was infringing on one of the most poignant moments in Bob's long life. Neither man spoke until the mood was broken when three boisterous middle-aged men entered the bar.

Al looked their way and said, "Done shirking my greeting duties. Good luck, Chris, with putting up with the tub of lard."

Bob watched Al head to the door. "And that's my friendly greeter."

I turned back to my cooling cheeseburger and Bob returned to his no-telling-what-number beer, when I heard a chair hitting the floor and Lawrence scream, "Oh shit!"

Bob moved quicker than I had ever seen him move. He was out of the booth, slammed two chairs out of his way, and was standing beside the prone shape of Al on the floor. One of the three men who had entered was bent down and checking for a pulse. He calmly looked up and told Lawrence he was a doctor and to call 911.

I grabbed a handful of bar towels and the doctor put them under Al's head. "Is he alive?" I asked.

The doctor ignored me and started CPR. My friend's eyes were closed, and I couldn't see signs of life. Bob stood back and muttered a plethora of profanities. I felt helpless. Had Charleston lost a true hero, and had I lost another friend?

CHAPTER TWENTY-FOUR

The doctor ordered us to step back and give Al air as he continued to press on his chest. Bob had given the doc a dirty look and I was afraid he was going to ignore the order and move closer, but instead he nodded and plopped down on a nearby chair. The two men who had accompanied the doctor had gone out front to make sure the ambulance found us, and Lawrence had turned on the overhead lights giving the doctor a better view of Al. It was the first time that I'd seen the inside of the bar with the lights on. It had always looked tired and rundown; now it looked exhausted and on its last legs. Lawrence had moved behind the bar and bowed his head. I didn't know if Lawrence was praying, but I was.

It only took a few minutes for the ambulance to rush the three blocks from the hospital, but it seemed like an eternity. Two paramedics walked in the room. They appeared confident, listened to what the doctor who had been administering CPR said, and focused their attention to Al. The doctor stepped aside and one of the paramedics took over the CPR. The other paramedic leaned over Al's head, but his body blocked my view, so I couldn't see what he was doing. Regardless, I felt Al was in good hands; all irrelevant if he was no longer with us.

It was then that I glanced over at Bob at the table beside me. His head was resting on the table and his breath was coming in gasps.

I scooted my chair over to his table. "Bob, are you okay?"

He didn't answer, and I moved around to see his face. Sweat was rolling down his face, his arms were shaking, and in the harsh fluorescent light he looked whiter than a bar of soap, and his skin looked as waxy.

I yelled to the doctor who was standing beside the paramedic administering CPR. He glanced over, took a quick look down at Al, and rushed to Bob's table. Bob had opened his eyes and mumbled, "I need air ... air." He tried to raise his head, but it fell back to the table. I moved back from the table and the doc took my place. He leaned close to Bob and asked if my friend could hear him. Bob said yes, and the doc asked him what he was feeling.

I closed my eyes, took a deep breath, and felt helpless. I was surprised to see Lawrence at my side offering me a glass of water. His hands trembled as he handed the glass to me and he never took his eyes off Al, still unmoving on the floor.

I don't know who called them, but a second set of paramedics burst through the door. One of them pushed a gurney and stopped at Al and the second one came over to Bob, conferred with the doc, and leaned down to talk to Bob. I wasn't close enough to hear what was being said, but it looked like Bob was responding to the questions; a good sign, I assumed. I walked across the room to be closer to Al and heard one of the paramedics say they needed to get him to the hospital stat.

I may have been fooling myself, but I took that as a good

sign—he's alive. But, he hadn't moved, and his eyes were closed as they were loading him on the stretcher and wheeled him out the door. I turned back to Bob and watched the EMT take his blood pressure and continued to ask him questions. Bob was becoming more animated.

He jerked his head back and looked over to where Al had been on. "Where's Al? Is he okay?"

The paramedic told him Al was on the way to the hospital, he was in good hands, and Bob needed to stay calm for them to figure out what was wrong with him. Bob mumbled a profanity. I smiled and thought he was getting back to normal. Bob became more agitated when the paramedic said they were going to take him to the hospital. Bob insisted there was nothing wrong and he was just upset about his friend.

"That may be, sir, but we've got to check you out. Keep taking deep breaths and we'll wheel another gurney in and give you a ride to the hospital."

I expected an expletive-filled explosion, but instead Bob lowered his head to the table and closed his eyes. Maybe his condition was worse than I had thought. Bob's gurney arrived, and the two paramedics maneuvered it around to get Bob's large body situated on it and to wheel him out. Lawrence and I moved three tables out of the way so they could get Bob to the ambulance.

I watched the ambulance as its siren stopped traffic as it made a U-turn and headed to the hospital. I wanted to rush to the ER but from experience with some of my friends who had made similar trips, knew it would have been fruitless. It would be a while before anything was known, or at least before the medical staff told me anything. The doc and his two friends were sitting at one of the tables and Lawrence was wandering through the room with a lost look on his face.

I thanked the good Samaritan for everything he had done. He gave me a sad smile and said, "All I wanted was a cheeseburger."

Lawrence heard him, hurried to the table, and asked what everyone wanted. He now had a purpose, something he could do. I didn't know if the men worried about how Lawrence would fix their food in his current state of mind or were no longer hungry, but two of them said they didn't need anything and the doc said they had a meeting to get to. Before they left, I asked the doctor how he thought Al and Bob were.

He nodded toward the table where Bob had been. "I think he had a panic attack. His vitals were normal—normal for an overweight diabetic. He'll probably be okay. The other gentleman is another story. Don't take this as gospel. I didn't have enough time or information to know for sure, but he was barely holding on when he left. Sorry."

Lawrence moved beside me and heard the prognostication. "Oh Lord, please help Al. He's such a dear sweet man. God, he's lived your wishes. Please help him."

I seconded that and realized I should contact someone from Al's family and Bob's wife, Betty. I also realized Tanesa, an ER doctor at the hospital, was the only member of Al's family that I knew. She had given me her cell number a couple of years ago; I was glad, since I doubted Lawrence, in his state of shock, would have been able to find it.

I was afraid Tanesa wasn't going to answer and had almost hung up when she answered. She was off work for a couple of days but said she'd head to the hospital and would be there in fifteen minutes.

I wasn't as lucky with Bob's wife. After six rings, I got Bob's cheerful, warm, friendly voice mail message that said: *What? If you haven't figured it out, we're not here. Leave a message and we might call you back.* I left a message for her to call me and kicked myself I didn't have her cell number.

Lawrence asked if I needed anything. I was tempted to say a liter or two of wine, but instead said I was fine. The part-time chef and I were the only two left in Al's and Lawrence stood behind the bar and stared at the door like he was expecting Al to walk through it. I moved to Bob's table and looked at the brass nameplate. I hadn't done anything but felt exhausted. My legs were weak as I plopped down in the booth. The jukebox was silent, and I missed the bickering between Bob and Al about the musical selections—Motown versus country. Al asking Bob if he liked any music created since Kennedy was president; Bob responding by asking Al if he liked any singers who had skin lighter than his. I smiled thinking how Al had salted the jukebox with songs only Bob would like and the harassment he had endured from most of his African-American customers.

I also remembered the countless words of wisdom that flowed from the bar owner; wisdom he hadn't gotten from formal schooling, for he had little, but from his many years of living in a world that many of us couldn't endure and the sacrifices he had made for the nine children he and his wife had adopted before her death several years ago.

And I thought about what Al had said only a little while earlier about friends and how the true ones would do anything for you. Bob and Al, each from a different world, were perfect examples of that. I hoped I could be that good of a friend to my friends. I was never big on symbolism, but as I sat and listened to silence coming from Al's jukebox, I prayed that wasn't telling me Al would never be punching in another song—Motown or country.

I turned my head, so Lawrence couldn't see the tears streaming down my cheek.

CHAPTER TWENTY-FIVE

Tanesa was waiting for me as I entered the hospital. She forced a smile and motioned for me to follow her to an empty row of seats off the side of the packed lobby.

"Is your dad—"

She squeezed my arm. "He's alive." She hesitated, and then continued, "Probably a heart attack, but with his declining health it could be complicated with any number of things. His vitals are sucking wind."

I didn't know what to say other than I was sorry.

Al's daughter stared at the double doors that led to the bowels of the hospital. She gave a slight nod and mumbled, "There's always hope." She looked up at me. "Chris, if that doctor hadn't been in the bar, we wouldn't be having this conversation." She grinned. "Dad always said he'd take luck any day over something going right just because people tried to do their best. It was pure luck that man was there."

I asked if she'd seen him. She said briefly but was moved out of the medical team's way. She knew she was too close to the patient to be much help.

"He's a stubborn man," I said. "If anyone can make it, your dad can."

She tilted her head in my direction. "Stubborn, you're not kidding, but with everything else going wrong with his aging body, stubbornness may not be enough." She snapped her fingers. "His—your—friend Bob Howard's in much better condition. There's nothing wrong with his heart." She hesitated and smiled. "Other than dad saying that he doesn't have one. Anyway, it was a panic attack. They're hanging on to him for another hour or so then kicking him out. He'll be fine."

I told her I was thankful for that, and I felt sorry for whoever was back there having to deal with him. She looked back at the double doors and chuckled. "Yeah, he told the poor nurse who was trying to take his blood pressure to 'take that damned squeezy thing off my arm and get the hell back to saving his good friend's life.'"

I smiled. "I'm surprised they haven't thrown him out."

"Folks back there are used to insults, abuse, and malcontents who frequent the ER. Bob'll fit right in. Has anyone called his wife?"

I told her I couldn't reach her and didn't have her cell phone number. She said she'd go back and see if Bob had called her or wanted me to. I suspected Tanesa wanted to see if there was anything new to report on Al.

She was gone longer than I had hoped, when I heard him before I saw him.

"I'll break his scrawny neck if he bothers Betty. Push faster!"

The doors to the treatment area swung open and out came a wheelchair being pushed by Tanesa and stuffed with the ample rear end of Bob. He glared at me. "Does Betty know I'm here?"

I returned his glare. "Not that I know of. What are you doing out here?"

"Hospitals are for sick people. I'm as healthy as a horse."

Substitute jackass, I thought. "So, they kicked you out?"

Before Bob responded, Tanesa said, "They wanted to keep him a couple more hours, but your friend here told them that unless they let him walk, roll, out of here in the next ten minutes he was going to call the cops and report he'd been kidnapped."

Bob uttered a profanity and repeated, "Hospitals are for sick people." He started to stand, but slowly lowered himself back in the wheelchair, took a deep breath, and said, "Now are you going to take me to my car or not?"

"Not," I said. "If I take you anywhere other than the psych ward, it'll be to your house. Take it or leave it."

Bob looked over his shoulder at Tanesa who was standing behind him and said, "See the insolence I have to put up with." He turned to me. "What in the hell are you waiting for? Get your car so sweetie pie here can wheel me to the door."

Sweetie pie, Tanesa, should have smacked him, but instead ruffled his already disarranged hair and kissed him on the cheek. Ten minutes later, I had helped Bob in the front seat and started to close the door. He held up his cell phone and said, "Tanesa, you promise, swear, and whatever else is holy to you, that you'll call me the second you hear anything?"

She said she'd call both of us and I headed to Bob's house. He closed his eyes and I thought he was asleep, but instead he said, "I've always been overweight, even when I was in grade school."

Where had that come from, I wondered, and nodded.

He stared straight ahead, and said, "Kids made fun of me but not nearly as much fun as they made of Jacob."

"Jacob?" I said.

"Jacob Bishop, only negro in my class. You may have noticed I'm an irreverent, loud, some might say, smart ass."

He could say that again, but I didn't say anything and waited to see where he was going with the story.

"The shit I say doesn't compare to what some of the kids said about, and to, Jacob. Cruel, damned cruel."

"Kids can be cruel, especially to someone who's different from them."

"Don't get all damned sociological or psychological on me. It's my story."

What's not to love about Bob?

"Anyway, I figured Jacob needed a friend and what better person to be that friend than chubby Bobby; yes, I was called Bobby way back then. I started palling around with him." Bob closed his eyes and nodded. "That was decades before that politically correct crap reared its damned ugly head. Jacob called me Fatso Bobby, and I called him Nigg—umm, Negro Jacob. We became best buds and the damned bullies had a harder time picking on Jacob or me. Bullies lose their bulliness when there is more than one person to pick on. I was the only kid in the school who knew Jacob was a great kid. He was funny, kind, and smart as a whip, whatever the hell that means. We spent hours together, having fun, and still insulted each other every chance we got. It was our way of saying we liked each other without getting all gooey about it." Bob's eyes closed again.

"What happened to Jacob?"

"Hell if I know. We went to different high schools and lost contact." He shook his head, "Oh God, please let Al be okay."

His story had begun to make sense. If anyone who didn't know him watched how he and Al had traded insults and talked about each other, it would have been hard to understand how they had been friends. I was wondering if I should ask him more about his childhood friend as we pulled in front of his impressive house.

He looked at me. "If Betty's here, keep your damned mouth shut. I'll do the talking. I don't want to worry her."

I agreed, as if I had a choice, but needn't have worried. Betty wasn't home. Bob settled in an oversized, leather recliner in the family room and asked me to get him a beer. I asked if he should have one, and he repeated, for the third time as I recall, that he was not sick. I returned with his beer and a bottled water for me.

Bob had his eyes shut but opened them when he heard me returning, and said, "Think we did well at Brian's fundraiser."

"It was a great event. I know Brian appreciated it."

"I know a few more realtors whose arms I can twist for a few more bucks for the campaign. They don't know Brian, crap, they're so uppity they don't know that Folly Beach exists. One of them—goes by Norvell, real name's Norm—has perfected a snooty British accent when he says Kiawah or Isle of Palms." Bob shook his head. "The guy's a jerk but has made oodles of bucks."

I was beginning to realize Bob was talking about anything but his friend Al. He was worried, and from what Tanesa had said, he had reason to be. We talked more about the fundraiser as Bob finished the beer and asked me to get him another. I wondered when Betty would get home and relieve me of Bob sitting.

Before I returned with his second beer, his strong voice blurted. "So, who killed Lauren?"

I delivered the beer and said, "Don't know."

He took a gulp, rested the bottle on the armrest. "Why the hell not? You're trying to figure it out, aren't you?"

"Bob, the death has been ruled accidental or self-inflicted. There's nothing to figure—"

"Blah, blah, blah. I didn't ask for the police version. I've known you too long for you to slide that crap by me. I'm not as good at it as Charles's gal Heather but let me slip on my psychic hat." He moved his hand to his head like he was putting on a hat. I swallowed a laugh as he continued. "Slimeball Joel Hurt was dating dead Lauren, correction, was dating the live Lauren. Slimeball Joel is running against your bud Brian. My colleagues the Holthouses told you that Slimeball Joel was badmouthing Brian. Some ancient proverb, said before even you were born, said the enemy of my enemy is my friend. The Holthouses were pissed at how Joel was talking which made him their enemy so Slimeball Joel is your enemy. Therefore, he must have kilt his gal friend Lauren."

Bob's psychic revelation or confusing lesson in logic held water up until he jumped to the conclusion that Joel must have killed—kilt—Lauren. Logical or not, it was what I was thinking based on more information than Bob had been privy to. "He may be my enemy, but why the big leap to him being a murderer?"

Bob smiled. "Nothing. Correct me if I'm wrong, you think her death was more than a mere overdose and Slimeball Joel jumps out as the best suspect. Does he have an alibi for when she was offed?"

Bob's question made me realize I hadn't heard, or if I had, didn't remember when she died. "Don't know. I'm not certain when she died."

"And you call yourself a detective. This old, chunky realtor knows that's important if you're going to solve the crime."

"Bob, I don't call myself a detective, and no one knows if there was a crime committed."

"Whatever. But when you wake up in the morning and put your britches and detective clothes on, check the alibi."

I wasn't about to admit it was a good idea, not only to check on Joel, but to eliminate my suspicions about Katelin, or possibly even Candice.

"I'll do that," I said, more to get him off the subject.

It wasn't necessary since Betty, Bob's angelic wife, came through the back door carrying two grocery bags and a bag from Walmart.

Betty glanced at Bob reclined in his chair and smiled at me. "Chris, did you pick up a runaway and bring him home?" She turned to her husband. "Where's your car?"

Bob stood and gave Betty a hug. I didn't want to be there when Bob told her about his trip to the hospital and told her I was late for a meeting. She didn't question who I could be meeting. Bob told her he would explain after "that little twerp skedaddles."

Before the fireworks began, I skedaddled.

CHAPTER TWENTY-SIX

The first thing in the morning, I called Cindy to see if she had the timeframe on Lauren's death. The chief answered with, "Hello, Mr. Landrum, how may I be of assistance?" It was her way of saying she was meeting with someone important and don't pester her. I asked her to call when she got a chance, and she said, "Of course." I hadn't received an update on Al and had waited as long as my patience would allow. I called Tanesa but it went to voicemail, so I said I was worried about her dad and asked her to call me if she got a chance.

I was O-for-two, so instead of pacing the floor waiting for the phone to ring, I walked next door to Bert's Market to grab a Danish and a cup of coffee. Two construction workers were ahead of me in the coffee line and Eric was waiting on a teenager dressed in a red bathing suit and a fisherman's vest. I grinned as I thought of how out of place that would have appeared most anywhere in the country. I poured my coffee and waited for Eric to wait on the customer in front of me, paid for the Danish, and said, "Eric, got a question."

"Make it simple. This morning's been a bear."

"Has anyone mentioned Lauren Craft's time of death?"

He tilted his head and ran his hand through his beard. "Might I assume you question her manner of demise?"

"Curious, that's all."

"Um-hum, whatever you say. To answer your question, asked out of curiosity, I heard it was around nine o'clock the night before they found her."

My phone rang before Eric could tell me he didn't believe me.

"Chris, this is Tanesa. Is this a good time to talk?"

That's the way to start a phone conversation, I thought, and realized why she had called. I tensed up but managed to say it was.

"I don't have much to report. He's still in critical condition. His vitals show hope, and then regress. From my perspective, that he's still alive is a good sign. The next twenty-four hours are critical. Sorry I can't offer more."

I told her I was pleased she had called and that he was still among the living. I asked if she was getting any rest. She said no, chuckled, and said that wasn't unusual for an ER doc. I thanked her for calling and she assured me she would let me know if there was any change.

Eric had overheard my half of the conversation and gave me an inquisitive glance. I shared what had happened with Al and a little about Bob. Eric had never met Al but knew Bob from a couple of encounters in the store. He told me he was sorry and that he'd pray for Al's speedy recovery. I said I would be satisfied for recovery, speedy or otherwise.

I still wasn't ready to go home and worry, so I walked around Bert's looking at various food items, items I would never buy, but were providing a distraction. I was further distracted when I saw Wayne Swan. He saw me and headed my way.

Wayne gave me a strong handshake and at the same time a politician's pat on the back. Instead of the navy blazer look from the previous two times I'd seen him, he was dressed like the construction worker that he was. He wore torn jeans, scuffed work boots, a tan T-shirt and his dark hair was speckled with sawdust.

"Good to see you, Chris. I was going to call you yesterday but got tied up with a challenging rehab on East Huron."

"You were going to tell me that your candidate was dropping out of the race and supporting Mayor Newman."

Wayne laughed, louder than necessary. "No such luck, my friend. I wanted to ask you to meet again with Joel."

"Sorry, Wayne, I don't see where it—"

He held his hand in front of my face and interrupted. "Come on, Chris. What harm could it cause?"

I was distracted and thinking about Al and Bob and didn't have the time or mental energy to play games with Brian's opponent. "Harm, none, but what good could it do? I've already said I was backing Brian."

"I know, I know," Wayne said, and looked around the store. "But Chris, if you give Joel a chance, I think you'll like him and his ideas for improving the community that you play such a critical part in."

Sucking-up at its best, I thought. "Wayne, I like Joel. He seems to be well-respected and I'm sure he has innovative ideas, but—"

Wayne interrupted. "No buts, Joel knows it will be hard to convince you to switch allegiance. He knows he might not succeed but asks to talk to you again about his ideas. You never know."

"Wayne—"

"One more thing, Chris. We know Dude Sloan held a fundraiser for Brian Newman. I've known Dude ever since I moved here, so I was surprised. Think it's the first thing he's done anything politically in all those years—yes, surprising. Anyway, I was in the surf shop talking to my good friend Katelin Hatchett when Dude came over. I took the opportunity to talk to him about Joel. Dude said he liked Brian and was supporting him, but after we talked a little about Joel's ideas, and about his deep-seated support of local businesses, Dude met with Joel. They sat down the next day and after it was over Dude said he liked some of Joel's ideas and might switch to Joel." Wayne smiled. "Of course, Dude didn't use those precise words, but I think that was the drift of what he'd said."

I guess Wayne did know Dude, at least how he talked. I doubted Dude would support Joel but had no interest in arguing with Wayne.

"I still don't see not supporting Brian, but I appreciate your efforts."

"Chris, I've known Joel for many years and would do anything for him. For him to have a chance, I must convince some of Mayor Newman's supporters to listen to Joel's platform. Give it one more chance, please."

I kept looking at my phone and wishing it to ring with updates on Al or Bob. Wayne was keeping me distracted, but not in a positive way.

"Okay, I'll meet with him," I said, more to get away from Wayne than to agree.

He shook my hand again and said, "Great, I'll talk to Joel and let you know when he can meet and I'll get back with you." He nodded like he'd won a major battle. "Better get back to my job site and keep my guys plugging away."

Hallelujah, I thought, and lied, "Nice talking to you."

"Havin' a political rally back there?" Eric asked, as I walked to the door.

"More like an arm-twisting session."

Eric laughed. "I don't recall there being so much politicin' this far before an election. If sheer persistence can win, Mayor Newman better keep an eye on Joel Hurt and his good bud Wayne."

I started to tell Eric it wasn't going to work with me when Cindy returned my call.

"When in the hell were you going to tell me about Al, and that damned, blustery, foul-mouth, fat realtor that for reasons beyond my comprehension you call a friend?" she said as way of a pleasant introduction.

"How'd you hear about them?"

"I'm the freakin' police chief. Give me a break. Besides, all I had to do was walk in the Dog and one of my bosses, Councilmember Salmon cornered me before I got coffee—a serious mistake, in case you're interested—to tell me. And no, I don't know who told him. Remember, I hadn't had my coffee."

I gave her an update, as sketchy as it was, and she said she was sorry and hoped Al made it. She didn't say the same about Bob, but to give her the benefit of the doubt, I assumed that was because he was already at home.

I thanked her for her concern and for returning my call and she thanked me for not calling her a dozen times after my first call. I asked if she had an estimated time of death for Lauren. She asked me why I wanted to know. I said I'd tell her after she gave me the time of death. She uttered an East Tennessee profanity, mumbled something about me being the death of her yet, but only if I didn't get killed first, and then got around to saying the coroner estimated the time of death being between seven and ten the evening before her body was discovered. Eric was right again.

"Now, why did you want to know?"

"I'm still thinking her death wasn't accidental."

"Chris, when are you going to get a life and stop butting in to police business? Crap, never mind, I know the answer is never. So, what's her time of death got to do with anything?"

"Have you checked Joel Hurt and Katelin Hatchett's alibis for that evening?"

There was silence on the other end of the line, and then Cindy mumbled something I couldn't understand, and said, "Gee Chris, I started checking everyone who lives on Folly's alibis but only got through the last names starting with *G*. Was going to start on the *H* this afternoon."

She finished ranting, and said, "Why in the holy blue blazes should I check their alibis? What aren't you telling me?"

"From what I've heard, their relationship with Lauren was fractured at best. Joel had dated Katelin and Lauren at the same time—seldom the formula for a healthy life. They each have said things about Lauren's drug use that contradicted the autopsy's findings."

"So, the motive was Katelin being jealous? That's all you have? What about Joel? Why would he want his girlfriend dead?"

"Cindy, they each lied about Lauren."

"Everyone lies."

"Maybe, and I don't have a better reason for either of them to have killed her. I don't know if she was murdered, but all I'm asking is someone checks their alibis."

"The sheriff's office has already ruled out homicide. What reason would I have for opening that can of sardines?"

"Because you're so wonderful, because one of your favorite citizens asked you to, because—"

"Enough, enough!" she interrupted. "I'll do it to shut you up." The phone went dead.

Cindy was right. There was no evidence the death was anything but an accidental overdose or possibly suicide, but it still bothered me. Was I projecting my distrust for Joel to Lauren's death? Did I want him to be a killer because he was running against Brian Newman and had lied to me about liking him? Why had both Joel and Katelin lied about Lauren getting back into drugs? And was a door handle without prints enough to think something sinister had taken place?

My phone rang and distracted me from my game of twenty questions. I was almost afraid to answer for fear of bad news about Al but was relieved to see Barb's name on the screen. I was more relieved when she asked if I wanted to meet her for supper. I said yes and figured it would be the perfect distraction.

CHAPTER TWENTY-SEVEN

I met Barb a block from her condo at Locklear's Beach City Grill. We were given a table inside but it had the same incredible view of the Folly Pier as did the outside seating. She wore light gray shorts and a red blouse. I complimented her appearance and she said that makeup could hide a plethora of ills. I told her I should try wearing some. She laughed and said, "No need." The optimist in me decided that she'd meant I looked good enough without it. The realist in me knew better.

I started to tell her about Al and Bob but didn't want to ruin what I had hoped was to be a pleasant, refreshing, and peaceful evening. She shared a couple of stories about some irritating customers in her bookstore and she told me a joke that a preteen girl had told her while the girl's parents perused the used collection. The joke was more silly than funny, but Barb seemed to need cheering up as much as I did.

She switched directions when she asked, "Heard anything more about Lauren's death?"

I was surprised she'd brought it up and asked her why.

"No reason," she said, and looked out the window at the pier.

I cocked my head to the side. "No reason?"

"Curious, I guess. Council member Salmon's wife was in today and said her husband was worried about Lauren's boyfriend and the slate of council candidates he was putting together. Marc complaint s about being on the council, but he still loves being there. I knew you were questioning Lauren's death, and hearing about Joel made me think about her."

This wasn't quite the distraction I was hoping for. "I still have bad feelings about it, but there's nothing specific to point to anything other than an OD or suicide."

She reached across the table and put her hand on my arm. "Good, you don't need to be worrying about something like that. Besides, you didn't know her?"

"True, but—"

"And you don't like her dad, and from what you've said, the feeling's mutual."

"Yes, but—"

"And you don't like Joel because he's running against your friend, so that makes you suspicious of him."

"Also true," I said and waited for her to interrupt.

She didn't have to, a waitress did when she asked if she could get us something to drink. We each ordered, and Barb still didn't say anything.

"I'll tell you what does bother me," I said. "Joel, and for that matter Katelin. Each of them lied to me about Lauren's drug use. Why would they have said she was using again when the coroner's report said there wasn't evidence of recent use except for the overdose in her system?"

"I don't know," Barb said. "But everyone tells less than the truth on occasion. Have you thought that they may have truly believed she was using?"

I shook my head. "That doesn't make sense. I don't know about Joel, but Katelin has been a user, she'd even been in rehab with Lauren, so she'd know the signs. On top of that, there's Joel lying to me about liking Brian and going behind Brian's back and telling near-strangers how horrible the mayor is."

"Chris, when I was practicing law in Harrisburg, I dealt with several politicians—which was several more than I wanted to—and learned that lying came as easy to some of them as breathing did. Yes, Joel might be a liar, but that doesn't mean he had anything to do with Lauren's death."

I agreed with Barb and saw her point, but it still bothered me. Besides, there was no point arguing with her. There were several people walking along the pier and pointed it out to Barb and said how good a time they seemed to be having. I was determined to have a peaceful evening and wanted to get away from talking about Lauren.

Barb followed my gaze and said it was great seeing people having a good time. Our food arrived and she took a bite and looked at me. "So, when were you going to tell me about your friends Al and Bob?"

There went the pleasant, peaceful evening.

"How did you hear?"

She pointed her fork at me. "You know the hardest thing I've had to adjust to since moving here?"

I didn't figure she wanted me to guess. "What?"

"You probably don't remember, but the first time I met you we were in the Lost Dog Cafe. Either you or I, I'm not sure which, said something about one of their menu items, and a woman at the next table leaned over and said how good it was. I'd never seen her before, and to my knowledge, she'd never seen me."

"I remember." How could I not have remembered? It was one

of the most traumatic mornings of my life. I had stumbled on a dead body in the alley behind Barb's Books and the foul-weather sanctuary of First Light Church.

She continued to point the fork at me. "My point is this is the first place I've lived where everyone seems super friendly. It's a bit disconcerting." She hesitated and smiled. "But it's endearing, I suppose endearing is the right word, regardless, that trait is beginning to grow on me."

"Good," I said, but still didn't know what that had to do with Al and Bob.

"What's slower to grow on me is how so many people figure it's their mission in life to share everything they know about everyone. Seems that boundaries are often crossed. I know I'm a bit off track, but where I'm going is that in addition to Marc Salmon's wife telling me about Joel and the candidates he was putting together to run against Marc, she told me since you and I were dating, she wanted me to know she was sorry to hear about your friends. She said Marc told her, and he'd heard it from Dude, who'd learned about it from Charles, who, may or may not have been with you when poor Al collapsed. Or something like that." She put the fork on her plate and stared at me.

I looked out the window and then at Barb. "To be honest, I was hoping I'd be distracted tonight and not have to think about Bob and Al. I haven't spent as much time with Al as I have Bob, but I consider both good friends." I updated her on their condition. I also apologized for not bringing it up earlier and repeated why I hadn't.

"I'm terribly sorry about your friends," she said and reached across the table and squeezed my hand. "I've become jaded from years of practicing law. I was always having to look past what people said and try to figure out what their angle was, what they wanted, and not what they said they wanted. It was exhausting. I was so sick of fake smiles, fake feelings, fake damned near everything." She shook her head like she was throwing out those thoughts. "Chris, one of the first things you told me was that newcomers to Folly either loved or hated it here. I didn't tell you, but at the time, it was looking like I was one of the haters. The world I came from was as different from Folly as, umm." She hesitated and looked at her fork. "This fork is from an ant colony. You'll never know how many times I wanted to pack up my belongings and slink out of town under the cover of darkness."

"You didn't appear happy, but I didn't know how bad it was."

She set the fork on her plate and grinned. "Know what turned me around?"

I smiled. "My charm, good looks, and wonderful personality?"

Barb laughed, not the reaction I had hoped for, but it looked good on her.

"You better add sense of humor to that list," she said.

I wasn't certain if it was an insult or compliment, but either way, her laughter went a long way to improving my mood.

She stopped laughing and said, "Dude."

"Dude what?"

"Dude turned me around. For being my brother—step-brother—we're as opposite two people can be. But, in his word-challenged way, he pointed out the good around us. I wasn't ready to listen at first, but I started seeing examples firsthand. Kindness I'd never experienced before appeared around every corner." She stopped and turned to the window.

"Folly is filled with wonderful people."

She nodded. "And when Rocky gave his life protecting me, a near stranger, I was rocked to the core. Chris, that poor man didn't know me from Eve, but out of blind devotion to Dude, he put himself between a bullet and me. That's a level of friendship

I'd never seen or experienced." Rocky had been one of Dude's two snarky employees who had learned that Barb's life was in danger and, because of his dedication to Dude, sacrificed his own life to save Barb. "From what you've said, Bob has little in common with Al, but they've been friends for years. And if what Marc's wife said was true, it was a friendship that was so strong that when Al suffered his heart attack, it affected Bob so much he had a panic attack."

"That's true," I said, not knowing anything to add.

We finished eating in silence and Barb suggested that we walk to the end of the pier. I felt the tension slipping away as she held my hand while we strolled past several visitors looking over the side toward the sun as it slid down behind the island.

We were seated on one of the wooden benches at the end of the pier when she said, "I'm glad I didn't slink away."

"Me too."

The rest of my tension left after she suggested I spend the night in her condo.

CHAPTER TWENTY-EIGHT

I was about to let the entire situation go, but it still bothered me that both Katelin and Joel had lied about Lauren using drugs. I wasn't ready to talk to Joel again, but figured it couldn't hurt if I asked Katelin one more time about Lauren's relationship with Joel. I didn't have her phone number, but she'd said she was between jobs so there was a chance I could catch her at home.

I parked in front of a large, wood frame house Katelin, Candice, and Lauren shared on East Ashley Avenue. I was surprised to see the house was new and large by Folly standards. It had a two-car garage, another rarity on the island. A red Mazda was in the drive so I figured someone was home.

Katelin met me at the door. She saw me and blinked a couple of times. I couldn't tell if she was just waking up or was leery of me being at her door. She hesitated and opened the door half way and looked past me toward the street.

"I hope I'm not intruding," I said. "I had a few questions to ask and didn't have your number. Could I come in?"

She glanced back in the room. "Umm, sure, I was surprised to see you. Come in." She was wearing cut-off jeans, an over-sized T-shirt, and was barefoot.

I stepped in the large entry hall and glanced into the living room on the right. She saw me looking, said for me to go in and have a seat, and asked if I wanted coffee or something else to drink. I had already reached my coffee limit and said I was fine. She said she still needed a cup and would be back. I sat in a wingback chair across from a large upholstered couch. The furniture was old but appeared to be high quality. I heard what sounded like floorboards creaking from the second floor but couldn't tell if it was someone up there or the wind that had picked up, rattling a shutter or some loose wood outside.

She returned and was taking a sip from a Black Magic Cafe mug and sat on the couch across from me. She had slipped on sandals and crossed her legs. "Questions, Mr. Landrum?"

I wished I had given more thought before I'd arrived to what I wanted to ask. "Again, Katelin, I'm sorry about Lauren. I know it must be difficult for you to lose a roommate that way."

She looked in her mug and shrugged. "Yeah. You know, I was afraid something like this might happen. She did it to herself, but I blame Joel for pushing her back to drugs and the dark path where they led."

"Why blame Joel?"

"You mean other than he's a complete asshole? You mean something other than because he was dating both of us at the same time—lying out his freakin' mouth to both of us and pretending it was our imagination? Or because of what happened to Candice, our other roommate?" She jumped off the couch. Some of the coffee sloshed out of her mug as she went to the window and looked toward the street. "Did you see anyone out there when you came in?"

"No. Are you expecting someone?"

Her hand trembled and I was afraid she was going to drop the mug. "Umm, no. Just wondering." She moved back to the couch and plopped down.

I didn't know which of her questions to respond to first but felt like I was walking on egg shells and didn't want to set her off more than she already was. I also wondered if she was on something.

"I was curious about what you'd said about Lauren being back on drugs. Someone said that she wasn't and I was confused." I didn't want to tell her that the someone who said Lauren wasn't on drugs was the coroner.

She stared at me and shook her head. "I thought the last time we'd gone through rehab together that she'd kicked it for sure. She was finally getting her life together, think she wanted to get closer to her parents." She looked back in her mug. "Then Joel came along and screwed both of us up. He got her back on drugs, I know he did. And now he wants to be the mayor. What a crock."

"Do you think he could have had something to do with her death?"

"Of course, he did. He got her hooked. She found out about him two timing her. He got her the drugs. What more could he have done to lead her over the edge?"

"I understand, but do you think he could have been more directly involved. Could he—"

Katelin interrupted. "You mean like killing her on purpose?"

I nodded.

"You don't think her death was accidental?"

"I don't know. I'm just looking at the possibility."

She looked at me and tilted her head. "What do the cops think? Do they think it was intentional? Oh my God, really?"

"I don't think so. They're working under the assumption it was either an accidental overdose or suicide."

Katelin exhaled and looked at the floor. "That's what I think happened."

"Overdose or suicide?"

"Crap, I don't know. Either way, it was Joel's fault. God, I wish he had never moved here."

"Why do you think Joel would have intentionally hurt Lauren?"

"Anti-drugs, anti-drugs! Isn't that Mr. High and Mighty's big campaign pitch? Isn't he telling everyone if elected mayor he'll crack down on illegal drugs and all the dastardly things they cause? How will it look if his little girlfriend's an addict? He had to get her out of the way before he started politicin' big time. The day before she died, I hear he was telling some people he'd broken up with her and their relationship hadn't been serious anyway." She pounded her mug on the coffee table. "Hadn't been serious, hah! He dumped me for her and had the nerve to say it wasn't serious. Let me tell you, I could say some things about him that'd keep him from getting elected to dogcatcher, much less mayor."

"You think he killed her so she wouldn't hurt his campaign?"

"Wouldn't surprise me one iota." She jumped up from the couch again and looked out the window. "You sure no one was out there?"

Wasn't paranoia a possible side effect of drug use? Did her bizarre behavior indicate Katelin was on something? I said, "Do you think someone's out there?"

She jerked her head around and glared at me. "They have been. Are you sure .... Never mind. Do you have other questions? I'm busy."

I remembered she had said something about the third roommate, Candice, but figured this wasn't the time to ask. My time was up. I thanked her for her time and saw myself out. I glanced back and saw her staring out the window. I walked to my car and looked around to see if there was anyone out here. I didn't see anyone.

Now what, I wondered as I drove to the house. Was Katelin being paranoid because of drugs or had someone been watching her? Were her comments about Joel being the reason for Lauren's death legitimate, or was she a jilted lover thinking the worst about Joel because he'd left her? Did Joel tell someone he had broken up with Lauren and that possibly caused her to end her life? Then another possibility struck me. Could Katelin have killed Lauren in hopes she could get Joel back, and because he didn't respond the way she wanted him to, she was throwing him under the bus?

I pulled in the drive, let the motor continue to run, and stared at my steering wheel. An hour ago, I was ready to accept the police version of what had happened. Yet now, I thought I could make a good argument that Katelin or Joel could have been responsible for Lauren's death. But, had she killed herself, either accidentally or on purpose, or had one of the others murdered her?

I would get yelled at but took the chance and called Cindy. Instead of getting voice mail where I could ask my question without her yelling at me, she answered.

"Yes and no," she said as way of a greeting.

It was now a tossup on which I hated the most: Caller ID or cryptic responses.

"Yes, that you think I'm the most wonderful person in the world," I said. "And no, even though you'd love to, you won't ditch Larry and run off with me."

"You calling from the psych ward?" Cindy laughed. "You've done gone loony."

I was glad I got a laugh out of her rather than one of her patented rants. "I'm calling from my driveway, and some may call it a psych ward."

"No argument from me," she said.

"Yes and no?" I said.

"It's been almost twenty-four hours since you asked about alibis, so I figured you couldn't wait a second longer before you started pestering me about them. Right?"

"You got me there."

"Of course, I did. So, the yes is I found out if Joel had an alibi, and no if Katelin had one."

I waited for her to elaborate, but her small amount of revenge was to force me to ask. "Yes, you found out about Joel, or yes he has an alibi?"

"Joel was holed up with his campaign manager during the timeframe we were given for Lauren's death. Unless he could be in two places at the same time, he's as innocent as baby Jesus."

"Did you confirm his story?"

"Golly, gee, Chris, why didn't I think of that?"

"I suppose that means you did."

"Of course, I confirmed it, numbskull. Remember, I'm the brilliant police chief. According to Wayne Swan, he and Joel spent several hours that evening working on a brochure for his campaign. And before you ask, no, Joel didn't leave Wayne's house that entire time. You can mark Joel off your list of imaginary killers of Lauren Craft who you, and only you, have imagined being killed."

I ignored the last comment. "What about Katelin?"

"I haven't talked to her yet. The phone number I had for her has been disconnected, so I'll try to catch her at home."

I told Cindy I'd left Katelin's and a little about her reactions to my questions and her thinking that someone was watching her. Cindy proceeded to express in strong, unkind words how stupid it was of me to visit Katelin, and I needed to learn to mind my own business. I crossed my fingers and told her she was right and that I would butt out.

Before the phone went dead, she responded like a highly-trained chief of police would by saying, "Liar, liar, pants on fire!"

CHAPTER TWENTY-NINE

The next morning I was drinking coffee and staring at my refrigerator as if I expected words of wisdom or a clue to what was going on to appear on it. None appeared but the phone did ring. It was barely seven o'clock so I tensed; seldom did good news come this early.

"Chris, this is Tanesa. Did I wake you up?"

I took a deep breath and closed my eyes expecting the worst. "I was awake."

"Good. With my screwy shifts around here, I lose track of when normal people get up. Anyway, I wanted to give you an update."

She sounded upbeat. *So far, so good*, I thought—I hoped. "How is your dad?"

"The best I can say is he's alive but still in a coma."

"I thought he had a heart attack. Can that cause a coma?"

"Without getting too technical, yes, he had a cardiac arrest and that led to a lack of oxygen to the brain which in turn caused the coma."

"Tanesa, I hate to ask, but what's your best guess about his chances?"

"To be honest, it doesn't look good. Even though he's alive, his body is frail. If he was thirty years younger, I'd have hope, but ... well, I don't know."

That's what I was afraid of. "I'm sorry."

I heard her sniffle and there was a long silence before she said, "But I'm not giving up. I've seen people come through these doors who didn't seem to have a chance in the world of surviving. Miracles can happen. Everything is being done medically that can be, but it'll take more. Even if he pulls out of the coma, he could have serious disabilities. It'll all depend on how long his brain was deprived of oxygen. Please pray for him."

"I will, Tanesa. He's lived through some terrible times. He's strong."

"And as stubborn as hell."

I chuckled. "I think he'll pull through just to be able to sit back and watch Bob battle with customers at Al's."

"He'd love that. I hope you're right."

I asked if she wanted me to come to the hospital and she said it wouldn't do any good. She'd let me know if there was any change and I thanked her for calling. She asked if I'd call Bob and fill him in.

I'd wait a couple of hours to call Bob. His mornings didn't start until around ten. Calling sooner would be like waking a bear out of hibernation, but more profane. Instead of incurring Bob's wrath, I walked to the Dog for breakfast. There were three vacant tables on the front patio, but I didn't need any of them. Charles was at a table and bent over exchanging kisses with a Labrador retriever attached to a leash held by a man at the adjacent table. I pulled out the chair opposite my friend before he noticed me. Nothing stands between Charles and a dog.

"Whoa, where did you come from?" Charles said after he bid farewell to his new canine friend that was following its master to the exit.

I was distressed about Al's condition, so I resisted offering a smart-aleck remark, and asked if I could join him for breakfast.

He stared at me and squinted. "What's wrong?"

"Why do you think something's wrong?"

"First, in the zillion years we've know each other, you've never asked if you could join me, and second, you passed up laying a smart remark on me when I asked where you came from."

He knew me too well. I told him about my conversation with Tanesa.

"Does Bob know?"

"Don't think so. Tanesa asked me to call him."

Charles put his hand over his face. "Make sure I'm a couple of miles away when you make that call."

A food delivery truck stopped in front of the restaurant and I couldn't hear what Charles said next. I doubt I missed much. The truck, and its loud diesel engine moved down the road and Charles was saying something about Marc Salmon. I asked him to repeat it.

He tilted his head toward the inside dining area. "I said, Marc said that one of his supporters told him Joel is holding fundraisers in West Ashley to get money for his council candidates to, as Marc put it, 'stomp my ass.' Marc said he'd never had to resort to begging for money to run for council, but if he wanted to stay on the job, he'd have to do something."

"I'm afraid Joel's going to do whatever he needs to do to beat Brian and to get his candidates on the council."

Amber appeared at the table with coffee for me and asked if I wanted granola and yogurt; I said French toast. She smiled and headed to the kitchen.

"Speaking of Joel," Charles said as if Amber hadn't been here, "you still think he had something to do with Lauren's death?"

I glanced around to see who was nearby. "I did, but now I'm not sure. Not even sure her death was anything more than what the coroner has ruled."

Charles started to say something but paused as a Folly Beach patrol car blasted down Center Street with its siren blaring. Seconds later, the distinct siren of one of the city's fire engines started dogs howling as it pulled out of the station a couple of blocks away.

Charles looked in the direction of the fire station, and said, "Don't suppose you want to call Cindy and see what's going on?"

I may have the smart-aleck gene, but Charles had the nosy gene in spades. "No but speaking of Cindy." I took a sip of coffee and shared my conversation with her and what she'd said about Joel's alibi. Before Charles interrupted with a hundred questions, I told him about my visit to Katelin and what she'd said about Joel.

"So, you figured Joel killed Lauren and Cindy blew it all by coming up with such a good alibi for Joel." Another patrol car's siren could be heard in the distance. "Sure, you don't want to call Cindy?"

"I'm sure."

Charles shrugged. "So, Wayne was Joel's alibi?

I nodded.

"That's the Wayne who's running Joel's campaign; the same

Wayne who's Joel's good friend. Was there anyone else at this brochure-creating meeting?"

"Cindy didn't mention anyone."

"So, this could be the same Wayne who would be the only person on earth who could vouch for being with Joel when Lauren met her maker."

I nodded, again, and said, "And could be the same Wayne who's such a good friend of Joel that he might lie about Joel being with him?"

Charles pointed his knife at me. "Now you're catching on. Lauren and Joel were dating, so it would make sense he would be with her that night. It had to be someone who knew her and that she trusted."

"Not necessarily. I've given it some thought. Anyone could have stuck a gun to her head and made her drive out there. And Charles, that's assuming she was murdered, which it seems that only I believe."

"Add me to that short list. Oh yeah, there's one other person who needs to be added."

"The killer," I said.

"Yep, and that could be the person you went to see yesterday."

"Katelin did seem intent on pointing fingers at Joel at the same time she was painting a picture of Lauren falling back into drugs."

"Throwing around stuff that would deflect attention from her. What's her alibi?"

"Cindy's still checking."

Amber arrived with my breakfast and Charles had taken the last bite of his eggs. "And you'll let me know the second you find out, right?"

I told him of course, and he said he had to meet Heather.

She'd said she needed to talk to him, and when Heather calls, Charles jumps. I was impressed by her control over him.

There was one other table occupied on the patio, so I decided to call Bob and get that unpleasant task out of the way. I was surprised when Betty answered Bob's cell phone. I told her who I was and asked if Bob was okay.

"Oh, Chris, I'm glad you called. I don't exactly know how to answer your question. I think his health is okay, or at least he hasn't complained since yesterday about feeling bad. And when it comes to his health, he's a big baby and will moan and groan about a splinter like someone was cutting his hand off. Anyway, I'm not worried about that, but I don't recall ever seeing him so down about anything as he is about Al."

"I'm sorry to hear it. Anything I can do?"

"Short of waving a magic wand and making Al well, I don't know what it could be."

It wouldn't help his mood, but I felt I needed to tell him what Tanesa had said. "Is he there now?"

Betty said yes, but he was still asleep. She was surprised he had slept that long but didn't want to disturb him. I shared what Tanesa had told me and asked if she wanted me to tell him when he woke up. She hesitated, but finally said it might be better if she told him. I deferred to her judgment and ended by saying I was sorry about Al and wished her luck in telling Bob. She said she'd need it.

Amber brought a refill on my coffee, looked around, and sat where Charles had been earlier. She said, "Are you okay?"

"Sure, why?"

She tapped her fingers on the table. "Because you look like someone stole your car and burned your house down. You may be able to fib to other folks, but remember, I know you better than anyone here. So, what's wrong?"

I told her about Al and Bob. She reached over the table and put her hand on my hand that was holding the mug, and said, "Oh Chris, I'm so sorry. I know how much friends mean to you, and I know they're two of your best. Anything I can do?"

I smiled, thanked her, and said she was doing it.

The couple at the other table waved for Amber to bring them the check. She nodded in their direction and said to me, "Let me know if you need anything, you hear?"

After she left, I started thinking about what she had said about friends. Would Wayne have lied about Joel's whereabouts? And I tried to remember what Katelin had said about her friend, and roommate, Candice. Wasn't it something about Lauren possibly killing herself because of what happened to Candice? I was busy trying to figure out Katelin's relationship with Lauren and why she may have killed her and didn't catch what Katelin had meant about Candice. All I knew about the third housemate was she was seldom home and Dude had said she had been fired from one of Joel's garden centers allegedly for theft but the rumor was that was actually because she had learned something about Joel that he didn't want known. She was now working at a real estate office in Charleston. Would it help if I talked to her to get her take on what happened to Lauren? Possibly, but I didn't know where she worked.

Instead of sitting at the Dog and asking myself questions, that I knew I had no answer for, I decided to go back to Katelin and Candice's house to see if Candice was there. I'd like to get her take on Joel and Lauren, and with luck, more about what had happened to her job at the garden center.

A block before I got to their rental, one earlier question was answered—an answer I didn't want to know.

CHAPTER THIRTY

Three police cars, two fire trucks, and an ambulance were parked at all angles in front of Katelin's house. Yellow crime-scene tape blocked the entrance to the open garage door and a glimpse of the rear of Katelin's Mazda was visible under a blue tarp on the other side of the tape. A gaggle of area residents were milling around the yard next door. One of the Folly Beach Public Safety officers was waving his arms at cars to keep moving on the busy street. One of the fire trucks blocked most of the garage as I slowly drove past the house so I parked in the next empty drive and walked to the group of people standing as close to Katelin's house as the police permitted.

It was easy to spot my friend, Chester Carr, in the group. Charles's late Aunt Melinda had said he was a "spittin' image of Mr. Magoo", and she wasn't far off. I'd known him for several years.

I asked him what was going on.

"Don't know much," he said and pointed to a woman on the

other side of the group, "Marge said they found a body in that red car in the garage. I just got here, was on my way to visit a friend who lives out past the Washout."

I was afraid I knew the answer, but asked, "Anyone know who it was?"

"Suppose the cops do, but I don't."

There was a black Ford Focus in the drive. "Know whose car that is?"

Chester turned his Coke bottle thick glasses my direction. "Chris, I just got here, and I ain't a reporter."

"I know, but I thought you—"

He stuck his hand in my face and said, "Hold on." He turned and waved for the woman he'd referred to as Marge to come over. She smiled at Chester, gave a quick glance at the garage, and walked over.

"Marge," said Chester. "You know Chris?"

She shook her head and Chester introduced me as the guy who used to have the photo gallery where Barb's Books is now located and that I've helped the police catch a few killers. I wished he'd left out the last part. She shook my hand and said she was Marge Monroe and lived in the house across from Katelin's. She was in her eighties but had a strong handshake and bounced on the balls of her feet with energy I hoped I had when I reached her age.

Chester pointed to Katelin's. "Marge, know who's dead?"

"Suspect it's one of those girls who lived there. Think her name's Katelin something. That's her red car and the EMTs hauled somebody out of it. Couldn't see much since they strung that blue tarp over the car."

That's what I was afraid of. "Know who the black car belongs to?"

Marge looked at the Ford Focus and back to me. "Candice

Richardson, she's the third gal who lives there. My goodness, that makes two of them dead. Hope nothing happens to Candice."

"Marge," I said, "how well do you know Candice?"

"Better than the other two, I suppose. She's seldom there, but I've run into her a couple of times in Bert's and she liked talking about flowers. I have a flower garden behind my house and Candice had planted some over there, so it was something we could talk about."

"Have you seen her since all this happened?"

"No, but I guess she's in the house since her car's there." She smiled and patted Chester on his bald head. "Gotta get back home. My hubby'll be wondering what happened to me. He's bedridden and I can't be gone long. Nice meeting you, Carl."

I told her it was nice meeting her as well. I didn't correct my name.

A patrol car was parked directly across the street from where we were standing and Officer Allen Spencer was walking to it from Katelin's house. I had known the six-foot tall, muscular officer since I had moved to Folly. He was new on the force at that time, and I was new to Folly so we had something to talk about. I excused myself from Chester and intercepted Allen as he reached the car door.

"Hey, Chris."

He'd always been cordial, polite, and helpful, characteristics that not all police had shared.

I shook his hand and said, "What happened?"

"Looks like suicide. Young lady who lived there." He glanced at something he'd written on his palm. "Her name's Katelin Hatchett. She was in her locked car in the garage, motor running."

"Who found her?"

"Housemate."

"Candice Richardson?"

Allen stared at me. "How'd you know?"

I told him a neighbor said the black car in the drive belonged to Candice and I knew she was the other housemate.

"Tragic," Allen said. "Such a young lady, so much life in front of her."

"Are you sure it was suicide?"

"That's what the EMTs said. No signs of foul play and the car was locked. She did have a big bruise on her forehead, but the guys think it was caused by the steering wheel her head hit when she passed out." He hesitated, looked at the name on his palm, and back at me. "Do you think it was something else?"

"Did you know Lauren Craft was a third housemate?"

"The woman found dead near the County Park?"

"Yes," I said. "Doesn't it seem strange both died this close together, both were found in their car, and both could have been suicides?"

Allen nodded. "I suppose. I'm sure the detectives from the Sheriff's office will get it sorted out. One of them should be here any minute."

"Do you know who's coming?"

"No."

I nodded toward the house. "Is the chief over there?"

"Yeah, she's waiting around for a detective. Chris, I've gotta run. I'm supposed to be on patrol."

I thanked him for the information, and he repeated they'll figure it out, before pulling out to make my island safer. I hoped they would figure it out but didn't have as much confidence as did Officer Spencer.

There wasn't anything I could do here but knew there was one thing I had to do, and that was to call Charles and let him know what'd happened. I would incur enormous quantities of grief if I didn't tell him within seconds of when I learned something important. Even then, I would be surprised if he didn't say, "What took you seconds to tell me?"

"Got something important to tell you," Charles blurted as way of greeting upon answering my call.

"So do I," I said.

"Not as important as what I have. I'm home, come over. It'll blow your mind away."

Since he didn't bombard me with questions about what I had to tell him, I figured whatever he had to say might blow my mind away. Besides, with everything cluttering up my mind, it wouldn't take much to make it explode.

Charles had been watching for me. He opened the door before my car had come to a stop in the gravel and shell parking lot of his small, book-filled apartment on Sandbar Lane. He wore a crimson and blue Samford University, long-sleeve T-shirt, navy shorts, and a wide smile.

"You're not going to believe my news," he said as I stepped in the book-filled living room.

I didn't waste my breath by saying something like *Hi, Charles*, nor did I step in the middle of his story to tell him about Katelin's death. I said, "What's the news?"

He raised both hands over his head. "I'm getting married!"

He's right; I didn't believe it. I headed to the kitchen that, if possible, was smaller than his tiny bathroom, and poured a glass of white wine out of the double-bottle he kept in his refrigerator for me. I asked if he wanted a beer. He said yes and told me to get back in the living room so he could tell me more about his nuptial plans.

I handed him the Budweiser and said, "Is that what Heather wanted to talk to you about yesterday?"

He took a sip, clinked the can down on a stack of books beside his chair, and scratched his stringy hair. "Sort of."

A couple of years back, Charles had proposed to Heather. Their marriage had been the final wish of his aunt before she'd succumbed to cancer. The proposal was more an emotional response to his aunt's request than something he'd thought out, and he'd later decided he wasn't ready for marriage, and may never be. Heather said she'd understood, but I was never certain she had accepted it.

"Sort of?" I said.

"She didn't come right out and say we should get hitched, but wanted me to know she wasn't getting younger, and now her dream of becoming a country music star had been stomped on, she was feeling like a failure. You know I can't do anything to make her a star, but I can help her meet her need to be married."

"Did you propose?"

"No. Most of the time she talked about feeling like a failure and something had to happen. I spent most of the rest of the time reassuring her she was a wonderful person and far from a failure. Besides, popping the question and making her Mrs. Charles Fowler came to me in the middle of the night. I can't imagine why she'd want to be that, but I'm going to make it happen. Chris, I'm excited."

"When are you going to ask her?"

"Tomorrow, and you're going to be there."

"Whoa," I said. "Why? That's a private moment between you two."

He shook his head. "Wrong. I've been reading up on this.

The latest thing in marriage proposals is for the groom to invite his friends and sneaks around and invites her friends and family to be wherever the question's to be popped. They even video the big knee-on-the-ground moment. Can you believe that?"

I couldn't, but didn't say anything before he continued, "You're my only friend, and I don't have any family left, and I couldn't figure out if Heather had anyone she would want to be there, so it's you. Yep, you'll be with us."

"Are you sure you want to propose, and if you are, about me being there?"

"Gerald Ford said, 'I know I am getting better at golf because I'm hitting fewer spectators.' I'm going to get this proposal thing right this time; yes, I am. I'm definitely positive that I'm sure."

"Okay. I'd be honored to share the moment with you." I also wondered what Heather would think about me crashing their intimate moment.

Charles took another sip. "Now with that settled, what's so important that you had to barge into my home and drink my wine for?"

No, I didn't remind him he'd invited me and the only reason he had wine in his apartment was for me. I did tell him where I'd been and what had happened.

The first sign he was distracted by his marriage plans was when he didn't chastise me for waiting so long to tell him. He also didn't ask who was there, what everyone watching the police action had said, and if any of them had their dogs with them.

"Strange," he said.

"That's all you have to say?"

He took another drag on his beer and said, "Think I need to get a ring before I pop the question?"

I said no, asked what time tomorrow, and where. He said

eleven o'clock in the morning, and that he wanted to "pop the question" on the Folly Pier because it provided a great view of the beach and that it was where he'd said his farewells to his aunt. He'd spread her ashes in the ocean from the end of the pier. I said I'd meet him there, and said I'd better be going.

I echoed his comment as I walked to the car. "Strange."

CHAPTER THIRTY-ONE

"Okay, nosy one, this is your duly appointed, highly competent, plum near able to walk on water police chief."

I may have missed a word or two from her telephonic wakeup call since I glanced at the window and saw it was dark outside and looked at the bedside clock and saw it was five thirty.

"Good morning Cindy."

"I figured since you're the one who wakes the roosters up each morning, that I'd catch you awake. You were, weren't you?"

I lied and said, "Of course. What have I done to be honored with your call?"

"Damned near nothing, but I figured you'd want to know what happened out on East Arctic yesterday since it involved someone you've taken an interest in."

I opened my sleep-filled eyes wide and said, "Katelin Hatchett's death?"

"You've already heard?"

I told her I was one of the inquisitive citizens at Katelin's house.

Cindy sighed, "Why am I not surprised? Then I can go about keeping your island free of crime. Adios."

"Cindy," I said, hoping to stop her from hanging up.

"What now?"

"Was it suicide?"

"Everything points to it."

"Did she leave a note?"

"No, but that doesn't mean anything. Less than half of suicide victims leave notes."

I carried the phone into the kitchen and started to fix coffee. I knew what Officer Spencer had told me, but asked Cindy anyway, "Were there any signs of a struggle?"

"What part of suicide don't you get? Not really. She had a bump on her head but it was probably caused by it hitting the steering wheel when she first passed out."

"Could she have been hit hard enough to knock her out?"

"Chris, how the hell would I know that? Tell you what, let me come over there and smack you on the head and see how big a bump it'll take to knock you out. A bump's a bump. But, I get your point. I'll check with the ME."

"Thanks," I said. "I hear her housemate found her."

"Yeah, Candice came home, changed clothes, and started to fix something to drink when she heard Katelin's car running in the garage. At first, she thought Katelin had come home, and Candice didn't hear the garage door open. She said she realized that she parked blocking the garage and her housemate couldn't have gotten around her car. She went to check, and the rest is history."

"Bear with me a second, Cindy. So, it's possible Candice

could have been home long enough to set it up to look like a suicide."

"Stop and hold your jackass. Why would Candice kill Katelin?"

Instead of answering, I asked, "Did you check if Candice had an alibi for when Lauren was killed?"

There was a moment of silence on the other end of the phone. "Not yet. Crap, I could have asked her yesterday, but had a more immediate death on my hands. Are you saying she killed both housemates? And I guess more importantly, I'm looking at one suicide and one either accidental overdose or possibly suicide. Why the bee in your Tilley about them being killed?"

"Cindy, I'm only asking questions. I have no idea what's happening. But don't you think it's mighty strange that they died so close together?"

"Yes, but because something is strange doesn't raise it to the level of homicide."

She was right, but I wasn't ready to let it go. "Could you do me one big favor?"

Another sigh on the other end of the line. She said, "What?" It sounded like an exclamation more than a question.

"See if Joel Hurt has an alibi for when Katelin was killed, umm, died."

The next thing I heard was a dial tone. I assumed that meant, *"Of course I will, Chris. Good suggestion."*

Charles had said eleven o'clock, so I knew that meant ten thirty, so I arrived at the pier a little after ten. It was a gorgeous day with light billowy clouds overhead and a temperature in the mid-seventies. The pier was busier than usual. Several men had cast lines and were waiting for the fish to grab the bait for an early lunch. Two children were giggling and pointing to three birds that were fighting over a potato chip the children had accidentally—on purpose—dropped on the deck. And an elderly couple leaned over the edge and watched a group of college age men playing volleyball.

My phone rang and I was surprised that Cindy was able to get back with me so quickly. There was no need to be surprised since it wasn't her.

"Thank god, you answered," Charles said, sounding out of breath. "Come to Heather's apartment. Now!"

For the second time this morning, I was hung up on. But Charles sounded much more distressed than Cindy. I was pulling up in front of Heather's dilapidated apartment building ten minutes later and saw Charles's car parked in front. Heather's apartment door was open but I knocked before entering.

Charles came out of the kitchen waving a piece of paper in his hand, and said, "She's gone. Everything's gone."

I glanced around and didn't see any of the knickknacks that had dotted every surface in the apartment. "What do you mean gone?"

He handed me the paper, flopped down on the couch, and bowed his head.

The note was in flowing script and read: *Chuckie, dear. I wanted to tell you this in person but chickened out. Sorry you must find out this way. My dream of singing is busted. It was squashed like an elephant stepping on an ant. My hopes of becoming your wife seem as far away as Spain. And I feel like I'm in one of those straitjacket things. I must leave. Honest to god, I must. I may be making a big mistake, but it's what I want to do. I'm taking all that I can carry. You can do whatever you want to do with the rest. I'm getting a cab to the bus station and by the time you read this, I'm long gone. PLEASE do not try to find me. Chuckie, this isn't your fault so don't start blaming yourself. xoxo forever, Heather*

Charles's hands covered his head. For the first time, I noticed he had on a white, long-sleeve T-shirt unadorned with any logos or school mascots.

"I'm sorry," I said, and felt helpless.

"No matter what she said, it's my fault. I couldn't do anything about her singing, but why didn't I go through with marrying her the first time, and why didn't I say something about getting hitched when she was feeling so bad the other night? Why, Chris, why?"

"There're no easy answers, Charles. Getting married had to be right for both of you. The last time it wasn't."

"I know, but was I being selfish, wanting everything my way?"

"You were wonderful to her and she knew it. Don't kick yourself. Any idea where she's headed?"

He looked at the door. "I don't know. Could be anywhere—except Nashville. She never mentioned wanting to be somewhere else." He put his head back down. "If she'd waited one more day, one more measly day, my proposal …"

I didn't say anything for a couple of minutes. Charles was deep in his thoughts and didn't need to be disturbed. I finally said, "Want to try to find out where she's going?"

He looked back at the door and at the note I still had in my hand. "She said for me not to. Chris, I've got to honor her wish. I've go to."

Tears formed in the corner of his eyes and he looked away.

And I felt helpless.

CHAPTER THIRTY-TWO

I'd tried every way I knew to help my grieving friend. Nothing worked. He said he needed to be alone. I didn't want to leave him, but his words had an edge of finality, so I told him to call me day or night if he needed anything. He said he would, but I'd be shocked if he did.

I called Bob on my way home and asked how he was doing.

"My best friend is about dead. I'm old and the idiot doctors tell me that I'm falling apart. I own a damned run-down bar that's losing money. And Betty said that unless I get my sorry butt out of the chair and do something worth a damn, she was going to put me in the wheelbarrow and dump me at the curb for the trash collector. How the hell you think I'm doing?"

I coughed to mask a giggle and said, "Poor little Bobby Howard."

"You're damned right, for a change."

Enough foolishness, I thought, as I pulled in my drive. "Any news about Al?"

"I called Tanesa an hour ago. She told me yesterday that

she'd call me if she learned anything, but I was damned tired of waiting. Anyway, she said there's slight improvement. He's still in that damned coma but his heart sounds stronger this morning."

"That's good news."

Bob said, "I suppose."

I debated whether to tell him about Katelin's alleged suicide and about Heather leaving but decided that Bob didn't need more unwelcome news.

"He's still alive, so that's good."

"Yeah," Bob said. "Betty yelled something, so unless you want to hear me bitch and groan more, I'd better go see what she wants. She's not that good with the wheelbarrow."

"Tell her I said hi."

For the third time today, I was hung up on. Fortunately, I'm not paranoid. What I did realize was that I was hungry and didn't feel like facing people in a restaurant. I walked next door to Bert's to grab whatever doughy delights they had in stock. I was pleased that they had a cinnamon Danish, but what I was not pleased to see was Wayne Swan heading my way.

"Chris Landrum, the person I wanted to see."

Wayne Swan, the last person I wanted to see, I thought but didn't say it. "Hi, Wayne. What'd you need?"

"Listen, Joel and I are going to be in the bar at Loggerheads this afternoon around four. Could you join us?"

I gave my best faux smile and said, "Why?"

"Joel would love to meet with you one more time. He has some things that might help you change your mind about supporting him."

I wanted to scream, "No!" but thought it may be a good idea to meet with Joel, so I said that I'd be there. I didn't tell Wayne that while I'd be there it wasn't why they wanted to meet me.

What better chance to learn more about Joel's relationship with Lauren and Katelin?

Home was my next destination, and I reached it without having to get in an extended discussion with anyone else. I thought about calling Tanesa, but after she'd endured a call from Bob, she probably needed peace and quiet. I'm not a big nap person, but after Cindy's early morning wakeup call, I managed to sleep for an hour before waking up regretting that I'd agreed to meet with Joel. What could I learn about his relationship with the two deceased housemates? I waffled between thinking he would reveal something that would lend support to my belief that he was responsible for their deaths, and that whatever he'd tell me couldn't be believed.

I had a hard time focusing on anything other than Charles and Heather. My friend was in pain and there was nothing to do to help. How would things have been different if Charles had proposed earlier? I had known him for a long time and on numerous occasions he had confided that he was afraid of marriage. And he and Heather had lived together during their short-lived, ill-fated move to Nashville. It would have been the opportune time to see if marriage would be right for him, yet he never mentioned the possibility while they were there or after their return to Folly.

Nothing was being accomplished by my analyzing Charles's situation and Joel's believability, so I walked to Loggerhead's. It was a half-hour before I was to meet Joel and Wayne and I smiled to myself as I headed up the steps to the elevated outside bar. I was becoming more like Charles than I ever imagined possible. The temperature was in the mid-eighties and a gray cloud-cover kept the sun from being intolerable, so the large outdoor seating area was packed. I wondered how long we would have to wait for a table when Ed, half of the husband and wife team owners of the restaurant, put his arm on my shoulder, welcomed me, and said that he was expecting me. I smiled and asked how he knew I'd be here.

He pointed to a table by the railing. "They said you were coming and if I saw you to point you their way."

Joel and Wayne were at a table that had the best view across the street to the Oceanfront Villas. A sliver of the ocean could be seen through the gap between the parking lot and the elevated condo complex. They leaned toward each other and appeared in deep conversation.

I thanked Ed, told him to give my regards to his wife Yvonne and weaved my way past the standing room only crowd to Joel's table. Wayne was flailing his arms around and saying something about not going to do it when Joel spotted me.

Joel waved his hand in front of Wayne, stood, smiled, and said, "You're early. You caught us discussing the landscaping on a big project Wayne is working on."

From the way Wayne was acting before I arrived, I would have used the word arguing rather than discussing, but whatever. I returned his smile and shook his hand. Wayne took a sip of his beer from a plastic cup and waved in my direction. He remained seated as I sat in the plastic chair facing the bar.

Joel looked at Wayne who hadn't spoken and turned back to me. "I've asked Wayne to join us, hope you don't mind." He gave me a politician's smile, baring all his teeth. "He can help keep me on track; I have a way of wandering in my conversations."

"Fine with me," I said, although I wanted Joel to wander.

A waitress had been at the table beside us and Wayne touched her back to get her attention. She pointed at the near-empty cups in front of Wayne and Joel. "Another round?"

Wayne said yes and ordered a glass of white wine for me. I

was impressed that he knew my drink of choice but irritated that he ordered without asking if that was what I wanted. After the waitress had headed to the bar, Wayne said, "Sorry, Chris, I should have asked before ordering for you. Was that okay?"

Partial redemption. I said that it was.

Wayne looked at Joel and turned back to me. "I'm being rude. Sorry. Joel and I were debating an issue about a remodel. The owner keeps changing what he wants but doesn't want to spend more money on it. We're trying to see how to cut costs while giving him what he's asking for."

That wasn't my impression of what they were arguing about, but I mumbled something about how it must be difficult to meet everyone's needs.

Joel interrupted. "Neither here nor there. Don't want to bore you with our work. I'm thrilled you agreed to meet with me again. Have you given more thought to supporting me in my Quixote-like quest to unseat Brian Newman?"

"A little," I said. Most of my thought has been trying to figure out how to prove he killed the two women but didn't think it would be wise to mention it.

"Good," Joel said. "I was afraid you were so deep in his camp that I wouldn't have a chance with you. And, before you say anything, I know that two of your friends have had fundraisers for Brian and you attended each of them. I understand friendship and am not a stranger to loyalty. In fact, I admire it, but I also know that you have the reputation of doing what you believe is right, regardless of what others may think. I also know about you getting involved in death investigations, often involving perilous situations." He chuckled. "I've even heard you're asking questions about the tragic death of Lauren Craft. I admire your gumption, although I'm afraid it's misplaced with Lauren. The poor girl couldn't handle the horrific dangers of drugs and overdosed." He paused, shook his head, and said, "So sad."

I couldn't decide if he was continuing to suck up to me or fishing to see how much I knew, or suspected, about Lauren's death. Either way, I saw this as an opening to the real reason I was here.

"It was terrible about her death. I offer my deepest condolences. I know you and she were close and her loss must be painful."

He glanced across the street toward the ocean and at me. "Yes, it is terrible, but we weren't that close. We went out a few times but it wasn't serious. Of course, I liked her, but didn't see it going anywhere, and when I learned about her renewing her affair with drugs, I had to sever our relationship. As you know, I have a strong anti-drug stance; I see the use of illegal drugs and the misuse of legal prescriptions as being one of the biggest problems facing our country, and yes, infiltrating our community. I cannot tolerate it. I believe that is where our current elected officials and I differ, and—"

I wasn't ready to listen to a campaign speech and interrupted, "I'm surprised. I was under the impression that you and Lauren were much closer than that."

The waitress returned with our drinks.

"See, Wayne," Joel said and pointed to me, "he doesn't beat around the bush. He doesn't hesitate to challenge things. I admire that." He smiled and turned back to me. "You and I have a lot in common, and that's why I'm asking you to support me."

The waitress returned with our drinks and I noticed how much louder it was than when I had arrived. The crowd had increased and groups were speaking louder to be heard over other groups.

I wanted to steer the conversation back to Lauren but didn't want to be obvious. "Joel, I'm honored that you are spending so much time with me and I think you have a lot of promising ideas, but I've known Brian Newman for a long time. I like and respect him. He's not been perfect, and I don't agree with all his positions, but he's been good for our community, and I will continue to support him."

Wayne was fiddling with his napkin and turned to Joel. "My friend, I don't think you're going to win Chris over. We should let him get on his way."

I wasn't ready to pass up this opportunity to pump Joel for information. "That's okay, Wayne, I'm not in a hurry, besides it's great to be outside."

Joel said, "I agree and even if I can't twist your arm, it's good getting to know you better."

I snapped my fingers like I'd thought of something. "Have you heard about Katelin Hatchett?"

Wayne glanced at Joel who gave a slight nod and said, "Just heard about it this morning. Can't imagine what would cause someone to end his or her own life."

"She was one of Lauren's housemates," I said. "Did you know her?"

Joel rubbed the side of his nose, and said, "Umm, we'd gone out a couple of times."

"Oh," I said. "Before you dated Lauren?"

"Yeah," he said and took a sip.

I didn't think he would say that he was at the same time. Might as well go for broke. "Her housemate found her. That must've been horrible. Her name's Candice something. You knew her, I hear?"

Wayne leaned toward the table. "Don't believe I do."

Joel mimicked Wayne's move. "Yeah, I knew her a little. She'd worked at one of my garden centers for a while. She found a better paying job, something where she could use her degree in accounting. Why?"

"Curious," I said. "It's amazing how rumors get started." I smiled.

"Rumors?" Joel asked.

"I heard that Candice had stolen money from your garden center and that she was fired, but now that you said she got a job in accounting, that couldn't be true or she wouldn't have gotten a good reference."

Joel laughed, but his hands were gripping his cup so tightly that I was afraid it would break. "You're right about rumors. No truth to that as far as I know, and since they're my businesses, I'd know."

I nodded like I believed him and decided to go for broke. "Speaking of rumors, I heard that Katelin's body was found yesterday morning, and someone said it was around dusk. Do you know when it was?"

"Don't know," Wayne said. "Didn't hear about it until today."

"I don't know for certain," said Joel. "But it was probably late morning when we heard sirens coming from everywhere. Wayne and I were a couple of blocks from here. I was pricing the landscaping for one of Wayne's new clients. He tore down an old shed and wants to extend his garden around the back of his house. We'd been there way longer than we should have been for the size job."

Wayne said, "That's probably what that racket was about."

"Enough about death," Joel said. "It's too pretty a day to be talking about depressing things."

Wayne agreed and we drifted into a benign discussion about the weather, the new restaurant on Center Street, and how much both were looking forward to fall and cooler weather. Joel said that he had to be going and we went our separate ways.

As I walked home, I thought about what I had learned. Joel had continued to lie about the depth of his relationship with Lauren, the reason that Candice had been fired, and adroitly avoided the subject of dating Lauren and Katelin at the same time. But the most significant revelation was that if it wasn't for Wayne, Joel wouldn't have had an alibi for the times either of the ladies had died. Interesting.

CHAPTER THIRTY-THREE

It'd been more than twenty-four hours since I left Charles. I hoped that he'd reach out to me, but that was not to be, so I made the first move and called. Instead of hearing his voice cheery or otherwise, I got his message: *This is Charles. I won't return your call, but if you want, leave a message in case I change my mind.* I almost yearned for his pre-Nashville sojourn when he didn't have a phone or answering machine. Should I go and knock on his door? No, if he wanted to talk, he knew how to reach me. He needed time to absorb Heather's departure and what it had meant, and more important, how he was going to proceed from here.

It had been even longer since I'd heard from Al's daughter, but was determined not to pester her. She'd said she would let me know if there was any change. It had also been a couple of days since I'd talked to Cindy. As chief of police, she was pulled in countless directions, her priorities changed minute by minute depending on what her department was involved in: vehicle accidents, burglaries, inappropriate actions of inebriated citizens and visitors alike, calls from irate residents, and the never-ending issues related to illegal parking. And that's not considering the wishes and desires of the city's elected officials. I decided to call and remind her of a couple of items I'd asked her to check into.

"No, Chris," were the first words out of her mouth.

"No what?"

"Don't know, but I figure whatever it is, the answer is no."

"Couldn't I be calling to wish you a pleasant day?"

She made a noise that sounded like a braying goat before she said, "Umm, no."

"So, alibis: Joel for when Katelin died and Candice for when Lauren died."

"I haven't talked to Joel yet, but Candice says she doesn't remember what she was doing when Lauren bit the dust."

I knew what Joel had told me about where he was and wished Candice could have been more specific with Cindy. I was mulling that over, when she added, "But, I did talk to Detective Callahan. He caught Katelin's case and is convinced that her death by asphyxiation was of her own doing. The coroner said the knot on the head was consistent with contact with the steering wheel and Callahan said that was good enough for him."

Detective Callahan and I had a few encounters, of which most were negative, when he investigated the death of a member of First Light Church. Callahan was young, but proved to be competent, although a bit stuffy.

"So, he's closing the case?"

"Yes and no," Cindy said and paused.

"Which means?"

"I shared the same questions you'd asked when you thought I wasn't paying attention. He agreed that having two deaths that close together, involving housemates, and with both having a history with Joel, seemed an unlikely coincidence."

"Good," I said.

"But, he didn't see enough evidence to conclude anything other than Lauren's death was either accidental or suicide, and that Katelin's was a suicide. Before you get all huffy, he said that before he moved on to the latest crop of murders, he would talk to Joel and anybody else whose name came up. He's doing that as a favor to me."

I thanked her and she said that whether I believed it or not she had more to do than take calls from a bald, nosy, senior citizen. I told her to spend my tax money wisely, and she reminded me that I was retired and was taking rather than paying tax money. She giggled and then was gone.

I started to check on Bob but decided that I had already endured enough grief for the day, so instead, I walked three blocks to Cal's for a late lunch and an earful of country music. Cal had owned the bar since taking over for its former owner who now resided in prison, the permanent address he'd earned after killing an attorney and framing my friend Sean Aker who was a law partner with the deceased attorney. Cal's could be described as the perfect country music bar. An antique Wurlitzer juke was full of country classics, the ambience included the strong smell of stale beer and burnt burgers, and tables and chairs that had seen their better days—a decade ago. It also included another country classic, Cal Ballew, who'd had a hit record, although it was popular before most of his customers were born.

From the jukebox, Barbara Mandrell was singing about "The Midnight Oil" as my eyes adjusted to the dim lighting. The bar was half full, or in the eyes of its owner who had to pay the bills, half empty, so I didn't have trouble finding a table nor finding a glass of wine. Cal had my drink to the table before I looked around to see who was there.

Along with the wine came the questions: "How's Al? How's

Bob? Did you hear about that gal who offed herself in the garage? How's that neighbor you don't like since his kid overdosed?"

I took a sip and waited for the gangly six-foot-three Texan to finish his litany of questions, and when he stopped to take a breath, said, "You forget to ask, 'How's Chris?'"

He smiled. "Don't think so, so how's Al?"

He must have figured that I was okay, so I gave him the meager update that I had been given and told him that Bob was fine. I ignored the questions about Katelin's death and about Lauren's parents.

"Since you're short on news, let me tell you what happened this morning."

Randy Travis's voice filled the room singing about what happened in "1982," and I nodded for Cal to tell me what happened more recently.

"When I'm in the mood to open for lunch, I come in at ten-o'clock. Figured there wouldn't be too many people in today so I let my cook have the day off. I can fix the customers anything they want to eat as long as it's a burger and fries. Most only want to drink beer."

I knew he was headed somewhere with the story and I didn't have anywhere else to be, so I let him ramble at his pace. Once again, I nodded for him to continue.

"I stuck my key in the lock when I saw Michigan by the side of the building leaning on his cane. He looked at his wrist and told me I was thirty minutes late. I asked him late for what, and he said I should've been here earlier."

One of Cal's less than endearing habits had been calling people by the name of their home state. Charles and I had been trying to break him of the habit and had come close to succeeding—but only close.

I smiled. "That sounds like Charles. What'd he want?"

"First he wanted to give me a hard time for being late. I didn't let it take, so I asked him one more time what he wanted. He followed me in, helped me turn on the lights, and straighten up the chairs from last night's non-interior-design-oriented customers, and said he wanted to have a party."

"What kind of party?"

A customer two tables over called for Cal to bring him another drink.

Cal unfolded himself from the chair and said, "Hold that question, I'll be back."

Jim Reeves's mellow voice was singing "He'll Have to Go," and Marc Salmon lowered his body in the chair previously occupied by the country crooner—Cal, not Jim Reeves.

"Mind if I join you?" he asked.

He was already seated so I thought the correct answer would be I didn't mind, and said, "My pleasure."

Cal had started back and saw Marc in his chair. He frowned and then put on his happy proprietor face and asked Marc if he could get him anything.

"Hi, Cal. How about a fish sandwich?"

Cal nodded and bit his lower lip like he was thinking, and said, "How about a hamburger?"

Marc said, "That the special of the day?"

"Only choice of the day," Cal said.

Marc said, "Sounds good."

Cal tipped his Stetson to the council member and headed to the grill.

Marc watched Cal go and said, "Heard any gossip about the election?"

Gossip and politics were to Marc like hydrogen and oxygen were to water.

"Nothing you don't already know, I suspect. What's the latest?"

He looked around the room and leaned closer like he was getting ready to divulge a state secret. "We don't have much formal polling over here, especially this far out from an election, but I was talking to a couple of local political tongue waggers who said that unless something drastic happens between now and the election, Brian's a shoo-in to get reelected."

I hoped that was the case, told Marc so, and asked what his tongue waggers, if there was such a word, had to say about the council races.

"They didn't say it, but it seems to me that if Brian wins reelection by a large margin, I should be okay. He and I don't always agree, but on most issues we're on the same page."

"What'd they say about Joel?"

Marc shook his head. "The newcomer's spreading manure about our mayor. If you listen to him, you'd think Brian's a serial-killer, rapist, who hangs around the barnyard with amorous intentions." Marc smiled. "Other than that, Joel thinks the world of our current leader."

"Any talk about Joel and Lauren or Joel and Katelin?"

Marc leaned close and whispered, "Why?"

I didn't think his question was worthy of a whisper. "Seems strange that he dated both and now they're dead."

"Don't the police think your neighbor's daughter's death was self-inflicted? And the latest gal killed herself, right?"

"That's what they're saying."

Marc leaned closer. "You don't think he had anything to do with their deaths, do you?"

I shrugged. "If you hear anything about Joel that involves them, let me know."

"You got it," Marc said as Cal slid a burger in front of the council member.

Cal pulled the chair out that was beside Marc and started to sit when another customer called for him.

"Hold your pony," Cal said, huffed, and headed to the demanding customer.

Marc took a large bite out of the burger and tilted his head. "Forgot to ask, how's your friend Al?"

There was a reason Marc had the reputation of being the biggest repository of news and gossip on the island. To my knowledge, he'd never met Al, and I wasn't certain that he knew that he existed. I asked how he'd heard and he said something vague like *word gets around*. I shared what little I knew and he expressed his sympathy and wish for a speedy recovery.

Marc looked at his watch. "I'm late for a meeting at city hall."

He looked around for Cal who was busy playing chef. I said I'd take care of the tab. Marc thanked me and rushed out, and I sat and reminded myself that everything he'd said about Joel was consistent with what I'd heard.

Cal returned mumbling something about pesky customers whittling into his fun time. He took off his Stetson, wiped his brow, and mumbled something else about chefin's hard work. He took a deep breath and said, "Where were we?"

I said he was about to tell me about Charles's party.

"Ah, yes. The boy said he wanted to have, let's see, what did he call it, oh yeah, a *happy journey party* for Heather. Cripes, I didn't even know that she was heading out on a journey, and he told me not only was she heading out but had done gone. I was flabbergasted."

I agreed. "Did he say why he wanted to hold it?"

"This is where it gets sad. The poor boy said that he hadn't done enough to keep her here, and the least he could do was to wish her the best on her journey to wherever. He told me that he didn't know where she was headed. Ain't that the pits?" He shook his head. "Not that I'll miss her singing in here, but I sure as hell will miss her bubbly personality, and it didn't take a psychiatrist to see how happy she made Charles. No, it didn't."

"When does he want to hold the, umm, party?"

"Saturday."

"That's the day after tomorrow."

Cal held out his hand and looked at his fingers like he was counting the days. "Sure is. Seemed soon to me, but that's what the boy said. I even asked if he didn't think that was too soon to put together a proper party."

"What'd he say?"

"Said he needed to do it soon before he chickened out."

Another customer demanded Cal's time and I called Charles, although I wasn't optimistic that he would answer. I was right. He did have a new message: *If you insist on seeing me, I'll be hosting a big Happy Journey Party for Heather at Cal's Saturday night. The shindig starts at eight.*

George and Tammy were singing about "My Elusive Dreams" as I left Cal's, sadder than when I arrived—and that was going some.

CHAPTER THIRTY-FOUR

I left Charles a couple of phone messages the next day and true to his word, he didn't return my calls. I also knocked on his door early Friday evening in hopes that he would acknowledge my existence. His car was there so I assumed he was holed up among his books. I called Tanesa and she was at work but in clipped, hurried phrases told me that there was no change in her dad's condition. I had no better luck when I called Bob and Betty answered and said that her more-cranky-than-usual hubby was taking a nap and if she'd learned one thing over the years it was not to awaken him unless she was ready to suffer the consequences. I told her I was calling to see how he was and she said, "Gruff, antsy, irritable, and boorish."

"So, he's back to normal."

Betty laughed. "You know him way too well."

"I share your pain. Let him sleep and if he wakes up in a good mood, tell him I called."

I had better luck when I called Barb, Dude, and Preacher Burl to invite them to Charles's party. Each said they'd be honored to attend—actually, Dude said, "Cool," which I assumed meant he'd surf over to the wingding.

Charles's message said the party was to start at eight, so I was outside Cal's at seven-thirty under the assumption that Charles would arrive around then. I wanted to see if there was anything I could do before he made it inside. Consistent with his normal behavior, I saw my friend approaching the bar at seven-thirty on the dot. He wore a long-sleeve University of Arkansas T-shirt and cargo shorts. Instead of his crooked smile, his face was squished up in a frown that would have been appropriate at a funeral. His shoulders were bent down and he leaned on his cane more than I had seen before.

"Hello, Chris," he said.

That ordinary by most people's standards salutation told me that he was hurting more than he would let on. I put my arm around his shoulder and asked how he was doing. He said fine which I knew was a lie. I asked if there was anything I could do to help.

"I wish there was," he said, and looked at the sidewalk.

His eyes were bloodshot and his hand on the cane was trembling.

He looked at Cal's door and pointed his cane to the vacant lot beside the restaurant and bar. I took the hint and followed him around the side.

"Remember how I told you Heather was so sad the other night?"

I told him that I did.

"She told me about a vision that she had, but I didn't pay much attention to it then. She said it came to her through her psychic powers."

"Has she done that often?"

"Not much, well not much as I remember. Some of the stuff

she says is so far out that I sort of tune some of it out. I'm not as big a believer in her psychic powers as she is." He stared at the light pole across the street.

"What'd she say?"

That jarred him back to the here and now. "She said it came to her when she was half awake, half asleep, and half in psychic mode. I didn't want to get in an argument with her about math, so I tried to do what you do. I nodded and told her to go on. She said that she was a baby bird, well, not that she was the bird, but seeing whatever was going on through the eyes of a bird. Apparently, the bird had a bad wing and somehow got separated from its mother. Heather, or the bird, felt lost in a large clump of trees near a river. She said, it may not have been too large a group of trees, but to a baby bird it seemed humongous."

"What was her mood when she was telling you this?"

"Strange. It was sort of like she was telling me about a show she saw on TV. She didn't seem happy or unhappy when she was talking. But the more I think about it, she could have been sounding all factual like so she wouldn't get swept into the vision, or whatever it was."

"I didn't mean to stop you. What else did she, umm, see, dream, or think?"

"Said the little bird knew it was supposed to be somewhere else doing something, but it didn't know what. It saw other birds fly away, but because of its bad wing it couldn't follow. Some of the other birds fluttered down and sat on one of the trees and tweeted like they were as happy as—happy as a lark. She didn't say lark. A couple of them came down and sat by the lame bird. They were nice, but the baby bird knew they couldn't help it fly." He looked down and back at me. "Chris, to be honest, I didn't hear everything she was saying. It didn't make sense, and I tuned some of it out. I started paying attention again when she said the one-wing bird saw a stubby log floating down the stream beside where it was sitting. The log was moving fast and the little bird decided to hop on and float wherever it was going. There was room on the log for the little bird, but not enough for any of the others. Suppose the big question was whether the little critter should get on the log and float away."

"What did it do?"

Charles smiled for the first time since he'd arrived. "Don't know. Heather woke up when the little thing was about to decide."

I said, "And you think Heather saw herself as the bird and decided to let the log take her away?"

He tilted his head toward the ocean. "There wasn't room on it for me."

"And you're blaming yourself for not understanding her vision, dream, whatever, and for doing something about it then."

"Yeah," he mumbled.

"Charles, there was no way to know she would leave."

"I should have. She takes her psychic stuff seriously."

Cal's front door opened and sounds of George Jones singing "The Grand Tour" laid a blanket of country sadness on us.

Charles looked at the building and offered a weak smile. "Nothing like George's moaning to cheer up a hurtin' soul."

As strange as it seemed, I understood. I said, "Time to get your party started," and ushered him to Cal's front door.

CHAPTER THIRTY-FIVE

It was still ten minutes before the party was to begin and there were already a dozen patrons in the bar. Each table had a balloon floating above it attached to a string that was held in place by a fist-sized rock. A variety of messages were printed on the multi-colored balloons. One read *Let's Celebrate*, three read *Bon Voyage*, and the rest read *Happy Birthday*. Cal met us at the door with a strong handshake and a pat on Charles' back. He was attired in his traditional, sweat-stained Stetson, his rhinestone-studded, white jacket, and in the spirit of Folly, red knee-length shorts.

The bar owner waved around the room. "What do you think, Charles?"

Charles faked a smile and said, "Festive."

"Yep," Cal said, "Tried to get all *Bon Voyage* balloons but the store just had three. I figured after a few drinks, nobody'll be able to read them anyhow. Got the rock idea from a party I sang at a few decades ago. They covered bricks with shiny paper and used them to hold down the balloons. Didn't have any shiny paper or bricks." Cal laughed. "Now I can say this ain't only a country bar, but a rock bar."

Charles smiled, sincerer this time. I told Cal it looked like he'd thought of everything.

Vern Gosdin was singing "Chiseled in Stone" from the jukebox and Cal said he would grab our drinks and for us to join the party. Dude was leaned against the bar talking to Preacher Burl. We walked over and Charles patted the back of Dude's tie-dyed T-shirt.

Dude smiled and said, "Here be the guest of honor. Aloha."

Preacher Burl took the more conservative route. "It's good to see you, Charles. Thank you for inviting me to this significant event."

"Glad you're here," Charles mumbled.

Cal handed Charles a beer and a plastic cup of wine to me. There were two men in deep conversation on the next two bar stools. I didn't recognize them, so I caught Cal's eye and nodded their direction.

Cal leaned close to me and said, "Couple of salesmen staying at the Tides. They're not part of our shindig, but I let them buy beer anyway."

Cal was generous like that. There were a few others in the bar I didn't recognize and figured they were also here for the drinks and not, as Cal had put it, our shindig.

Cal had pulled a couple of the tables together in the center of the room, covered them with a Happy Birthday paper tablecloth and had placed a large bowl of chips in the center. Two smaller containers held salsa. Chester Carr was munching on a chip and talking to Cindy LaMond and her husband, Larry. I started to walk over to talk to them when Dude said, "Where be H?"

I had wondered how Charles would handle questions about Heather's departure.

Charles looked around the room and back at Dude. "I don't know, but I wish her well wherever it is."

So far, so good, I thought.

Dude nodded. "Me be praying to sun god for H to have boss surfin'."

Preacher Burl took a step closer to Charles. "My prayers are with her."

I suppose he didn't want his god to be left out. Barb walked in with Amber. They headed to the chips, and I asked Charles if he wanted to greet the latest arrivals. He told Dude and Burl he'd get back with them and followed me to the center of the room where he was mobbed by the chip munchers. Cal reached the group at the same time and asked who wanted drinks. The Charles lovefest was put on hold while everyone told Cal what they wanted. Fortunately, everyone said beer, so Cal could handle the orders. Amber hugged Charles; Barb gave me a peck on the cheek and was next to hug Charles. The chief hugged him next, and the men in the group forsook hugs and shook his hand. Charles thanked them for coming and from the jukebox the piano genius of Floyd Cramer played "Last Date."

Several more of Charles's acquaintances came in while he was with the salsa group. I knew most of them, but a couple were strangers; but since they seemed to know the others, I assumed they knew Charles and weren't here just for drinks.

I moved away from the group and Cindy followed me. The decibel level increased with everyone talking over the music. The chief and I moved to the quietest corner.

"Talked with Joel about his alibis," she said and took a sip of beer.

"And?"

"Cool your jets, impatient one. Give this chick a chance to enjoy Cal's generosity." She took another sip, and continued,

"Joel, a charming snake that boy is. Know what he told someone whose name I will not divulge?"

I had no idea, so I shrugged.

"Said the first thing he would do as mayor would be to fire the director of public safety. Since that's the highfalutin title on my business card, I didn't take too kindly to it. But, you'd be proud of me. When I was talking to him about his alibis, I didn't once pull my gun and shoot him in the, let's say, male body parts. I was tempted but figured it could possibly look bad on my record."

I rolled my eyes. "Alibis?"

I didn't think it possible, but the room was getting noisier. Several more of Charles's friends arrived and gathered around him. It looked like a herd of cattle surrounding a food trough— figuratively speaking, of course. I moved closer to the chief to hear what she was saying. Nearby, Chester Carr was talking to David Darnell, an insurance agent who had moved to Folly a couple of years ago and was a member of a walking group Chester had formed around that time, but they weren't as loud as most of the others in the room.

Cindy repeated in great detail what I had already known about Joel and the strategy session he was holding with Wayne at the time Lauren had died.

I wanted to move her along. "What about when Katelin was murd ... umm, died?"

"Take a patience pill," she said and sipped her beer. "That's where the story gets a bit fuzzy. Joel said he had three yard crews working on the island that day. Said he spent most of the time going from crew to crew. Also said he may have been at one of his buddy's remodeling job sites working on a land-scaping bid."

"Wayne Swan?" I asked.

Cindy nodded. "He wasn't sure exactly when he and Wayne were meeting, nor when he was with his other crews."

"Times that couldn't be accounted for?"

"Yes, but don't get all suspicious about that. I think most days, most of us would have a tough time accounting for every hour."

"True," I said. "But it still doesn't get him off the hook. I wish it'd been more definitive."

"Chris, I agree. Heck, I'd like to plant a little-ole chip in everyone's head so we could track every movement around the island, but the mayor keeps throwing in my face that pesky thing called the Constitution and says I'd better stick to catching crooks the old-fashioned way. Bosses!"

As often is the case, she got a smile out of me, and said she'd better get back to her hubby before he started boring everyone with hardware store gobbledygook. Cindy moved away to save the non-hardware store obsessed public and Chester told David that he'd talk to him later and moved in front of me.

"Chris, I'm not the nosy, busybody type, but I couldn't help overhearing parts of your conversation with the police chief."

Chester was right. Among my friends and acquaintances, he was one of the least nosy—the key word being least, which, of course, still made him nosy.

"And?" I said.

"Did the chief say something about Joel Hurt meeting with someone during the time that poor Brad Burton's daughter died?"

"Yes, he was meeting at Wayne Swan's house, something about working on a campaign brochure."

"Funny."

"Why funny?" I asked.

"Maybe I have the time she died wrong, but I'd asked a

couple of people and they said it was between eight and ten o'clock."

I said, "I was told between seven and ten, but you're close."

"Where does Wayne live?"

"Somewhere near the Washout. Why?"

"That night I was sitting on my front porch talking on the phone to a cousin in Maine. Name's Sally. I seldom get to talk to her, see we're not close. Anyway, I saw Joel's big truck speed by the house like a bat out of hell, can't miss it, it's got all that writing on the door bragging about his company. You know I'm less than a block off Center Street and it gets crowded that time of night."

I interrupted. "What time was it?"

"Oh yeah, I hadn't mentioned. Exactly nine-fifteen, Sally's favorite show came on at nine-thirty and she only had fifteen minutes to talk. Anyway, I was irritated Joel was driving that fast; could've killed someone walking up the street. So, if he said he was meeting all that time with someone in the other direction, he's not telling the truth."

"You sure?"

"Yes, sir. I remember it was the next day that all the police cars and two television trucks went right in front of the house on their way toward the County Park and poor Brad Burton's daughter." Chester looked toward the entrance. "Speaking of Brad."

I turned and was surprised to see Brad and Hazel Burton stepping into the bar and looking lost. I told Chester I'd talk to him later and went to the door to greet the Burtons.

"Brad, Hazel, thanks for coming."

Hazel stepped in front of her husband and reached to shake my hand. Her hand was warm and clammy. Brad stayed behind her and gazed around the room. He looked as comfortable as a typewriter in an Apple store.

Hazel reached back and pulled Brad forward, turned to me, and said, "I was in Mr. John's Beach Store yesterday and got in a conversation with a young lady buying a beach towel. She told me about this party and how the community sticks together whenever something bad has happened. Said everyone fights like dogs and cats unless there's a crisis. She said she didn't personally know Charles or Heather, but her boyfriend did and they were going to come out tonight to support Charles."

"That was nice of her," I said.

Hazel nodded. "So, I told Brad it was what we'd experienced since, umm, losing Lauren and maybe it'd be good if we came tonight. If for no other reason than getting us out of the house and not think all the time about our loss. Isn't that right, Brad?"

Brad smiled and said yes, but he still looked like he'd rather be somewhere else.

I pointed toward the bar. "Follow me, and let's get you something to drink."

Hazel followed and Brad lingered a couple of steps behind us. Cal was quick to hand each of them a beer and Hazel said she saw the woman from Mr. John's on the other side of the room and she and Brad should go over and thank her for inviting them.

Gene Watson was singing "Between This Time and the Next Time," the smell of beer and burnt hamburgers filled the air, and I stood beside the bar and agreed with Hazel's new acquaintance about the community gathering together in time of crisis or need. I also started thinking about what Chester had said about seeing Joel during the time he was allegedly with his friend working on the campaign. Did it prove he had something to do with Lauren's death? Not really, but what it did was say he was a liar, and that was something I already knew.

The jukebox went silent, and Cal tapped on the softball-sized, silver microphone in the middle of the small stage. "Attention," said the bar's owner. "Y'all focus up here for a few."

Most of the conflicting conversations ended but three people leaning against the bar kept talking. Cal tapped the mic again, and Brad, who was grabbing a second beer at the bar, grabbed one of the talkers by the shoulder and motioned for silence. It was probably a hold Brad hadn't used since he was with the Sheriff's office. It worked and Cal had everyone's attention.

He held his forefinger in the air. "First, I want to thank all of you for coming out. It's only been two days since my buddy Charles there," Cal pointed at his buddy, "approached me about having this party. He's going to say a few words in a minute, but I wanted to hog the stage for a few first." Cal gave a stage grin. "For those of you who have been begging me to sing a few hits tonight, Charles said it was okay and I'll croon a few later. But now you need to know why we're gathered. As I suspect most of you know, Miss Heather's not only a singer; heck, she'd used this here mic many a night to entertain many a happy customer, but she's also a psychic. Now I know some of you aren't believers in what psychics do, but I know Heather, and she's a powerful believer. She's not with us in body tonight, and I'm not certain where she is. But what I am certain of, is wherever she is, she's using her psychic power to learn about this here big party in her honor, and knows all our good thoughts," Cal paused, looked at Preacher Burl, and continued, "and our prayers go with her on her journey. And Miss Heather, you're missed a heap here and are welcome back anytime."

Cal stopped and looked out on the gathering like he was waiting for a response. I wasn't certain what response would be appropriate, but Dude must have. He applauded, and everyone followed his lead.

Cal nodded. "Thank y'all. Now Charles, want to say a few words?"

Charles was standing directly in front of the bandstand, whispered something to Cal, and Cal stepped back to the mic. "Charles'll say a few words to us a little later. Drink up."

And we did.

CHAPTER THIRTY-SIX

Hazel was still talking to the woman who told her about the party. I had seen her working in Mr. John's but didn't know her name. Brad grabbed a third beer and looked around the room and headed my way.

"I had no idea how many friends Lauren had here," he said as he stopped beside me. "You wouldn't believe how many people have come by the house or stopped Hazel or me on the street to offer condolences. Most of them I'd never seen before. Know what else surprised me?"

"What?"

"Every one of them expressed everything from surprise to shock about Lauren overdosing. Now some of them did say they knew her back when she was using, and even they said she'd kicked drugs and became vocal about not using whenever the topic came up. Two of her friends said that she swore to them there was no way she would ever use again."

"I'd heard that too."

"Chris, you and I have never seen eye to eye on, well, most

everything, but the one thing I keep hearing about you is that you're loyal to your friends and can keep a secret."

"I like to think so," I said wondering where he was going with this.

"I was a cop for a long time, way too long a time," he said and closed his eyes. "During that time, I investigated numerous suicides. Kneeling down and looking at a body with half its head blown away or looking up at someone who'd hanged himself... or herself...was no picnic, but you know the hardest part?"

I guessed. "Breaking the news to their loved ones?"

Brad nodded. "Nearly every one of them swore the death couldn't have been suicide. Their dear sweet daughter, son, husband, wife, or whatever couldn't possibly have done it. It had to be something else, usually murder, and I as a cop had better find the killer and find him quick. Regardless how obvious the cause of death, they were in total denial." He looked around and said, "I'll be back," and headed to the bar for beer number four.

What he'd said didn't surprise me, but why was he telling me? He was back with a fresh beer in hand so I didn't have to wait long for an answer.

He took a deep breath and sighed. "Chris, when I heard about Lauren, every one of those notifications flooded my mind. I was determined not to fall into the same state of denial as did all those family members. So, even after her friends said she was clean, and the coroner found little, if any, drugs in her system, I told myself not to do what those other people had done. I bought into the suicide or accidental overdose explanation." He hesitated and looked at the floor. "I think I was wrong."

"I do too," I said to the top of his head.

His head jerked up. "Really?"

I said yes and told him what I had learned about Joel from Chester, and about my suspicions about him having something to do with Katelin's death. Brad's hand gripped the beer so hard his knuckles turned red. He took a step toward the bar but turned and came back to me.

He pointed the empty beer bottle at me. "First thing Monday, I'm going to contact my friends in the Sheriff's office and push them, push them hard, to pursue her death—her murder."

From the comments I had heard from his colleagues, I'd be surprised if he had any friends left in the office but was glad to hear someone felt as strongly about it as I did.

"Good."

"If they don't want to do their job, I'm going to figure it out myself. Damned if I'm going to let my little girl's killer get away."

My phone rang before I could respond. The screen indicated it was Tanesa. I excused myself and moved to the sidewalk where I could hear better. I noticed my hand shaking as I touched the answer button. Please let this be good news.

"Chris, this is Tanesa. Can you talk?"

I said I could.

"I wanted to tell you Dad has pulled out of his coma."

"Wonderful," I interrupted.

"Yes, he's talking some, but not making any sense. That's not necessarily bad. It's understandable that his brain's a bit scrambled after what he's been through."

I told her I remembered how a couple of months earlier Cal had confused timeframes after he awoke from his coma after being hit in the head. It took him a couple of weeks to get back to normal—Cal normal.

"I hope that's the case," Tanesa said. "But it'll be a while before we know if dad has suffered permanent damage. The flow of blood had been restricted for a long time, and some, hopefully minor, damage is likely."

"The good news is he's still alive."

"Where there's life, there's hope," Tanesa said, sounding more like a philosopher than an ER doc.

I agreed, thanked her for calling, and asked if he could be having visitors anytime soon. She said she'd let me know, but it might be a while. I asked if she had called Bob to let him know. She said no and she had to get back to work and asked if I'd call him.

I made a quick call to Bob before I returned to the party. I felt I was talking to a total stranger rather than Bob. He was civil, almost polite, thrilled about Al, and for the cherry on top of the soda, he thanked me for calling. I hit end call and glanced at the screen to make sure I had called the same Bob Howard I had learned to love, despite himself.

I returned to the bar and found Barb to tell her the good news. She was talking to her step-brother Dude and from the slice of conversation I overheard they were sharing a story from their childhood in Pennsylvania.

I heard Dude say, "You be weird sis."

Barb laughed and said, "You calling me weird's like a frill-necked lizard calling a rabbit weird."

Dude looked at her and ran his hand through his long, stringy hair. "Me no know what naked lizard be."

Barb chuckled, "Frill-necked lizard. Take my word for it, it's weirder than a rabbit."

Dude rubbed his hair again. "Me take word of lawyerster even weirder."

Barb said, "I'm no longer a lawyer; I'm a simple bookstore owner."

"Cool."

I'd heard enough about weird and moved closer to Barb and put my arm around her waist.

Dude said, "Ewe, mushy. Me leave and let you mush-away."

I watched Dude move in Charles's direction and asked if Barb needed another drink.

"You had to ask if I wanted more beer after you saw me talking with Dude?"

I smiled and headed to the bar to get her another beer and refill my wine. Brad had another beer in his hand and was leaning on the bar; to be closer to Chester Carr who he was talking to, and to stay balanced. I heard him slur something about murder and going to catch the killer. I also saw Hazel headed his way, hopefully to rein him in.

I handed Barb her drink and told her about my call from Tanesa. She said that was great and pointed the neck of her bottle at Brad. "See you and your good bud have been powwowing."

"Good bud, no; powwowing, sort of. He's coming around to believing his daughter's death was not by her own hand." I told her what I had learned from Chester that shot down Joel's alibi. Barb asked if I had told Chief LaMond. I said, "Not yet."

She gave me a stern look and tilted her head in Cindy's direction. "You haven't asked my advice, but if you had, I'd tell you to tell the police what Chester told you and then butt out." She held out her hand before I could respond. "I know, I know. The odds on you doing that are as great as Dude playing Hamlet in a theatre production in town. So, please be careful. I'm getting accustomed to spending time with you, time with you alive."

"To show how much I pay attention to your advice, I'll tell Cindy now."

I started toward Cindy and Larry when Cal tapped on the classic microphone. I stopped and returned to Barb's side.

"Okay ladies and gentlemen," said Cal in his Texas accent. "Here's what you've been waiting for. Charles, come on up."

Charles looked at Cal, and turned to look at the crowd, before stepping behind the mic. He wiped the back of his hand on his shorts and gently touched the mic with his other hand and said, "I want to, umm, I want to thank …" He lowered his head and coughed back a tear. He wiped his eyes and said, "Thank you for coming." He stepped back and Cal rushed over to him, put his arm on Charles's shoulder and leaned toward the mic.

"Folks, Charles wants to thank all of you for being so kind to him and to Heather before she left. He knows with all your fine thoughts she's bound to be okay, wherever she is. Now before some of you drift off, and before I sing a tune or two to honor Heather, let's all move closer to the stage."

Cal grabbed one of the chairs from the front table and set it behind the mic. He had Chester bring a long-handled, silver flashlight to the stage and told him where to stand with it. Cal asked Larry to hit the light switches so the only illumination in the room came from the neon beer sign over the bar. The room became eerily silent and Cal said something to Chester who turned the flashlight on and pointed it at the empty chair.

Cal said, "This is for you, Heather. Safe travels." He started singing Heather's favorite song, and one she had sung at every performance in Cal's. "Crazy."

I began to feel like I was at a funeral, and in some way, I suppose I was.

CHAPTER THIRTY-SEVEN

Cal's tribute was well intentioned. He had a huge heart and wanted to do everything in his power to smooth Heather's departure and to show Charles he and many others cared. Unfortunately, it had the opposite effect on my friend. After Cal's flashlight moment, he slid into a set of traditional country songs, and Charles came close to sliding off the stage. Even before the lights were turned back on, I saw Charles slump and grab his knees. I rushed to the stage and gave him a shoulder to lean on as he moved to the nearest table. He was hurting. I got him a glass of water and asked if he was okay to walk. He didn't need to stay in the bar any longer. I motioned for Barb to help me clear the way to the exit and Charles walked, with the aid of each of us, out the door where he sucked in the fresh air and regained his composure. Several people who had come for the sole purpose of supporting Charles saw us, wanted to say something to him, but instead respected his privacy as we left.

Charles had driven the seven blocks from his apartment to

Cal's, but said he'd feel better if he walked around a while before walking home. I asked if I could go with him, and I was pleased when he said yes. Barb headed to her condo, and Charles and I inched our way to the Folly Pier. It was in the opposite direction from his apartment, but I could tell he wanted the peaceful walk to the end of the structure. It was in the mid-eighties but a brisk breeze blew off the ocean and made the walk comfortable. I didn't know what to say, and Charles seemed caught up in his thoughts and didn't speak.

We reached the end of the pier, Charles flopped down on one of the wooden benches, and I sat beside him and waited for him to start the conversation. No words came as we both stared at the lights of the Tides Hotel and the large Charleston Oceanfront Villas condo complex beside the hotel. A few small groups of people walked along the beach swinging flashlights toward the sand as they went along.

"Nice tribute Cal put together," Charles said, the first words he'd spoken in fifteen minutes.

"It was," I said.

"Wouldn't be surprised if Heather didn't see it however she gets the vibes. Hope she did."

"She knows we all care."

Charles stared at the shore and said, "Chris, I thought I was as messed up as a person could be after Melinda died two years ago." He turned to me. "I didn't know what screwed up was until now. Why didn't I ask Heather to marry me earlier? Why?"

No answer would be adequate, so I said, "Sorry. You know she did what she had to do. Maybe she'll come back. You never know."

He shook his head like he was flailing out bad thoughts. "Heard anything about Al?"

I was glad he'd changed the subject. What else could be said about Heather? I was also glad to tell him about Tanesa's call and Al's improved condition.

He sat up straighter. "When were you going to tell me?"

Charles was getting back to being Charles. I told him this was the first opportunity. He didn't agree or disagree; he huffed.

"Want to know what I heard about Joel's alibi for the time Lauren Kraft died?"

"Duh!"

I told him about what Chester had said and that I was going to share that information with Cindy in the morning. I hesitated and told him what Barb had said about me about me butting out. Charles asked why? I said because I didn't know how I could find out more and was leaving it to the police.

He looked at the Tides and at me. "Teddy Roosevelt said, 'Whenever you are asked if you can do a job, tell'em, *Certainly, I can!* Then get busy and find out how to do it.' You've got to find out how to catch that sleazeball who killed Lauren, and who's trying to stomp Brian's chance of getting reelected."

"Tomorrow," I said. "I'll deal with it tomorrow."

Charles nodded, and said, "Think I need to get this weary sack of bones home."

"I'll walk with you."

"Out of your way, besides, I need to be alone."

Charles stood, grabbed his cane from the deck, and left me seated on the pier.

The faint sounds of music coming from the bars on Center Street combined with an occasional slap of waves against the pier's pilings were the only sounds I heard. Most of the noise came from thoughts and questions rattling around in my mind. Tonight's party, even though it was the creation of Charles himself, showed him how much support he had and how much everyone missed Heather, but I was afraid that instead of cheering him up, it put him deeper into a funk. Charles was hurting and there was nothing I could do for him. I would be there for him if he asked for anything, but was that enough? Al had broken free from his coma, but could have significant brain damage, a condition possibly worse than if he had died. Bob now had a bar to run; a career change that would tax anyone, so no telling how it would affect my burly, aging, iconoclastic friend. There were way more downsides than positives. And I still had the nagging feeling Lauren's and Katelin's deaths were at the hands of the person who was trying to unseat my friend as mayor, instead of suicide or resulting from an overdose.

It was too late to call Cindy and tell her what I'd learned about Joel. Too late to do anything to help Charles. And there was nothing I could do to help Al. I started to tell myself things couldn't get worse but reminded myself that every time I had thought that, I was proven wrong. The wisest thing for me to do would be to go home, get some sleep, and contact Cindy first thing in the morning.

For once, I did the wise thing.

A light rain was falling the next morning as I crawled out of bed. My head was fuzzy from having more wine at Cal's party than food or sense. I was hungry and certain there was nothing in the house to eat; or at least, nothing intended to be eaten this early in the morning. I wasn't ready to face anyone in the Dog, so I walked next door to Bert's to grab coffee and a muffin. I was half-asleep as I left the house, but the steady rain served the same purpose as a shower, and I was fully awake as I stepped through the double door of the iconic store.

"Hear there was quite a bash at Cal's last night," boomed the cheerful voice of Eric as I headed to the coffee urn. "Suppose you were there." He threw the hand towel he'd been using to wipe crumbs off the counter over his shoulder and walked my way.

Somehow, our conversation had passed the *good morning* phase, so I smiled and said, "Yes, it was nice."

"How's Charles? Must have been a mixed bag for him."

I said he was pleased that so many people had turned out but was still in shock about Heather leaving.

"Sorry to hear it," Eric said, and tilted his head in the direction of my house. "Also hear your neighbor showed a side we haven't seen around here."

"Brad Burton?"

"That would be the one."

"What'd he do?" I asked.

Eric smoothed out his beard and nodded. "Let's see. First, I hear he tried to drink Cal's dry. Came close, from the word that's been spreading around here."

I looked at my watch. It wasn't yet eight o'clock, fewer than seven hours after the party ended. "Who'd you hear that from?"

"Chester Carr about a half hour ago, and Janice, she left right before you came in. That's all so far. I also hear he was nearly screaming before his wife dragged him out."

"Screaming about what?"

Eric looked around and even though we were the only two in the store, he leaned closer and said, "Screaming that Joel Hurt killed his little girl and he was going to prove it and make sure Hurt burns. You were there, didn't you hear him?"

I explained that Charles and I had left before it was over and missed Brad's outbursts.

"By now, you're probably the only two on Folly who haven't

heard about it." Eric waved his arms around. "Speed of light and speed of rumors are about the same."

Eric was right and I told him so, when Preacher Burl strolled in, saw Eric and me, and gave a big Sunday morning smile. He wore a wrinkled white shirt, black suit slacks, and a food-stained tie.

"How is my favorite Bert's employee and my favorite retired, former photo gallery owner this fine Sabbath morn?"

Eric told the preacher he was "as fine as frog hair," a simile I understood, but had never been a fan of since frogs don't have hair, fine or otherwise. I simply said I was okay.

"Brother Chris, did you and Charles leave the gala early? I looked for you and no one seemed to know where you had gone."

"Charles needed fresh air, so we walked to the pier." Not quite the whole truth, but close.

"I thought it was as such. Brother Charles didn't appear chipper after Cal performed his moving rendition of Heather's favorite song. Is Charles okay?"

Eric excused himself to wait on a new customer.

I lowered my voice and said, "I'm glad you asked, Preacher. It might be helpful if you'd talk to Charles. He's pretty torn up about Heather leaving. I think it's worse than he was when his Aunt passed away."

"I will try to engage him in conversation after this morning's service. Of course, that's if he attends. Looks like we'll have to meet in the foul-weather sanctuary rather than on the beach. Will you be joining us?"

I hadn't planned to but couldn't think of a good excuse not to. "I hope to."

"Excellent, and I will do whatever I can to help Charles. He's lucky to have such a good friend as you. Of course, true friend-ship goes both ways."

"I agree, Preacher. I don't know how I would have survived over here without Charles."

Burl smiled and said, "I wish I had such close friends during my times of need."

"One question," I said, "did my neighbor, Brad Burton, say anything, umm, unusual after I left the party?"

Burl looked down at the concrete floor. "Now, Brother Chris, you know I'm not prone to gossip and am uncomfortable saying anything negative about someone, especially after the tragic loss of his daughter."

That said enough. "I understand Preacher."

"I need to prepare for this morning's service. See you in church."

I nodded, more uncommitted than affirmative.

CHAPTER THIRTY-EIGHT

The rain intensified and I rooted through the hall closet to find my seldom-used umbrella before I headed out to First Light Church's harsh weather meeting spot in a former storefront on Center Street. Preacher Burl had come to Folly from Indianapolis and founded the church under the sun and over the sand on the beach close to the Folly Pier. Because of its unique location and endearing personality of its minister, First Light had grown and met needs of residents the city's traditional houses of worship failed to attract. Charles was a regular, and I, for lack of a better term, had become an irregular in attendance.

I shook water off the umbrella and set it inside the door. The rain, combined with meeting in the least popular of the church's sanctuaries, had taken its toll on attendance. There were fewer than a couple of dozen people gathered around the lemonade cooler in the front corner of the storefront. Charles was talking to the preacher but before I could speak to them, Burl moved to the school lectern that served as his common-man's pulpit.

"Please take your seats and silence thy portable communication devices," Burl said, using the words that had started every service. I joined Charles on the second row and looked around. I was surprised to see Joel Hurt moving to the front pew. He had a *look at me, I'm important* smirk on his face and took his time being seated to make sure everyone saw him.

I must confess—something that's wise to do in church, but not the best route in the courtroom—that I didn't pay much attention to Preacher Burl's Bible readings and homily. My thoughts kept going back to Lauren, Katelin, Joel, and how devastated Brad and Hazel Burton must have been and Brad's outburst that Chester Carr had told me about. Something else kept nagging at me, something I couldn't put my finger on, but something that seemed important at the time. What was it?"

As Burl's flock, as he called us, stood to sing one of my favorite hymns, "How Great Thou Art," to conclude the service, I still couldn't get my mind off Joel and my hostile feelings toward him.

"Chris, earth to Chris," Charles said and tapped my arm.

"Sorry," I said. "What?"

Several of the worshippers had left and Charles and I were standing beside the pew. "Burl wants to talk to me, but I told him you and I were heading to the hospital to sneak in and see Al."

It was the first I'd heard about "our" plan. "We are?"

He answered my question when he said, "Ready to go?"

The ride to the hospital on the edge of downtown Charleston was miserable. The rain was so intense that layers of water covered more of the roadway than remained clear. Charles stared out the side window and didn't say anything about last night's party. He never mentioned Heather and had the defeated look of someone wallowing in misery. My focus was on keeping the car from sliding off the road.

I wasn't any more optimistic as we entered the automatic

front doors of the hospital. I couldn't imagine that they would let us see Al, making the trip a total waste. My fears were partially realized. Outside the intensive care unit, a harried nurse stopped us and said there was no way Al Washington could have visitors. I asked her if Dr. Tanesa Washington was on duty. She said she didn't know but was kind enough to check and told us Al's daughter was in the hospital and for us to go to the ER and ask if Dr. Washington was available.

We had waited fifteen minutes before Tanesa was able to meet us in the corridor outside the emergency room. Her shoulders were slumped, her eyes bloodshot, and it looked like she'd aged a decade since I'd seen her last.

She managed a smile and said she was glad to see us. I asked if she was okay and she said, "Not really. We lost someone on the table." She bit her lower lip and shook her head. "Not a damned thing I could do to save him."

I told her I was sorry and she said it was part of the job. I didn't know how she did it and told her so.

"Thanks. I suppose you came to see Dad."

"You bet," Charles said. "How can we sneak in?"

"It's better if you didn't. He's in bad shape, still not making sense. Sorry."

I told her we were sorry as well and were praying for him.

"I'll tell you something you can do," she said.

Charles asked what.

"Bob Howard was over a couple of hours ago. I told him the same thing I told you about seeing Dad. He was on his way to open the bar. He's been a godsend and allowing him to keep his pride and joy open. The bar's been Dad's life, and Bob's truly been Dad's savior." She hesitated and scraped her shoe on the tile. "But, umm, how can I say it, I worry about the, umm, cultural differences between Dad's customers and, umm, Mr. Howard."

"Got it," I said and smiled.

Tanesa returned the smile. "I know Lawrence, Dad's cook, will be there and helps more than Dad would admit, but, well, you know."

I did and told her getting a cheeseburger was next on our agenda.

She thanked us and said she needed to get back to work. She shuffled back into the ER and we left to make the short three block drive to Al's Bar and Gourmet Grill.

The sounds of Marvin Gaye singing "I Heard It Through the Grapevine" reached us before I reached for the door to the tired bar. We stepped in the dark room and waited for our eyes to adjust before trying to find Bob. From what I could see, the crowd appeared as sparse as it had been at the First Light service. There were groups at three tables and two men leaned against the bar. Lawrence was facing the grill and the most unlikely bar owner in the United States and probably on the continent leaned against the wall beside the grill.

Bob had on frayed navy-blue shorts, a sweat-stained Hawaiian flowery shirt, and a frown the size of a football. Sweat rolled down his cheeks.

I smiled as I approached him. "See you have everything under control."

Bob wiped the sweat from his cheeks. "You're a damned smart ass."

"Is that anyway to address your fine customers?" I said.

"Hell no, and if a fine customer ever comes in, I'll treat him different."

Charles couldn't stand being left out, even if it was a conversation of insults. "How are things going, Bob?"

Bob pointed his chubby forefinger at the jukebox where Stevie Wonder was singing "Superstition." He pointed to his ear. "Is blood pouring out?"

Charles studied Bob's ear like it was an archeological find. "Don't see any."

"Damned sure feels like it. That frickin' crap these deaf-eared customers call music is making my head explode."

"What happened to all your country classics Al had added to the jukebox?"

Over the wishes of most of the bar's regulars, Al had added several of Bob's favorite country songs to his Motown-oriented jukebox. Bob and Al's friendship defied all logic, but it was real, "damned real" according to Bob.

"When you came in, did you see a damned picket line in front? Did you see angry, hungry hordes flinging signs around and chanting 'Down with Country Music!?'"

We said no.

"Know why you didn't?" Bob asked.

I played along. "Why?"

"Because that damned Al's afro, black, negro, African American, or whatever they want to be called today, customers said unless I kept the jukebox playing good music and not country crap, they were going to picket. Chris, I've been in here less than a week and have already had to squelch a damned race riot. Hell, I had one former Black Panther member scoot in on a walker and threaten to punch me in my happy, smiling, ivory-colored face."

And I'd wondered why Tanesa was worried!

Lawrence delivered burgers to the nearby table and came over and asked if we wanted anything to eat.

I started to answer when Bob said, "Lawrence, get your bony butt back to the grill. You're messin' in my job."

I was surprised when Lawrence smiled. "Yes, Master Bob, whatever you say." He walked away.

"He's a good guy," Bob said. "I'm thrilled he's here."

"And it shows," I said, oozing sarcasm.

"Yep," Bob said. "I'm a natural at this customer and employee relations schmoozing." He looked around the room like he didn't know what to do with us. Finally, he said, sit anywhere and don't mess up anything. Cleaning's not my strength."

Not like customer and employee schmoozing, I thought as we moved to the booth with Bob's plaque on it.

"Think he'll make it?" Charles asked.

"Al or Bob?"

Charles looked toward the grill. "Bob. Al's in good hands."

"If someone doesn't kill him first, he has a chance," I said.

"Those two opposites would do anything for each other," Charles said and shook his head, more in admiration than anything negative.

I tapped my fingers on the table. I realized what had been nagging at my unconscious: Joel's alibi, more accurately, his alibis.

"Charles," I said, "What were you doing three days ago in the middle of the afternoon?"

"Don't know, why?"

"That's the point."

"What on earth are you talking about?"

"If someone asked me what I had been doing let's say last Thursday at two o'clock, I would have been hard pressed to remember. You just said you couldn't remember three days ago. I suspect that'd be true if you asked most people about a day and time farther back than yesterday. Times get muddled, the order in which we do things can get turned around, and whether we admit it, much of what we do is so inconsequential that we don't remember it."

Charles looked down at the table and blinked twice. "Yeah, a couple of days before Heather wanted to talk to me—you know, before she decided to leave, I thought about talking to her about marriage. I forgot all about it and look what happened. She's gone."

That wasn't what I had meant, but my friend was having a tough time focusing. What had happened with Heather was weighing on him. I tried again, "My point is we forget our actions quicker than we think that we do."

He said, "True, so what?"

"Joel told Cindy that he had been meeting with his campaign manager at the time Lauren died."

"Yes."

"And Wayne confirmed Joel's alibi. That means—"

"So?" Charles interrupted.

"Let me finish. When Katelin allegedly killed herself, Joel told the chief he was with one of his landscape crews, or possibly pricing a landscape job at one of Wayne's remodel sites, or he could have been driving between some of those locations."

"Come on Chris, I've got a headache. One more time, so what?"

Lawrence brought our cheeseburgers before I got to the *so what*. The soothing aroma from the still-sizzling burgers made me realize how hungry I was and I took a bite before continuing. Charles ignored his food and stared at me. Waiting was not one of his strengths.

"So, Joel has one airtight alibi, and one that wouldn't hold up in court. If the police had suspected that Katelin's death wasn't a suicide, Joel would be the prime suspect. He may be a liar, but he's not stupid. He would have known he would be a suspect and would have concocted a better alibi."

"I don't follow," Charles said and waved his hand in my face. "Got a question, do you think Heather heard how good everyone was talking about her at the party?"

Charles was able to change direction on a pinhead, but whenever we had been talking in the past about something as serious as murder, he was the first not to let the conversation drift.

"I'm sure she knows how much everyone there loves her," I said, hoping that satisfied his concern.

"I think so too. Sorry, what were you saying about Joel's alibis?"

I repeated what I'd said and Charles looked toward the door, before he said, "Are you still thinking Joel killed both?"

"He's obsessed about getting elected mayor. He's started an aggressive political campaign much earlier than anyone ever has. He's proven himself to be a liar and backstabber. And one of the foundations of his campaign is to stamp out illegal drugs on Folly."

Charles made eye contact. "And his girlfriend's thought to be a druggie, not quite the poster child for his campaign." Charles nodded. "So, Joel killed Lauren and Katelin, we already suspected that."

"But," I hesitated, "I don't think he did. He could have killed Lauren, or maybe he didn't."

Charles continued to ignore his lunch, but took a long draw on his Budweiser, and said, "So let me see if I have this right. You think Joel killed Lauren because he had an airtight alibi during her time of death. And that he didn't kill Katelin because he didn't have a good alibi? What am I missing?"

"Yes and no. What if we're looking at it backwards?"

Charles shook his head. "I feel like I'm talking to Dude. I

know my mind's been operating at half-speed, but what in the hell are you talking about?"

The country sound of Roger Miller's "When Two Worlds Collide" flowed from the jukebox, and a chorus of groans came from two tables when Miller started singing. I glanced over at Bob who was standing by the door. He had a huge grin on his face.

I turned back to Charles. "In the last week Burl, Cal, and someone else have made comments about how good friends do anything for each other. Look at Al and Bob, or Cal and Burl; and, you don't look that far, how about you and me. I'd do anything for you, and suspect you'd do the same."

Charles nodded but didn't say anything.

"I think it was Wayne."

"Whoa, Wayne. Why?"

"He and Joel have been friends long before they moved to Folly. Wayne is Joel's campaign manager and is as intent on getting Joel elected as Joel appears to be. Wayne alibied for Joel, but it also provided him an alibi at the same time. And, as far as I know, we don't know what Wayne's alibi is for the time when Katelin died, was killed."

Charles closed his eyes and tilted his head left and then right. "I still don't get why it was Wayne instead of Joel."

"Joel would have created a better alibi if he killed Katelin. From what everyone said, he was closer to Lauren than he let on after her death. I simply don't think he would have killed her."

"But you think Wayne could have because he wasn't close to her."

"Yes. I think my feelings about Joel have been biased because he's challenging my friend Brian."

Charles looked at his cheeseburger and at me. "I'm not convinced."

"I'm not sure I am either, but it makes more sense to me than the other way around."

"If Wayne did it, wouldn't Joel have known since he was Wayne's alibi?"

"Known maybe, suspected possibly. I don't know."

"So, what are we going to do about it?"

"I'm going to find Cindy after we leave here and tell her what Chester said about seeing Joel driving by his house when he was supposed to be with Wayne."

"And tell her your suspicions about Wayne?"

"Maybe."

I had been so intent on convincing Charles about the possibility of Wayne being a killer while trying to keep his focus off Heather long enough so we could discuss the killings, that I didn't notice Bob until he scooted into the booth and shoved me against the wall so he would have enough room to fit his ample rear on the seat.

Bob looked at Charles's plate and said, "What's wrong with your food? Hell, I didn't spit on it."

I knew Charles was in no mood for kidding, but Bob didn't.

Charles gave him a nasty look. "It's fine. I'm not hungry."

"Well excuse my helpful ass," Bob said and wrinkled up his nose. He turned to me. His shoulder rammed into my arm as he turned. He said, "Forgot to tell you something. I got a call last night from Jeff Holthouse."

"Jeff Holthouse?" I said.

"You getting senile? You met him and his wife at the fundraiser at my mansion."

"The realtors," I said.

Bob nodded. "Anyway, Jeff called to say he had met with Joel Hurt again about the landscape job he told you about at the party. Joel started talking about how corrupt your buddy Brian

Newman was. Joel had told him the same thing earlier, and Jeff wanted to change the subject and said something about hearing about the woman who killed herself in the garage and wondered if Joel knew her. Know what Joel told Jeff?"

I wondered how I would have known. "What?"

"Joel told Jeff he barely knew her, but his best friend had dated her but dumped her because she was crazy."

"Did Joel say who his best friend was?"

"Damn, Chris, do I have to do everything for you? I figured that might be a clue but I don't know a clue about what. And don't say you're not getting involved in whatever's going on over there. You always say that, but you get sucked in anyway."

I started to thank Bob for whatever, when one of the customers at a table by the window yelled, "What's it take to get another beer around here?"

"Hold your damned horses!" Bob said and mumbled something I couldn't understand.

"Customer   schmoozing,   Bob,"   I   said.   "Customer schmoozing."

He cocked his head in my direction. "Smart ass." He pushed himself up from the table and ambled to the thirsty customer to do some customer schmoozing.

"Interesting," I said to Charles.

Charles watched Bob go and said, "Don't suppose Joel's best friend is Wayne."

"I'd put money on it."

CHAPTER THIRTY-NINE

There was no break in the rain as I headed back to Folly. There was also no break in Charles's despondency. I tried to talk about Joel and Wayne and anything either of us may have heard that would help point a finger at one or the other, but I would have had better luck talking to Bob's customer who wanted another beer. I understood Charles's pain, but didn't know what I could say to help. I decided silence was the best approach and listened to the wipers slapping against the windshield as they rhythmically moved back and forth, barely keeping up with the downpour.

The rain had eased as I pulled in Charles's parking lot. I asked if there was anything I could do for him and he mumbled something about nothing could be done. I reached over to pat his arm, but he opened the door and hopped out of the car before I could say anything else. He opened his apartment door and went in without looking back, and I sat in the car staring at his closed door.

I couldn't do anything to help my friend but did have some

thoughts I wanted to share with Chief LaMond about the two deaths. I called her cell phone and was rewarded when she answered. I asked if she had a few minutes to spare. She said no, but it had never stopped me from interrupting her in the past so she didn't see any reason for me not to interrupt now. She was at her office and said she was stuck under a "three-foot high pile of elephant poop" and I could stop by and help her dig herself out. I assumed she'd meant it figuratively, and said I was surprised she was at the office Sunday evening.

"Twenty-four seven, twenty-four seven," she said and I said I'd be there in a few minutes.

Her office was on the second floor of the relatively new police and fire addition to the back of the coral-colored city hall. I knocked on her door and she yelled for me to come in. I was relieved to see that the three-foot high pile of elephant poop was a foot of file folders and loose papers.

She looked up. "There'd be less paperwork if we shot everybody who got drunk or parked the wrong way on the streets." She threw a piece of paper in the air. "I'm stuck in report hell."

"The glamour of chiefdom," I said and moved a pile of file folders off the chair in front of her desk and sat. I looked out the large window behind her that looked out on the Surf Bar. The rain had returned and the expression on Cindy's face was as gloomy as the weather.

She moved the stack of folders to the side of the desk and said, "Okay, this ain't national *invite yourself to the office day*, so why are you here and how are you going to ruin what's already a crappy day?"

Bob and Cindy could use a lesson, or two, or a million, in schmoozing, but I didn't figure this was the time to start. Instead, I began telling her what I had learned from Chester about Joel's alleged alibi.

She stuck both palms out like she was stopping traffic. "Halt! If you're going to try to get my brain working by spinning some convoluted story, I need bourbon." She rolled her eyes. "Since I'm stuck in report hell, coffee'll have to do. Want some?"

I said yes and she scurried out of the office and left me staring at the rain and wondering what I was going to say next that could possibly convince the chief I hadn't lost my mind. She returned before I'd figured it out and was carrying two white mugs with FB in blue letters on the outside and steaming hot coffee on the inside.

She handed me one of the mugs, lowered herself in her chair with a sigh, and said, "Let's hear it."

I spent the next ten minutes telling her everything I knew and everything I suspected. She shifted from exasperated bureaucrat to attentive police chief and even took notes during my monologue. I finished and realized I hadn't convinced myself of Wayne's guilt, so I doubted Cindy had been swayed.

The chief nodded, looked down in her coffee mug, and then back at me. "Chris, I've known you for a long time, going on eight years if my finger counting is accurate. During that time, you and your collection of quirky pals have defied all odds and have stumbled into some terrible situations and even more odds defying have helped catch some really, really bad people."

I shrugged.

"You've also accused folks of dastardly deeds who were as innocent as, umm, I don't know any spiffy analogies, but they were innocent."

I couldn't argue with that. I nodded.

"We've had two tragic deaths in the last few days, and both were investigated by the Sheriff's office. You know, I don't take too fondly to some of the sanctimonious, egotistic, know-it-all folks in that office, but most of the time they're right. They say one of the deaths was suicide and the other either a suicide or a self-inflicted drug overdose."

"I know, but…"

Cindy interrupted. "Hold that but. Here's my but. I tend to half-way agree with you, a practice that will be the end of me yet. I believe their deaths were caused by someone else, but I think it was Joel. Before you say it, it's not because he wants to kick me out of this high-paid, sexy, all-powerful, fun-filled job, but because, if Chester is right, Joel loses his alibi and he had the most reason to want Lauren out of the way. I don't know what happened with Katelin, but suspect she knew something about Joel and he was getting antsy about whatever it was getting out."

I couldn't argue with Cindy's logic, but still felt Joel would have done a better job establishing his alibi.

"You may be right, but could you at least check to see if you can pin down Wayne's whereabouts at the time Katelin died? And, I believe Chester did see Joel during that time frame. If he did, that means Wayne's story about being in a strategy session with Joel is bogus."

Cindy fumed, hemmed and hawed, and mumbled a couple of profanities, but in the end, agreed to talk to Chester, and again with Wayne and Joel. I thanked her and headed to the door before she changed her mind.

I wasn't quick enough. "Hit the brakes, troublemaker."

I stopped and turned back to the chief. She ruffled through a stack of papers and pulled one from near the bottom. She slipped on reading glasses and said, "Think you'll find this interesting. At zero two hundred—that's two this morning to you civilian types—Officer McCormick stopped a *Caucasian Male, age sixty-five, walking in a staggering pattern, along the two hundred block of East Arctic Avenue.* I'll skip the rest of the professional police jargon and'll dumb it down for you. Officer McCormick said the man was clearly inebriated and while staggering isn't against the law public intoxication is. The staggerer was alternating between mumbling and yelling words that sounded like, 'I'll get the son of a bitch if it's the last thing I'll do.' That may not be an exact quote, but it conveys the message."

"Who?" I asked.

"Chill. I'm on my way there. Now, if we arrested every citizen who's walking the streets, sidewalks, and beach under the technical definition of intoxicated, we'd have to rent the Tides to hold all of them in. For that reason, and another less ethical one, Officer McCormick ushered the individual far off the roadway and out of the way of moving vehicles and let him off with a warning."

"Then why the report?"

"Good question," Cindy said, and turned the report face down and slid it back in the pile of papers. "Officer McCormick, being an astute officer and one who didn't want me to be caught with my pants down—figuratively—thought he'd better write it up and give it to me. To shred or not to shred, that is the question."

I was ready to reach over the desk and grab the report, but Cindy decided she'd teased me enough. "You want to know who it was?"

"Of course."

"I believe you know him. After all, he's your neighbor."

"Brad Burton?"

"Bingo."

I shared how I'd mentioned at the party what I'd learned about Joel's alibi falling apart, and how Brad had reacted. Cindy said it must have eaten on him the more he'd thought about it. She also said Officer McCormick had taken extra time patrolling near where he'd stopped Burton. Her officer knew who Burton was and wanted to extend as much "fellow officer courtesy" as possible, even though Burton was retired. She ended with saying McCormick only saw Burton one more time, and he appeared to be near his house. I thanked her for letting me know and left her office. This time she didn't stop me.

The rain was stronger than it had been on the ride back to Folly and I had left the umbrella in the car. I was soaked before I reached the dry confines of the car. What now? I agreed with Cindy's need for a bourbon, or wine in my case, but decided it was too early for that and headed home. Besides, I needed to get out of these wet clothes.

I pulled in the drive and looked over at Brad and Hazel's house. I had only a few conversations with Hazel, and although I had spent much more time than that with Brad, we weren't friends. He was hurting and I was surprised by his early morning behavior after Charles's party. I could understand his anger, but he'd never struck me as someone who would become that agitated. Common sense told me I should butt out. I had shared what I had learned with the police chief. It was up to them to follow up. But Brad was my neighbor now, and wasn't checking to see how he was the neighborly thing to do? Maybe, but most neighbors didn't have as strained a relationship as I had with the former detective. But, that was in the past, and in the last few weeks he had confided some things in me he wouldn't have broached in the past. And, I kept coming back to the fact he was my neighbor.

So what harm could come from changing into dry clothes and walking next door to see how he was doing?

Had I only known!

CHAPTER FORTY

I t was still raining as hard as ever, but this time I had my umbrella, as I walked through the wet grass and hopped over a couple of puddles on my way to the Burton's door. I figured someone was home since I could see the rear of Brad's car sticking out from around the side of the house. I couldn't see if Hazel's vehicle was there. After three knocks, I was beginning to doubt my initial assessment. Perhaps Brad had gone somewhere with Hazel.

I heard what sounded like a piece of furniture hitting the floor, and the sound of a door slamming at the back of the house. I rushed around the house and saw the back of a man jogging toward the yard behind the Burton's. More accurately, I saw Wayne Swan running away.

Do I chase him? Do I see what had happened in the house? He had a head start and twenty years of youth on me, so the odds on me catching him were minimal. And what would I do if I caught him? I turned and headed to the back door. It was standing open a couple of inches.

I started to knock, but instead pushed the door the rest of the way open and yelled, "Brad, Hazel?"

The rain was making so much noise that I didn't hear anything, so I stepped in out of the deluge and yelled again. I was in the kitchen and everything appeared normal. There were a couple of supper plates in the strainer beside the sink and two magazines open on the small island on the far side of the room. "Brad, Hazel?" I tried again.

This time I heard a faint noise on the other side of the island that sounded like someone moaning. I moved around the island. Brad on the floor, on his side, his arm was bent over his head, and a trickle of blood oozed out from under his arm. His left leg moved—he was alive.

I knelt beside him and asked if he could hear me. He mumbled something I couldn't understand and I leaned close to his head and asked him to repeat it.

"Hazel," he said, "shit … call." He mumbled something else, but again, I didn't understand.

I stood, careful not to move Brad, and grabbed a dishtowel off the island and moved his arm away from his head wound. It was bleeding but the flow had eased. I covered the wound with the towel and moved his arm back over it.

"Brad, put pressure on the towel. I'll call for help."

"Hazel," he mumbled.

I pulled my phone out of my pocket and tapped in 911, as I looked around the kitchen for Brad's wife. I told the professional sounding 911 operator where I was and that she needed to dispatch an ambulance and the cops. She told me to stay on the line until help arrived; I said I'd try, but finding Hazel was more important than maintaining phone contact.

I told Brad not to move and that help was on the way. He

didn't respond and I didn't think there was anything I could do for him, so I headed to the other rooms to find his wife.

The two small bedrooms were on the left side of the house and I did a quick canvas of each of them. No Hazel. The bathroom was between the bedrooms and again, no one was there. I had glanced in the living room on my way to the bedrooms and hadn't seen anyone but had to look more closely. After all, I wouldn't have seen Brad hidden by the kitchen island if I hadn't heard him.

In the living room, I looked behind the couch and the two chairs. I heard the sirens from the emergency vehicles heading in our direction as I concluded Hazel wasn't at home. I started back to check on Brad when I noticed a red, nylon NIKE backpack in front of the couch. It had to have been there when I first looked in the living room, but I didn't notice it. I wouldn't have now if it didn't seem out of place. I couldn't picture either of the Burton's taking long walks, much less backpacking anywhere.

I knelt beside the backpack and unzipped the top zipper. What I saw made me thankful I had a strong heart. Five sticks of what looked like dynamite were wrapped together by duct tape. Taped to the top was a small digital clock with a display that showed minutes on the top and seconds in smaller numbers at the bottom.

The hour and minutes display read 0; the second display clicked from 59 to 58. Crap!

Now what? The wires attaching the clock to the dynamite were taped so I couldn't see them; and even if I could, I had no idea which ones to try to unhook.

The seconds display read: 53. Probably not enough time to take the backpack to anywhere safely. The emergency vehicle sirens were closer, but not close enough to do anything.

I had to get Brad out of the house.

47 seconds!

I ran to the kitchen and leaned down over Brad. "Brad, can you hear me?"

He moved his arm and moaned.

"Can you get up?"

No reaction, and there wasn't time to ask again. I grabbed him under the arms and tried to pull him toward the door. He wasn't a large man but lifting him was like lifting three sacks of concrete. It was all dead weight. I managed to slide him around the island and to within a few feet of the back door.

He moaned louder and I was afraid I was hurting him, more than he already was. The alternative was worse, so I ignored his moans and dragged him to the door. I stepped off the back porch and yanked him out the door and into the yard. He gave a loud guttural sound and opened his eyes and gave me a look like he thought I was killing him.

I ignored him and continued to drag him away from the house. My back felt like it was on fire and my arms were numb. We were twenty feet from the house when all hell broke loose.

I was facing the house with my arms wrapped around his chest. It looked like a bolt of lightning. The white flash blinded me, before the shock waves from the explosion slammed into us. I was knocked on my back and Brad didn't move. The kitchen window shattered into a zillion particles and covered the yard like a hailstorm. The door flew off its hinges and landed three feet to our left. Everything happened at the same time and I couldn't comprehend it. I think I saw the back-wall buckle and fall; part of the roof fell with it.

The sound of the explosion was deafening—literally. I saw parts of the house flying around but didn't hear a thing. The rain was joined by pieces of the house pelting down on the yard. It wasn't until someone held a large golf umbrella over our head, that I realized others were there.

The entire back half of the house was demolished. There was little fire after the explosion, but the fire department was hosing down the house. I don't know why it came to me, but I smiled thinking the hoses weren't needed; the rain was doing a good job of soaking everything.

I slid out from under Brad and two paramedics began working on me. One of the firefighters asked if I was okay. He pointed to my head and said I was bleeding. Other than feeling like I had been run over by one of the fire engines, I said I was fine, but he insisted one of the EMTs look me over. He also asked if anyone else was in the house. I said no but wondered what Brad had meant when he kept saying Hazel.

Cindy arrived next and shoved her officer out of the way so she could get to me. I assured her I was okay, and told her what had happened, and who I had seen running from the house moments before the explosion. She asked if I was sure. I nodded, and she stepped away and called someone on her radio.

Brad was loaded on a stretcher and they were loading him in the ambulance. I was concerned about Hazel and saw Brad talking to the EMT. Thank God, he was okay—or close. I tapped the medic on the arm and asked if I could ask Brad a question.

"Make it quick."

Brad's eyes were blinking and his head was wrapped in gauze. He saw me and said, "What happened?"

"I'll tell you later. Where's Hazel? You kept mentioning her name when we were in the house."

"I wanted you to call her. She'll worry."

"I will, but, where is she?"

"The mall. She's buying drapery for the living room."

And we had nearly gotten ourselves killed because I spent so much time looking for her.

Brad reached over and squeezed my arm. I leaned closer, and he said, "I think we'll need more than drapery."

CHAPTER FORTY-ONE

I t had been eight days since the Burton's attractive wood-framed cottage had become a pile of kindling; the same number of days that it'd been since Hazel Burton arrived home with three sets of tan and green drapery and nowhere to hang them.

Six days had come and gone since Joel Hurt, faced with charges of murder, decided he would rather flip on his long-time friend, to avoid a long, protracted trial. While Mr. Hurt admitted that Wayne Swan had concocted an alibi for each of them for the time of death of Lauren Craft, he swore he didn't know Swan had killed Ms. Craft until Swan told him so, the day he decided to leave town.

Five days had passed since Trooper Marcel Samuels of the Massachusetts State Police pulled over a late model Dodge Ram Pick-up truck near Worcester and with a hand on his firearm asked the driver if he was aware the folks in the Charleston County, South Carolina's Sheriff's office had a keen interest in talking to him. In fact, the interest was so keen Trooper Samuels asked the driver, identified as Wayne L. Swan, to step out of the truck where he was cuffed and taken into custody.

Two days had passed since Al Washington had started speaking in coherent sentences and asking about how Bob was doing running Al's Bar and Gourmet Grill. I had gotten to see him for a few minutes and joined in a lengthy line of visitors who had lied to him about how wonderful things were at the bar but were truthful when we said he was sorely missed.

And, it had been twenty-four hours since Bob decided to hold a party at Al's bar to celebrate Al rejoining reality. Another reason became apparent when he said, "Since I've got to be at that damned run-down shack anyway, I want some of my friends suffering along with me."

I hesitated for several hours before calling Charles to see if he wanted to go with me. I had talked to him once since the explosion and had left three messages he hadn't returned. In the off-kilter spirit of Folly, apparently four times was the charm instead of three. Charles answered the phone. It was three in the afternoon but he sounded like he had been asleep. I told him about Bob's misery loves company party, and was surprised when he said, "Sure, nothing else to do."

It was Monday, a traditionally slow night for bars and restaurants, and Al's wasn't bucking the trend. Four elderly gentlemen were seated around the table closest to the door. Each held a beer bottle and a hand of cards. There was a pile of matchsticks on the middle of the table that I suspected had some value other than cheap wood. Two other tables were occupied with couples. I had seen most of the diners in Al's but didn't know their names. Bob had told us the party was to begin at eight, so of course, Charles insisted we arrive by seven-thirty, so, other than Bob, we were the only partygoers present.

Lawrence greeted us at the door. "Thank God, some of Bob's

white friends finally got here. He's been pestering me ever since six wondering if anyone would show."

I told him that Bob told us the event started at eight.

Lawrence held out his hands. "Don't tell me anything about him. Lord, he's your friend. He only inherited me."

The only sound in the room was laughter coming from the card players. Bob looked over at us and walked to the side of the jukebox and hit some buttons. Willie Nelson began his version of "Faded Love," and an audible groan arose from the men at the card table.

Bob yelled over Willie's singing, "The party's on. Drinks are on me!"

That immediately stopped the card game and three of the four men raised their hands for more beer.

The door opened and Cal, followed by Chester Carr, stuck their heads in and stepped the rest of their bodies into the room, deciding it was safe. Cal had on his Stetson, his rhinestone-studded jacket, and jeans. Chester wore a navy blue, starched, dress shirt and gray dress slacks.

Bob saw them enter and said, "Look everybody, it's Hank Williams Sr. himself. And they thought you were dead."

The regulars had learned how much credence to put into anything Bob said; they ignored him. Rickey Van Shelton and "Somebody Lied," followed Willie on the jukebox and I heard one of the men at one of the other tables say something about grabbing the picket signs. Bob laughed, and Lawrence brought each of the newcomers a drink. It didn't look like the party's host was going to do it, so Charles and I pulled three tables together and slid chairs up to them.

It was Chester's first visit, and he looked around and took the chair closest to the back of the room. "How's Al doing?" he asked, to no one in particular.

Bob smiled and said, "He'll be back sitting over by the door in a couple of weeks. We'll try to find a chair for him or make him bring his own if we're crowded."

Right, I thought.

The Four Tops began "Reach Out I'll Be There," and an on-key chorus of Hallelujah came from the card players. Bob made a choking motion and asked Charles how he was doing. Charles mumbled a neutral response and then Chester asked him if he knew anything about what was happening with Joel and Wayne.

"According to Marc Salmon, Wayne doesn't have a snow-balls chance in that fryer over there." Charles pointed to the small kitchen. "And, while there isn't much to pin on Joel, he started his campaign as a dark horse candidate, and now would have a tough time finding a snail to ride to the polls on."

Bob had moved behind Charles. "That mean I can have my campaign contributions back?"

"No," I said.

"That's okay, my commission from finding the Burtons somewhere to live after Chris blew their house up will make up for it."

Cal tipped his Stetson in Bob's direction. "I hear finding them a house was easy. Didn't four people volunteer somewhere for them to live?"

"So, what's your point?" asked the Realtor.

Cal smiled. "My point is Folly has the kindest, most giving folks in the world and the Burtons are lucky to live there."

Chester didn't want to be left out. "And Chris is mighty lucky too. He ain't got Brad Burton next door anymore."

"Until they rebuild," Charles added.

Thanks for the reminder, friend.

Lawrence brought a second round of drinks to our table, and no telling what round to the card players. From the corner of my eye, I saw one of the players head to the jukebox and another member of the group move behind Bob.

The Four Tops blared, "Can't Help Myself," the man behind Bob twisted him around and walked him to the center of the room, where they were joined by the man who had gone to the jukebox.

Sugar pie honey bunch I'm weaker than a man should be, sang the man on each side of Bob.

Bob smiled and blurted out, *"I can't help myself, I'm a fool in love you see."*

I found myself somewhere between shock and amusement—not a bad place to be.

Can't help myself, no I can't help myself.

ABOUT THE AUTHOR

Bill Noel is the best-selling author of fourteen novels in the popular Folly Beach Mystery series. Besides being an award-winning novelist, Noel is a fine arts photographer and lives in Louisville, Kentucky, with his wife, Susan, and his off-kilter imagination. Learn more about the series, and the author by visiting www.billnoel.com.

91256230R00165

Made in the USA
Lexington, KY
19 June 2018